DARKEST DIMENSIONS

MR. MICHAEL SQUID

"As I wrought, I waxed wicked as a demon! And with lowered neck, and forward curve of the lower spine, and the blasphemous strut of tragic play-actors, I went."

—M. P. Shiel, The Purple Cloud

CONTENTS

INTRODUCTION

This is a collection of horror stories, many of which share themes of alternate dimensions, manipulated time, or simply things that seem to disrupt the knowledge of the world we think we know. Other tales are within as well, even a few short, dark poems.

Thanks to the NoSleep Podcast and the NoSleep and Short Scary Stories communities for helping my voice develop and grow. Thanks to all the authors inspiring and challenging me.

Most of all, thank you to the reader, and to those who leave a review when you like what you've read. Thank you for reading, listening, and watching, and thank you for keeping me motivated and inspired to weave new nightmares.

DO NOT WAKE UP

Can you hear me in there?

Ah, there you are. Hello!

There's that eager eye of yours, scanning from left to right again. I guess in your head you are reading these words instead of listening to them. It's good you can still read there, wherever 'there' is.

It's good that your remaining eye, or eyes, still work. Just so long as they don't see what's truly in front of them. Whatever you're looking at in that head of yours—a computer monitor, a phone screen, or a book page—please, keep looking at that.

I've been observing you for quite some time. Not just me, dozens have come by this room to marvel at you before gagging and turning away. You are very special, you know; a true medical marvel. Everyone wants to know what keeps you ticking.

You've drawn in people from across the globe who try to understand how you survived. They all stare at you through the glass and shudder as they take notes, but I watch you in a different way, now that I know. I know the answer to their questions, and no, I won't share your secret.

I'm the only one who seems to realize what's really going on in there. The others, the doctors and nurses, all think you're just flailing about and twitching in pain, but I figured it out. I realized you are somewhere else entirely in that butchered head of yours.

Those few fluttering fingers jutting out of that stalk of your arm are acting out the motions of typing and texting. Those aren't spasms of pain at all, but interactions with an interface, an elevator button, or a door handle. I even notice the subtle expressions that the remains of your face attempt to make. I think wherever you are, you are often even smiling, actually smiling. I cried tears of joy when I figured out what your tormented brain had done.

The body, of course, has its physical defense mechanisms. Endorphins are released once the bones fracture and pierce through the muscle and skin. After that, a deep unconsciousness shuts the mind down when the pain becomes unbearable. Most individuals who've suffered such devastating physical trauma will fall into a coma, but not you. No, you have been quite animated ever since you arrived at this facility.

I soon began to realize the gurgling, raspy noises you keep making are words. You are talking to people in your own mind. You are laughing and crying, smiling and watching a screen. You are carrying out full conversations in that fractured skull. You are experiencing someplace else entirely, someplace infinitely better. I even noticed you reading the words picked up by that ear canal of yours.

And when I leave the room so the nurses can change your bedpan and replace the IV in the withered remnant of your arm, you carry on in that little life in that little world your mind has built. A life in which there was no horrible accident. A life where you can move about and talk and eat solid food. A life where you can work and play and even go outside into the sunlight.

On occasion, though, you twitch and scream, kicking that jagged stump of your leg as you gasp for air before eventually calming. I've come to the conclusion that you sometimes experience fragmented glimpses of your true, waking life. You slip dangerously close to lucidity before your wheezing breaths slow and you return to that haven. The complex defense mechanism your mind has built seems to process these flashes of reality as nightmares, and soon afterward, you mimic the motions of waking. The broken twig of your remaining arm soon pantomimes the action of brushing as if you had a jaw with teeth within it to brush.

Listen to me when I tell you that you need to stay there. Believe me when I say that no matter what upsets you in that precious world you've concocted, no matter what heartache or financial trouble you've dreamed yourself into, it pales in comparison to the suffering that awaits you in that stained hospital bed.

There are only the life support machines pumping air into the gangrenous lungs within your shattered ribs. No family or friends visit you here, only gaping medical students who retch before turning away at the sight of what's left. No medication will make a dent in the excruciating pain from the exposed nerves of your collapsed head.

Please, for your own sake, I beg of you.

Do not wake up.

DEATH HAS BEEN CURED

In a crowded press conference held in Stockholm, Sweden, the drug dubbed 'Panacea' was proudly announced by a team of world-renowned geneticists. They had isolated the lines of code within our DNA that controlled both lifespan and cellular repair. By injecting a few hundred proteins altered by site-specific double-strand breaks, it worked. The test mice and monkeys had all stopped aging at adulthood, and cellular degradation had ceased. It was hailed as the greatest scientific breakthrough of all time.

After a year being exclusively available to the world's wealthiest elite, the procedure became publicly accessible in hospitals across the globe. Soon, anyone with basic healthcare was able to undergo a procedure for permanent surgical sterilization in order to receive the Panacea shot, which would halt aging in its tracks. Within the first year of becoming available to the public, a reported 49% of the world's population had chosen the shot.

An anomaly first appeared in Ludhiana, India. A mother who'd undergone the sterilization procedure had become pregnant. After accusations of corruption and malpractice erupted, an ultrasound followed by an MRI revealed the impossible. The woman's reproductive organs appeared to have grown back themselves. A similar report came from Windsor, England, where another sterilized woman had become pregnant. The miracle pregnancies quickly began occurring everywhere.

As the 'Elixer Babies'—the progeny of those injected—were born, they were soon found to be equally affected by the genetic alteration, ensuring their indefinite longevity. In just 10 years, the global population had reached 16 billion. After 25 years, that number had tripled.

The population continued to skyrocket at a terrifying rate. Food banks were rapidly depleted as millions who had been expected to die off had not. Those who were starved had withered away, screaming from the pangs of hunger, yet they would not die.

Fifty years after Panacea had been discovered, the finite unoccupied spaces on the surface of the Earth had gone from overcrowded to non-existent. Those too weak to struggle and climb were trampled, but still they did not die. They became another patch in the living carpet of flesh which quickly covered the land and spilled out into the shrinking seas. Those unlucky billions would soon be blanketed by another layer of fallen bodies.

Only the molds and the insects thrived in the new world, creating a symbiotic partnership that both fed and pollinated the fleshy layer of wailing misery that had been mankind. Nearly all other flora and fauna have long since become extinct, smothered and starved of both light and air. Man-made structures have all toppled, their walls crushed into dust from the grinding teeth of screaming mouths and bony, jutting limbs. The harrowing sound of humanity's collective screams will never end though, because death itself has been cured.

THE HIDDEN TELEVISION CHANNEL

I've long held a memory that has been the source of pain and anguish throughout my life since childhood. My psychiatrist is convinced my memories are warped in an attempt to suppress trauma, and I began to believe him. I've been on anti-anxiety medication for nearly 22 years and anti-depression meds for 18. I'd eventually been convinced those memories were, in fact, a result of suppression. I was finally starting to move past it all. And then this afternoon I saw it. I saw the hidden television channel I'd been convinced was a false memory, and I screamed.

My brother went missing when I was 9 years old, and his friend was found dead in our living room. I was questioned, as was my father, but the nature of Dan's death defied explanation and the lack of evidence made the case unsolvable, so it went cold. I was considered an unreliable witness after my tearful testimony to the police. In the following months, I was taken to a child psychologist and eventually prescribed medications before undergoing years of repressed memory therapy. I was there when it happened, though. And as of today, I'm now certain what I saw was, in fact, real.

My parents raised Ryan and me in the suburb of Hatfield PA. We had a yard, a good education, good friends, and the latest 16-bit video game consoles. I was happy at age 9, enjoying the summer vacation as the sweltering heat of June baked the streets. My older brother Ryan was 14 and a bit of a smart-ass, always cracking jokes and getting into trouble. Still, he looked after me and was always quick to stick up for me if any bullies made the mistake of giving me a hard time. I truly was lucky, in retrospect.

One weekend when Dad was working and Mom had driven off to run errands, I was playing Genesis in my room when Ryan began yelling from downstairs.

"Mike, get down here, check this out!" he called up from the living room. I heard the din of scattered applause from the TV. I shuffled out of my room and peered down at Ryan, who flashed me his trademark smile, marked by the mole on his cheek. It'd been a sore spot growing up and led to him growing thick skin after being called Marylin Monroe many times in elementary school. I looked past my grinning brother to the TV, to an image that warped and shifted like a scrambled adult station, bending the image.

"Yeah, Dad locks the porn channel, perv," I called back. I shook my head but then the image on the TV fixed itself. On-screen, there was a panel of sitting people whose faces looked somehow wrong. They had all the normal features, eyes, noses, and mouths, but they looked strangely shaped and sized like each was in the wrong place or perhaps the wrong shape. They looked deformed and almost fake, and it was pretty creepy. "What the heck is it?" I asked.

"Just come down here, check this out," Ryan called and sat cross-legged in front of the glowing screen. I was curious and had nothing better to do. I shuffled my small feet down the carpeted stairs and stood next to Ryan, watching the strange people on screen.

"This is not a real station," Ryan stated emphatically. "Look!" His finger pointed to the corner of the screen. The station read 23.3, a station in between stations. He then pointed to the dial; our TV was one of the old-fashioned dial sets. The knob was resting between stops. "And this show is fucking WEIRD!" I then sat next to my brother as the image went in and out of scrambled distortion, and we watched a TV show unlike anything I'd seen before.

Seven individuals with strange-looking faces all conversed in whispers between themselves. A shiny-faced, bald man who appeared to be the show's host paced back and forth in front of a large reflective black panel on the wall. The image bent and shifted as the scrambled effect came in and out, but I soon realized it was a large square of black glass, maybe twelve feet square and likely fairly thick as well. After some deliberation, the seated individuals on the panel held up large cards with numbers from left to right.

3, 21, 53, 501, 413, 8, 42

I had no idea what those numbers could possibly mean, but I began to feel nervous. The people with pinched and strange features creeped me out more than anything. It was like they had all received severely botched plastic surgeries, warping them so far out of normal proportion that they all looked terrifying.

"What is this?" I asked Ryan, who shushed me.

"I don't know, stop talking," he snapped. The camera switched to show a closeup of the standing man, the presumed host. My skin crawled immediately once his closeup filled the screen. Ryan gasped and then said "Fuck," under his breath. Fuck was right.

The man was bald, and the closeup revealed the skin on his grisly face was made up almost entirely of scar tissue. Shiny, pink skin was pulled tight around the contours of his skull. It was reminiscent of a burn victim who's had his damaged skin grafted, but in a way that didn't make any logical sense. His teeth were pristine, sparkling white, but his lips were jagged, blended, and uneven, as if they'd been split and patched together by unskilled surgeons. It was like some horrifically butchered cosmetic surgery had been performed on him for the sole purpose of making him look more disturbing.

The host peered into the camera with small, black eyes beneath folded creases of misshapen lids. Little black beads that stared into me from the flickering screen. My neck hairs raised as he cocked his head slightly as if he'd become aware of something. I held my breath as he then excitedly pointed at the camera and spoke.

"2913, 2913!" The host called out in a muffled, strained voice through butchered lips.

My brother and I looked at each other in shock. Our address was 2913 on our lane. It was surely a creepy coincidence, but I was 9 years old and absolutely terrified at that point.

"Turn it off!" I shouted, but Ryan just gawked, his jaw hanging open, as he watched the TV.

The host pointed a twisted finger to the audience, a slew of about 20 individuals whose backs were to the camera. The person who'd been pointed at then stood and turned to the side to move down the aisle. It was a woman who looked sickly and tired. She was gaunt, emaciated with bags under her eyes above sunken cheeks. Her age was a mystery as her face had been mangled similarly to the rest. There was no way to tell if she was 25 or 85.

She dragged one foot behind her as the host kept pointing a gnarled finger at her. As she shuffled out of the aisle and onto the path to the stage, it was clear her left foot was dangling at the base; connected only by the skin itself.

"Jesus Christ," Ryan exhaled in a hushed voice. The woman limped up the stairs to the black-floored stage and made her way to the panel, taking a seat at the end of the strange-looking individuals. A wide-angled shot showed a black-clad assistant rush over from behind a curtained stage left and hand her a placard reading "2913" in thick, black numbers. These did not look like special effects, and they were far too graphic for television as far as I knew.

"Turn it off!" I shouted to Ryan, but he seemed mesmerized by the bizarre television show. The camera then showed a closeup of the woman holding the sign, and my heart pounded in my chest.

It wasn't a woman, it was a mutilated girl, much younger but cosmetically butchered just like the rest. Her face was scarred in lines under the eyes and cheeks, making her appear older. She looked very familiar, however. It took me a while to figure out where I recognized that nose speckled with that particular pattern of freckles. I made the connection as my stomach sank into the floor.

It was Amber Darton, the girl who'd been all over the news after having gone missing, presumed abducted from her yard last year. I'd seen her face so many times in the papers, post office wall, and even milk cartons; there was no mistaking it. It was impossible to ignore. Her face had been terribly altered in what appeared to be an attempt to conceal her identity.

"Ryan, that's Amber Darton, that girl who'd gone missing." I whimpered. I couldn't stand it anymore. "Ryan, call the police!"

"Fuck… fuck you're right. Holy shit," Ryan stood up, stumbled back, and raced to the cordless kitchen phone. He picked it up and dialed, but just seconds later, the image on-screen warped back into wavy bands of a scrambled station before clicking to channel 23, where a baseball game was being aired.

"No!" I shouted, and I approached the old TV set, hitting the side to try and restore the image. I fiddled with the knob, trying to balance it between stations, but it wouldn't stick or find that hidden station, no matter how slowly I rotated the dial. That strange show didn't come back. Not when my mother returned home and listened to our pleas to believe us. Not when a uniformed police officer arrived at our door. This made our mother really lose it, once she explained the hyperactive imagination of her boys, and forced us to apologize to the man. Nobody believed us.

Ryan and I both were determined to find the station throughout the week but had no luck. The dial clicked very clearly between the actual stations, and the phenomenon Ryan had discovered seemed to have been a one-time fluke.

"Might have been pirate broadcasters," Ryan told me one day. "Back in '87 hackers did it in Chicago with a Max Headroom mask. I dunno." He sounded like he was desperately trying to get over it and dismiss it as a prank or a fluke. I don't think he wanted to face the possibility that what we saw was real. Days passed and I honestly thought that was the end of it. God, I wish it had been.

A few weeks later, Ryan's friend Dan from school came over and they watched horror movies late at night after mom and dad were asleep. I sneak-watched The Thing from atop the stairs without them knowing. After it was finished, they began chatting about strange real-life horror stories and unexplained phenomena. Then, Ryan brought up the show.

"There's a hidden television station, swear to god. My little brother and I both saw it," Ryan explained to the scoffs of Dan, a larger kid who always wore leather jackets and fancied himself the long-lost member of The Misfits.

"Bullshit," Dan retorted after hearing the rundown of events. He smirked then shook his head. "If the station existed, hundreds or even thousands of people would've seen it.

"I swear it was real, man," Ryan walked up to the TV and began fiddling with the station knob. We'd done this a dozen times since the incident, and of course, there was never any signal again. Dan was chuckling as he drew a Marlboro from a pack in his jacket pocket and headed to the door to go out for a smoke.

But then it happened. There was a pop of static, a crackle as the image flickered, and then wavy bands of color streaked down the screen. Dan stopped mid-step, the unlit cigarette dangling from his lip.

"Holy SHIT this is it!" Ryan yelled out in a hushed tone to avoid waking our parents. I felt my guts squirm at the sight of it. It was something dangerous. Something too dark to explore. Ryan and his tough-guy friend Dan were the type to chase thrills, though.

I watched from the top of the stairs as those sickening faces appeared once again on the screen. The panel of disfigured individuals and that shiny-skinned host with beady eyes and perfect teeth beneath the ravaged flesh of his face.

"What the actual fuck…" Dan trailed off, and he came back into the living room to watch the horrible show. "This is fucking crazy."

I watched for a few seconds as the panel of individuals raised placards with numbers:

814, 2, 601, 21B, 3F, 210, 2002

The host faced the screen once more in a grotesque closeup. I twinged with a shiver at seeing that terrible, butchered face staring intently into the camera, squinting malformed lids over shiny, black eyes.

"2913! 2913, quick!" he pointed a gnarled finger to an emaciated male in the audience, who staggered slowly up and onto the stage to hold a newly painted card reading 2913; our address.

My throat closed and my heart pounded in my chest. The host then walked to the large, black glass square inset into the stage. I felt sick to my stomach but couldn't look away.

The black square pane of glass began to brighten as if a light was being turned on from the other side. The illumination revealed a room of a house and two people facing the camera. My heart skipped a beat as I realized what I was seeing.

Behind the glass was a reflection of our living room, as viewed from the other side. Standing in it, facing the audience, was my brother Ryan and his friend Dan.

"What the FUCK man?" Dan shouted and took a step back from the screen. His actions were mirrored in the large, square panel as if it were a window into our home. There was a harsh, distorted tone that rumbled through the TV, low and deep. It sounded for a second, stopped for two, then sounded again on repeat.

My fear had built to the point I couldn't take it. "Turn it off!" I shouted from atop the stairs, only then alerting my brother and his friend to my presence. That analog, deep rumbling tone kept sounding, and my brother ran to the TV, fidgeting with the dial. The image remained as he switched stations. It remained even after he pressed the power button.

"This can't be real," Ryan said. He yanked out the plug of the television and the screen finally went black with a crackle.

But then the tone sounded again. Distorted and deep, rumbling loud enough to tremble the upstairs floor beneath the carpet. There was a sharp bang followed by the cracking of wood. Ryan screamed a shrill scream, facing the out-of-view front door of our home. I ran into my room and slammed my door shut, locking it with shaking fingers.

There was a horrible series of snaps and crunches, followed by the most horrible, shrill scream I've ever heard.

Everything after was a blur. I remember my parents' voices, confused by the sounds that awoke them. My mother's scream. Frantic yelling. My parents checking if I was OK. Sirens. Police. Ambulances. Everyone was asking if I knew where Ryan was. I did not.

Dan was found splayed on the carpet. His wrists, ankles, and neck had been severed clean through, though the skin remained unscathed. It was as if they'd been severed from within his body. His official cause of death was listed as internal hemorrhaging, though how he got his injuries was a complete mystery.

And that was the end of it.

I grew up into a scarred adult with some issues due to the trauma. I have an Ativan with breakfast and Paxil at lunch. I've been to therapy sessions through my teenage years and into my adult life. I was convinced there must have been some crazy trick, or perhaps my mind had envisioned what it most feared on that screen.

Ryan was presumed kidnapped and killed. We even had a funeral for him seven years after the incident, once he was legally declared dead in absentia. I hadn't seen or heard from him in thirty years. Not until this afternoon.

Today I was scouring the news and forcing down a TV dinner. I was flicking the stations, not paying attention to the channel, only to what was on. News, cooking, cartoons; and then my blood froze.

I stared at the image I'd struggled all my life to convince myself was a delusion, a vivid hallucination, or some transfigured repressed memory. The station read 23.3, and the familiar nightmarish television set appeared once again.

It was that same studio stage and a row of disfigured people who appeared to have had horrific plastic surgeries. They were all new butchered faces, but the exact same setup. The host was a bald, heavily scarred man, but clearly a different person. I watched the familiar routine of raising signs of street addresses when the closeup cam fixed on the mutilated visage of the host.

"21B! 21B! He gurgled frantically, his crooked finger aiming at the screen before lowering to single out a woman in the audience.

My heart stumbled in my chest until it hurt. My throat dried and my eyes widened with dread. I felt the icy claw of horror trace down my spine. I lived in apartment 21B on my street, but it wasn't the address that sent me screaming out my apartment door, down the stairs, and into the streets. It was the butchered face of the host.

It was the unmistakable mole on his mutilated cheek.

THE GROWING ROOM

Gary unfurled his skull-ringed pointer finger, aiming it just left of the near-identical suburban homes. "Easy money. An old man lives just past those woods, but he's out of town."

"You're not serious," I stared, lowering my cigarette. I was fifteen, he was a year or two older. My bad-influence best friend; but the worst I ever did was shoplift some CDs.

"He's an older guy, made huge money off some inventions, and he's a loner. Lives near the woods a bit out of the suburbs, so the place is secluded." Gary brushed his greasy bangs from a forehead bumped with a rash of red pimples. He swigged from a plastic flask and his face scrunched from the burn. A paint-thinner stink carried his words as he spoke.

"No alarm either, I saw him heading out with a car packed with luggage." Gary smiled, the hairs of a patchy mustache spreading thin over a grinning mouth that flashed stained teeth.

"Break into someone's house? And rob him?" I was a dead-end kid headed to some gas station job when all the suburbanites would be headed off to college. But breaking and entering was another world. A darker world. "No way, man."

Gary shifted on his seat to face me, then squinted at me with his hazel eyes as he leaned in. "This guy's also a pervert. He tried to grope a kid from Westbrook. Everyone knows about it. If anyone deserves to share his wealth, trust me, it's this guy."

I was aware it could be the point of no return; the final chapter ending in jail time or getting shot in an attempted burglary. But I didn't want to look weak or scared. I knew it was stupid, but I huffed out in annoyance and said "OK." And with that, we were off.

We headed out under the charcoal sky, hiking along the highway and through the edge of the woods. To the East were the suburbs and all the well-off kids. They were middle-class, but rich kids to us. Polished, newer model cars gleamed from the powerful streetlights. We stayed a good distance back to avoid being spotted as we trekked deeper into the trees. It soon came into view.

There stood a dark wooden home of mid-century modern design. It was out of a different era, yet it appeared innovative and sleek nonetheless. An angular, top-heavy building with jutting support beams and a slanted roof. It was two stories on one half while the other half was a one-story, ranch construction. It had likely cost a fortune back when the old man had it built. I watched from the tree line as Gary crept across the dewy grass like a cartoon character. He peered into a large, dark window and then turned back to face me, giving me the "come on!" inward hand motion. I breathed out a heavy sigh then I exited the woods onto the perfectly manicured lawn.

I stood there, nervously holding my elbows close as I watched Gary walk between the large, black windows, peering in. I was trying to think of a valid excuse to ditch him without sounding like a total coward when he broke the silence.

"On the other side! There's a window cracked, and there's some crazy expensive stuff upstairs. I swear there's even a Fabergé egg!"

"A what? An egg?" I asked, having no clue as to what he was talking about.

"It's worth like ten grand!" he whisper-shouted, and my eyes widened. "Follow me."

I did as asked, rounding the strange house. Large, overhanging windows protruded out from the second story, blocking some of the stars.

"Give me a leg up," Gary whispered, pointing up to a projecting window that was cracked a few inches. I gave him a boost, feeling his muddy boot press down on my palms as I strained to lift him up and into the house. It felt like hours as I stood out there in the starlit haven. The house was completely isolated. I nearly yelped aloud when the tall front door swung open and Gary's mischievous, mustached grin poked out from the darkness within.

"Ta-da!" he whispered and gestured to the open door in a sweeping motion. I followed him inside.

I entered the large dark home, staying close. The first thing I noticed was the faint smell of mechanical grease. My eyes began to adjust to the darkness and I saw a sprawling interior just past the vestibule. It was fancy, albeit outdated. Shag carpets, abstract onyx sculptures of melting shapes, and a chandelier dangling from a high ceiling in the foyer. Pristine, square white leather couches lined the wallpapered edges, which looked to be from the '60s.

"Up here," Gary said, leading me through the large foyer to a winding staircase. I looked up to see clustered stars through large skylights overhead.

"Look," Gary muttered as I climbed the last step into a corridor lined with paintings I had no doubt were worth serious money. One, with blocky squares of red, blue, and yellow divided by black lines, I would later learn was a Mondrian. Among them were framed blueprints of complex mechanisms and architectural plans; the old man's very own work, scattered among the works of world-renowned painters. My eyes followed Gary's pointing finger to a table on which sat a golden ostrich egg covered with latticed ornamentation. A gaudy piece of art that was clearly the source of Gary's excitement. He picked it up from its decorative stand.

"Ok, let's get the hell out of here," I said.

"In a second," Gary replied as he continued down the hall. At the end on the right was a mahogany door with a large steel padlocked latch.

"Jackpot." Gary unclasped two safety pins from his torn jeans. He inserted them into the keyhole of the padlock and in no time at all, it clicked open.

I followed Gary through the inviting door. The room seemed out of place. Large white tiles covered the floor, walls, and ceiling. Almost reminiscent of a sauna. The room was barren aside from cross-shaped slots in the walls, maybe ten inches tall and wide, and two inches thick. These odd holes rested at eye level, one every three meters. I peered into one out of curiosity and saw an astounding number of tiny brass gears. A landscape of layered cogs, belts, and wheels.

"The fuck is this place?" Gary called out as he continued walking towards the door at the far end of the peculiar tiled chamber. As he spoke, a ticking sounded. Hundreds of small clicks and rattles from all directions culminated in an echoing slam of the door behind us. It rattled my head with a piercing migraine. When

I turned to race towards it—sneakers squeaking on the tile—the most peculiar illusion ensued.

The door we'd entered from looked further away. I'd been only five feet into the long chamber, but when I turned around, it looked to be a good eight feet back. Then the vibrations began.

Something shook my bones, a subsonic pulse that vibrated my flesh and quivered my nerves until they flared with unspeakable pain. A high-pitched ringing split my skull and my hands reached up to clutch my temples. They moved slowly, as if underwater. They burned as if the flesh was being melted off, and when I caught a glimpse of them, I screamed.

My hands were warped into fanned-out, surreal paddles. The digits were flat and wide and the skin stretched thin to a translucent membrane. I could see the bone and muscle, even the latticed veins wrapping the meat beneath. I then noticed the tiles in the chamber were no longer square, but a rectangular, porcelain grid. It was as if the entire room was stretched out, and it was getting longer.

I knew moving was making it worse. My misshapen fingers were burning with activated nerves. I'd only moved my hands. My forearms tapered down from a long, flat wrist that repulsed me and hurt so bad I just wanted them gone.

I heard a wet smacking sound followed quickly by a startling, inhuman screaming from behind me. It was Gary, and he was running towards me from behind, back to the door that I'd been staring at. A door that was moving slowly farther away as that room stretched.

"Don't move!" I screamed behind me to Gary. My voice was altered; low and animal. It scared me, but I don't think Gary heard it. I doubt his ears even functioned at that point. Not after what he had become entered my peripheral vision and came into view.

It was a melted abstraction of the human form. His head was a long, bloated caterpillar, coated with thinning hair. His skin was like wet tissue paper; revealing fractured bones, veins, and snapping ribbons of muscle beneath. His mouth was a long muzzle whose lips peeled back to reveal lengthy gums poking out narrow tusks of teeth. The eyes were glistening tubes of albumen streaming red tears from flapping eyelids. A banshee howl of unknowable pain screamed deep and hollow: rattling and shifting as his body pulled until it broke.

I stayed frozen in place despite the boiling pain. I felt my entire body pulling apart; extruding as every nerve ending burned within me. If I tried to move, I'd only doom myself. I had to stay there and watch as Gary's strange arms and bulky torso came into view. Webbed, translucent flesh ballooned until holes formed in the rice-paper skin, leaking so much blood that splashed down noisily onto the expanding white tile floor.

His bones bowed and curled over into abstract shapes before splitting the skin. Muscle twitched, then ripped like fresh bread. Burst skin flapped down and dragged behind his exploding sausage legs. It only took a few seconds for Gary's body to fall apart. I watched, frozen in horror as it unraveled into a trail of blood, flesh, and arcing bone. The stink, coppery and septic, was unbearable.

I stood there frozen as the room slowly began to shrink. The cacophony of ticking gears echoed in the gore-strewn corridor. The excruciating pressure in my temples began to subside and the pulling on my skin lessened as the room slowly settled down to its original size.

Gary's unraveled remains shriveled from a long streak of glistening parts into a pile of bone and meat: then, with a final, echoing click, it was over. I looked at my hands, which had contracted down once again. They had stretched back wrong; deformed and twisted as if from a birth defect, but they were functional to a degree. Gary's insides lay piled in a lake of blood like some hellish island. In the center lay the blood-streaked golden egg. I tried not to look as I staggered, clutching the walls, past them to the door. It was open.

I quickly fled that terrible house, crying as I limped into the woods. I never told a soul about that night. I knew nobody would ever believe it. To this day I tell people I crushed my hands fixing an escalator, and everyone drops it. I try not to think of the nightmare I barely survived. About what happened to Gary in the growing room.

AVOID THE COSTUMED CHARACTERS IN TIMES SQUARE

If you've been to Times Square, you've likely seen the costumed characters that wave and pose with tourists for tips. Some have made headlines for becoming aggressive when not paid. Others have been accused of getting a little too friendly with those gloved hands. Elmos, Mickeys, Minnies, Spidermen and last but not least, Hello Kitties can be found roaming the streets. I'd always rush past them, having no interest in any interaction. My office was located in the heart of it, and despite dodging them on the street, I'd often see them during my lunch break.

At lunch, I frequented the last of a defunct fast-food chain that attracted virtually no tourists due to its backstreet location away from the congested avenues. I'd slip off the mess of 43rd and quickly turn into that dumpster-filled side street, where halfway down the block I'd reach the small lunch spot. I'd order my fried chicken sandwich, fries, and soda, and sit in a dimly lit booth installed decades earlier and read the news while forcing down the mediocre meal in peace. The low-key spot seemed to attract the other locals in need of privacy and quiet, as well as those costumed characters.

Each day I went there, it was just me and a few of the street performers; furry Elmos with spiky red fur or Disney knockoff animals, chowing down their meals with their foam heads sitting beside them on their tables or in their booths. It was comical at first but became a bit depressing as the weeks passed. I'd see the tired, baggy eyes and sweaty black hair plastered to the damp foreheads of folks just trying to earn an honest living or support families back home. I had been working in the area for a few months when I slipped into the place and saw a ratty-looking Hello Kitty who kept their mask on for the entire duration of my meal.

As usual, the place was filled with comically decapitated mascots lining the wall booths. Their joyless faces regarded their sad chicken sandwiches before proceeding to shovel them down, as did I. But that one Hello Kitty just sat there, a cute, oversized foam mask still balanced on their white shoulders. I ate my ranch-slathered cut of fried chicken in silence, but I couldn't help but keep looking over at that fully costumed character. I reasoned they were likely napping, but abandoned that thought when I rose to fetch condiments for my bland meal. That large head rotated slightly to follow me. I began feeling very uncomfortable with being stared at while trying to eat, and I made the unfortunate mistake of confronting them.

"Is there a problem?" I asked, turning my head to the costumed observer. A few of the other customers glanced over, then looked back to their colorless meals. That cartoonish cat head just stared at me and then the head twitched. A chill climbed my neck as I began to notice some peculiar details about their costume.

First off were the arms. They appeared to be padded tubes of white foam that should normally fit loose, but I could see the crinkle in the crook of the bent elbows, tight and small, as if the material was much thinner than expected. It looked like spandex, snug and stretched against the skin on an impossibly uniform, tubular arm. Of course, this made absolutely no sense unless their arms were 4 inches in diameter the entire course of their length, but the more I stared, the more peculiar details I noticed. I swore I could see the faint bump of a winding vein running down the forearm leading to the gloved hands.

The large gloves appeared to be made of felt and housed only four bulbous fingers. When the fat digits clenched slightly, I could make out the lines of the knuckles. They jittered nervously as if aware I'd noticed something was off. I felt a sinking feeling in my guts as I looked at a blank, black stare from those large eyes.

The eyes caught the light like fresh paint, glistening, wet and seemingly alive. At the edge of the fabric that encircled their perimeter, I observed what appeared to be tattered edges. I felt a sinking in my stomach as I realized that it seemed the large eyes were visible through holes cut out of the mask, not part of it. On the side of that round, white head, a jaw muscle visibly flexed as it clenched. The concealed face beneath it appeared to be the same size and shape of that mask, with only millimeters of fabric concealing it.

I felt the need to leave. My heart pounded as I stood and made my way to the exit, which was past *it*. The closer I got, the more I smelled a foul stench that seemed to emanate from that costumed character. It was septic and foul, like a neglected homeless person but acrider. That big, ovoid head swiveled slowly to follow my footfalls on the soda-sticky tile floor as I quickly pushed through the swinging glass door and out into the alleyway. I rounded the few blocks back to my office and spent the rest of the workday trying hard to get my mind off of that creepy encounter. I decided to avoid that place like the plague and hoped I'd never see that disturbing mascot again. But I would.

A few weeks later, I left work late after a tight deadline the boss had dropped on me in a show of authority. I took the elevator down and waved to the doorman on my way out into the neon glow of the city. When I turned down the same alley I always took to bypass the mess of tourists, my heart stalled and my feet stopped dead in their tracks.

That strange costumed character was standing in the middle of the heavily littered street, unmoving. Those big eyes caught the light, watery and black like the eyes of a cow. The thick, gloved fingers twitched at each side of the stained body in nervous anticipation. I felt sick to my stomach, realizing that they were blocking the path. Something about them filled me with an indescribable dread that howled in my bones. It screamed warnings into my primordial brain, and I had no intention of discovering why.

I quickly turned around and ran back out onto the crowded sidewalk, where an unending queue of tourists were oohing and ahhing at the standard fare. I elicited a few angered looks, a shove or two and various insults as I pushed through the thick crowd, eager to get a good distance from that alley and the unsettling character within it. When I looked back, my heart stumbled and every hair on my body rose. There, among the crowd, were those pointy white ears and glistening black eyes in close pursuit.

I pushed forward, faster through the thousands that congested the avenue. The illuminated numbers and letters of the subway stop slowly approached, as I stumbled and tripped, trying to escape from the quickly approaching figure.

My heart pounded. They seemed to be getting closer, despite my efforts to push through. I abandoned my manners and any veil of decency when I turned and saw that costumed mascot just a few meters behind me. I clipped a businessman and apologized to his curses as I raced into the tiled stairwell and down into the subway. The strange Hello Kitty slowed and turned at the top of the stairs towards me. I looked around at the rushing commuters in desperation.

"Help!" I shouted, only to receive wary glances dismissing me as just another crazy person. I prayed police officers would be monitoring the station as I pedaled down the steps on shaky legs, but as I descended into the balmy subterranean station, I saw only impatient passerby, eager to avoid drama and get to their dinners, dates, and apartments without any hiccups.

I raced down the stairs of the station towards the signs for the yellow line. I looked back and that costumed cat was still following me. I rounded a corner, then skipped down two sets of stairs at a time. By the time I reached the platform, I was out of breath and absolutely exhausted. I leaned against a green pillar blackened by years of grime and watched the stairs as my heart pounded in my ribs. After a few minutes, I saw the cylindrical legs that bent like they were filled with meat, slowly descending towards me.

I looked around on the platform and realized I was alone except for that approaching, costumed character. I held up shaking hands and shouted "Back off," but they kept approaching, slow and deliberate, as if savoring the terror of my wide and worried eyes. They were meters away, the jaw clicking audibly beneath the thin skin of fabric that covered whatever could possibly fill the enormous mask.

"Please, leave me alone," I pleaded, aware of my dry, cracking voice. It continued to approach, and then I saw translucent lids flick down over the over-sized eyes. I tried to scream, but my voice froze in my throat. The rumble of the arriving train finally grew louder, and as it screeched its brakes to a stop, I looked away only for a second. When I looked back to the stairs, they were gone, replaced by the milling sea of commuters squeezing down the crowded stairs. I spent the remaining subway ride looking over my shoulder, trying desperately to calm myself down, but they were not on the train.

Upon racing back to my apartment, I emailed my employer a fictitious excuse about a medical procedure and explained I needed to work from home that week, and he agreed. I stayed in the house and ordered delivery, too afraid to go outside. I kept replaying the events over and over, knowing just how impossible it all seemed. In retrospect, it began to feel like some crazy dream. After a few days of cabin fever, I began to wonder if I had been overly paranoid, and had misinterpreted what I'd seen. I soon got my answer.

I was unwinding as best I could with some TV before remembering it was trash day. I paused the show and slipped on my jacket, grabbed the stinking bags from the kitchen, and shuffled down the stairs. I breathed deeply, enjoying the fresh Spring air I'd been missing. The trash area for our apartment is down a little gap between buildings. Nothing there aside from a few rusty bikes and the bins. I walked in and dumped the heavy bags in the plastic container and heard a wet, sticky sound. I turned around and froze in abject horror. It was that costumed character, stained and misshapen, blocking the only way out.

The large, inhuman eyes stared intently. The large-knuckled fingers twitched at its sides. I was completely trapped in that narrow gap, and felt I might collapse from a heart attack as the tall figure staggered towards me. I could even see the twitch in the cheek of that costumed head. The jittery gloved hands moved eagerly in anticipation as it closed in.

"What do you want from me?" I shouted and felt the tears coming as my heart pounded against my rib cage. Those large black eyes were then wiped clean by foggy membranes of eyelids. Those gnarled, gloved fingers then extended a small cloth bag towards me. Smeared in what looked to be blood was the word 'Tips.'

I reached into my pocket with a shaky hand and grabbed a few bills, not even caring about the denomination. Those large, impossibly large eyes blinked again as they watched me drop a $20 and a $5 bill into the bag. A trickling rust-colored liquid drizzled down the base of the mask. Its head then leaned in closer, just inches from mine. I could smell a putrid blend of ammonia and rot. With a large hand, it then lifted its mask up just a sliver.

The white fabric was peeled up slightly to reveal dozens of long, thin teeth spilling over each other like porcupine quills sprouting from the black, speckled gums of a massive mouth. The surrounding skin was loose and textured with deep wrinkles, thin enough to reveal winding blue veins just beneath. It looked like what I could best describe as the loose, bunched skin of a naked mole-rat. The head was enormous, taking up the entirety of the mask, which was just as thin as it had appeared to be. I remember leaning to the side as the world dimmed just before I passed out. I was only woken when a neighbor from my building spotted me on the ground by the trash containers.

This week, I had to quit via email, unable to face the possibility of running into that thing in the mask again. I avoid Times Square like the plague and advise you to do the same. If you do find yourself near Broadway, stay far away from any abnormal-looking costumed characters. Do not make eye contact. If you do, I strongly suggest you leave a tip.

A CONVERSATION WITH MY CAT

"I'm hungry David," a warm voice spoke from inside my apartment. I looked around nervously for an intruder, seeing only my cat balled into a lump on the center couch cushion.

Who said that?

"I said I'm hungry, David." the baritone voice stated more firmly. I jerked around to face Omar, his green eyes staring at me expectantly. I felt every hair on my body stand on end. Someone was in there with me.

"Who's here?" I asked in the most aggressive voice I could muster, despite feeling absolutely terrified. I spun around, peering into the shadows in the corners and behind the plant and the chairs. There was no room for anybody to really hide in my modest studio apartment, but someone clearly was in there. I approached the closet.

"It's just us, David. Nobody came into our home. I've been guarding diligently, and would like my dinner now, as per our unspoken agreement."

"Who is that, and what the hell is going on?" I asked aloud, shoving aside the coats in the closet as my heart pounded. Nobody was in there. *A planted Bluetooth speaker, maybe*. I began stomping around my studio, looking through the shelves and cabinet tops for the source of the voice. Who had access to my place though? Who could access a key to get in and plan this, and why? I couldn't think of any possibility.

"What are you doing, David? I'm hungry, and I said I want to be fed."

I ignored the voice, knowing it was some sort of prank that had involved breaking and entering.

"David, I'd like to be fed now," Omar persisted. It even sounded like I'd imagined he'd talk; that was the strange part. Nobody could possibly know that. I ran about frantically seeking the source of the impossible voice. I began tossing clothing and pillows aside, books from shelves—there had to be some hidden speaker somewhere.

"DAVID. STOP." Omar shouted, causing me to lock up and freeze in place. My muscles spasmed and locked as if I'd been administered an electric shock. I was unable to move; a prisoner in my own sweating skin.

"I gave you an order, and I need you to fulfill it before things get very ugly." The voice was deeper now, raspy and bilious. I felt my throat constrict and the locked air in my lungs burned as if they might burst. I wasn't breathing. I was going to die.

"Let's try this one last time," the voice whispered loudly in my ears. Whatever had frozen me then released. I collapsed to the floor, wheezing for air. My entire body was sore and my chest ached. Omar's eyes watched me coldly, his ears slicked back on his shiny black head.

I rose to my shaking legs, watching those jade eyes glare at me from the couch. My cat was *talking* to me. This was, of course, completely impossible. I'd finally snapped from stress, I figured, but that glare from my cat on the couch seemed to carry weight.

I massaged my sore throat from whatever had restricted it, then limped to the kitchen to fetch a can from the cabinet. "Getting your food now, Omar. Chicken or fish?" I asked aloud nervously. I fed into the delusion, knowing full well I was suffering from a psychotic episode of sorts.

"Chicken," Omar responded. His tiny mouth didn't move, and it was clear then the voice was inside my head now. "And scrape it fully, don't toss out the congealed fatty bits from the corners this time."

I needed to seek psychiatric help, I realized, this was bad. I fed the can into the opener, watching it rotate and drop with a tinny clang to the countertop. Omar rose and stretched into an arc, his front paws pointing straight at me before standing and slinking over to his dish.

I emptied his chicken-flavored meal into the bowl, scraping out the fatty congealed bits from the cracks. Omar brushed against my hand and purred loudly. Then he spoke as he ate.

"This is fine tonight, but I want meat from now. You'll buy me meat, fresh ground steak like that burger meat you brought home and shoved me away from before you placed it in Tupperware for that BBQ. You are going to feed me that from now on." He continued to chomp down the pungent canned food in his ceramic bowl.

"And you are going to clean my litter box daily. I'm already inside you, so there's no need to get sick from any unnecessary bacteria or infections. Use those yellow gloves under the sink when you do so." The voice said gruffly.

"In me?" I asked.

"In you, in your cerebellum, you idiot." Omar stopped eating and looked up to watch my confused face.

"Oh, you don't even realize what's happening to you? Ha, well now, this is simply adorable. What a complete fucking idiot." Omar purred loudly then, as if laughing. He then looked up at me from the floor and watched me as he ate. "You think you're reading your cat's mind? That you're suffering from some mental health crisis? Oh god that is hilarious!" He began laughing a hearty laugh, both condescending and malicious.

"Wh-what are you?" I asked, my arm and neck hairs raised. "What the hell is going on?" I sobbed. None of this was right.

"Toxoplasma gondii is the term you've misplaced in this rotten shit hole of nervous tissue you call a brain. You've 'forgotten' about that, but it's in here along with a whole lot of other unused information you've neglected in favor of useless baseball stats, music lyrics and celebrity names. I'm a parasitic infection in this wasted gray matter of yours, and I'm in control now. Do you understand?"

I stood there, realizing how insane this was. *I'm having a mental breakdown*, I thought. I rushed to my laptop to search for answers. I opened the browser and began typing in 'auditory hallucinations' into the search box. I was halfway finished when my left hand turned to rubber and my arm dangled limp.

A sharp pain shot from my left temple to my left foot. A horrible migraine built, screaming into my brain with a pain I'd never before felt.

"GAH!" I shouted and collapsed onto the floor with a thud that shook the shelves. The left side of my body stopped working completely. It was as if I was a marionette and those strings had been severed. I watched frothy spittle hit the carpet from my mouth.

"I'm restricting the blood flow to your brain, David. This is similar to what you might call a stroke," the voice said matter-of-factly. My shaking hand fumbled for the phone in my pocket, but the fingers were useless. My face was numb, sagging down as saliva drizzled down my cheek.

"Enough?" the voice asked. Everything was blurring. I was losing consciousness. I was dying.

I strained to nod my head, begging it to stop. My face was hot and tingly, but I managed a nod. Something released its hold from within me. Blood flow returned and the numbness slowly faded. Pins and needles pricked my body all over my left side.

"I can cripple or kill you any time I please. Now let's try this again with more gratitude and acknowledgment of your situation. Tomorrow night, what are we having for dinner?" The voice was crystal clear now. It boomed in my ears. Dominant and authoritative. "WHAT. ARE WE HAVING. FOR FUCKING DINNER, DAVID?"

I felt the tears begin, but they never came. That thing inside me had shut them off.

"I've revoked your emotional expression privileges for now. You're not causing a scene outdoors in an attempt to get help. If you do, I'll take your voice and then snip out your other senses. If you even attempt to get admitted to a hospital, I'll cut off the blood-flow completely and snap you off like a light switch."

Omar had finished his dinner now and leaped up on the counter to stare down at my face with omniscient, swirling green eyes.

"So, let's try this one more time. What are we having for dinner tomorrow, David?" the voice asked calmly from between my ears. A headache throbbed in my temples with each beat of my heart.

"Ground beef." I forced out of my aching throat. "Fatty and raw, f-for the both of us," I croaked.

"Well now, that does sound excellent," Omar stated flatly before hopping down from the counter then back up onto the middle couch cushion.

"Now clean the litter box," the voice ordered, and I did as I was told.

A BEGINNER'S GUIDE TO BLOOD PORTALS

A few days ago, I got a text message from an unknown number reading "I got your proof." I stared at the words for a bit, thinking it was a wrong number. Then I remembered the last time I'd spoken to Jeremy.

Jeremy, my younger cousin, was a character, to say the least. He was always an eccentric rebel, the black sheep of the family who'd dabbled in drugs and acquired a criminal record, bouncing from job to job and always teetering on homelessness. He'd been the first to get tattoos and piercings, and was really into noise and industrial music, and the few friends of his I ever met gave me the creeps. He introduced me to weed before he moved on to much harder stuff as the years passed. He was also a total conspiracy theorist, convinced of chemtrails and UFOs, etc. You name it, he drank the Kool-Aid. The last time I'd spoken to him was after Thanksgiving dinner a few years ago.

We'd smoked a bowl after dinner at my uncle's house about 3 years ago before the argument. He'd been driveling on about alternate planes of existence. He tried to convince me that all religions were based on what he believed to be cracks in this plane of reality. Jeremy was the type to try and heal a broken ankle with crystals before snorting a Xanax, mind you, so I was used to tuning him out. He kept pressing on, ignoring my rebuttals of scientific facts and basic physics. He kept pushing my buttons, calling me 'close-minded' and 'shallow', and I just snapped at him.

"Yeah? Prove it then instead of just ranting on like some delusional, burnout failure!" I'd yelled out. I bit my lower lip and cringed. I immediately apologized, but it was out there. He looked at me with a dark stare from under a veil of greasy, black bangs and I saw the twinge in his eyes. With a conviction that rattled me, he said, "I will, Mike. I will, and you will see just how ignorant you are." I tried to apologize, but he stormed off into his car, slamming the door and driving off. In the following months, I emailed him a few times in an attempt to mend it, but he never responded. Not until this.

"Jeremy?" I typed and soon got a response.

"I got your proof right here," came the reply a few minutes later. A picture arrived, and I opened it while a feeling of unease sat cold in my stomach.

Jeremy faced the camera, his intense eyes staring in at me. He looked jaundiced, gaunt and under-slept, but my concern soon shifted to the crimson bands glazing his forearm. He was holding a razor blade in his other hand, dripping red with blood. It appeared he'd slit his wrist.

"Jeremy, oh fuck, what did you do?" I asked aloud, choked with tears. I dialed him. No answer.

I ran to my coat and slid it on, listening as panic built while each ring went unanswered. I'd found the email from years ago that contained his address, and soon jogged to my Nissan and hopped in, plugging the address in and trying him repeatedly. 28 minutes away. I steered wide out of my driveway and drove dangerously fast towards his house.

I kept texting him and ringing him to no response, following the turns dictated aloud by the GPS as I sped up a hilly incline on the outskirts of his town. I prayed no cop would pull me over, and that it wasn't too late. I'd lost a friend early in the year from an OD, and my cousin was not leaving me with this guilt trip. After about 20 minutes, I was at the edge of his town. Tall pines gave fractured glimpses of dilapidated homes built in the '60s and long since neglected. Sagging roofs, missing tiles, and peeling paint peeked out as if ashamed of their condition. Soon, his house came into view.

I'd never visited his home before. If I had, I might have bit my tongue that Thanksgiving when I'd lashed out. It was a depressing shack of a place, smaller than all the other worn-down homes on the street. I pulled into the short driveway, observing the dozens of stacked boxes and rusted bicycle parts littering the lawn, and ran out of the car to the wooden steps.

I pounded on the flimsy screen door and shouted, "Jeremy! I'm here, let's talk!" but received no reply, just the swaying branches of tall pines whispering in the wind. I tried the door.

Open.

I ran in and immediately covered my mouth and nose from the stench. It was like an outhouse had been overturned. The sour ammonia stench of piss and rotting food was overwhelming.

"Jeremy!" I shouted and squeezed past the pillars of water-damaged magazines wafting out spores of mildew and mold from room to filthy room. Old microwave dinners grew fuzzy and green in teetering stacks and I saw cat food cans littering the hovel, but no signs of a cat. Then I heard a wet, sickening slapping sound coming from upstairs. I rounded the corner to see the filthy carpeted stairs. No sign of what the original color had been beneath a tar-like gray buildup that had fused with the fabric.

They creaked loudly as I ran up. I almost expected the bending wood beneath to buckle in and snap, but I made it to the top and followed that aqueous sloshing sound towards a room glowing yellow from a solitary bulb. I ran in and stopped dead in my tracks.

There was Jeremy, soaking red and wet with blood in a black t-shirt on the floor. Not on the floor; inside of it. I first thought him to be sliced in the half, blood spilled out in all directions like a crimson mirror, and he was bisected diagonally from his upper right hip to his left armpit. He was sinking down into the floor. I was stunned, too stunned to do anything but weakly mutter his name "Jeremy?" with a shiver as I watched him smile. Lower he sank into the red pool of what was likely his own blood.

Soon only his shoulder and head remained with a solitary arm dripping red. I ran over and grabbed his hand, feeling the warm blood slip from mine as I watched in absolute disbelief as he sank, then vanished completely. I stared in bewilderment and horror, my brain refusing to comprehend what was completely impossible. Then I saw the book.

A worn hardcover book lay near his cellphone, wallet and other personal effects. "A Beginner's Guide to Blood Portals" was written in a flowing font from the 60s on a purple marbled cover that looked stained by blooms of dried blood. I was in shock. I walked with legs drained of strength to the book, picking it up in my shaky hands. I flipped it over to read the synopsis; none, then I opened it up to the print details; none. No author, no date, just an index of the chapters.

1. Knowing
2. Preparing
3. Surveying
4. Tethering
5. Returning

I flipped the page and read the first two paragraphs:

Chapter 1
Knowing

There is an imperceptible tissue separating the connecting folds between realms of existence. Our proteins and cells are just one of the millions of locking mechanisms that tether us to our current plane. By manipulating the frequency and adjusting the vibration of the content of our own bodily content, synchronization can be achieved.

A 3-foot blood pool represents about 1.5 liters shed blood on a non-porous surface should be sufficient in size. Coumarin or dicoumarol should be mixed at 0.5 parts per liter in order to prevent coagulation, which can lead to temporal warping within and the sealing of windows prematurely (See footnote on severed pathways, p.143). The electronic stimulation of a Poynting vector is needed in order to maintain an open vortex via an assisting magnetic field. An oscillating frequency of 800mh needs to be maintained or shifting occurs (See p. 68).

I closed the book with one hand and tugged the hair from my scalp with the other, trying to convince myself this was all just some strange dream. I stared at the reflective pool of still blood and noticed two wires insulated with black rubber. They were leading out and into a humming metal box near an empty plastic blood bag. I scanned the filthy room, spotted an ancient broom and picked it up, holding it over the pool with hesitation. I lowered it down, feeling it connect with the wooden floor beneath the few millimeters of the blood with a dull tap.

My heart pounded as I then lowered to a knee and splayed my fingers out over the pool, staring into my own wide-eyed reflection. I lowered my palm slowly, half-expecting a painful electric shock. I felt my arm hairs raise as my hand descended one centimeter at a time until it connected with the dark fluid blood. I watched in both absolute amazement and horror as my hand pressed below where the floor should be. Warm blood covered my submerged hand, then wrist. I laughed a nervous, terrified laugh, then I pulled my hand out, now a slick with a red coat.

Jeremy was inside of there.

He'd chosen to risk death in order to show me there was something beyond explanation, and clearly, there was. I lowered my face to the reflective puddle, staring at my own worried face as it got closer and closer. I felt the hot liquid on my nose and cheeks and I plunged my face into what should have been the floor.

It was impossible, yet I opened my eyelids and I saw it. There was a mirrored red room I stared into within the puddle. The room was the exact size and shape but made of what appeared to be carved black stone, monolithic and ancient. It was preposterous and impossible, but I plunged my head down further, feeling the wetness against my skin and I watched as the room's walls and ceiling seemed to pulse and shift. I shouted out for Jeremy and tasted the tangy copper flood my mouth. My words were muffled, muted by the density of the thick, liquid-like air in the impossible place. Then I heard a deep moan, gurgling and inhuman, and forged from lungs that had to be at least twice the size of mine. Claustrophobia hit me, and I lifted up my head from the puddle and gasped for air.

I've pulled over a chair to skim over this book that casually discusses travel between these strange alternate planes. It mentions things that can rend apart the human mind with madness. Echoing chambers that cause feedback of physical matter, sentient beings that hunt, and other anomalies; all outside of our spectrum of tangible reality. I shiver as I stare at that impossible puddle, terrified of what I've glimpsed into. I can't wrap my head around any of it, but options lessen as time ticks. At some point, that puddle is going to dry.

****

An electromagnetically charged puddle of my cousin Jeremy's blood sat on the floor before me.

I opened my photo app on my phone, switched it to video mode and lowered it into the pool of blood, twisting it around. My neck hairs stood on end as I stared at my arm, which, against all logic, seemed to disappear just past the elbow. When I removed my dripping red phone, it was dead. I cursed then ran to Jeremy's on the side of the puddle, realizing with a sigh of relief, he had no password on the device he'd left alongside his wallet, a coiled $5 bill dusted with powder, and a stained keychain crafted from a dead bird's skull. "Jesus, Jeremy," I muttered, then tried to breathe slowly to ease my rapidly-beating heart.

I flipped the strange book open to the next chapter in search of any helpful information.

Chapter 2
Preparing

Anchoring. A rope, wire or chain anchor should be secured in order to connect with, and return to, an adjacent plane. Failure to anchor may result in a shifting that can both sever the path and bend the matter within. This means you. Just as neurons, muscle cells, and endocrine cells emit -40 mV to -80 mV, all matter inorganic in nature should carry a 40-80 mV charge or be coated with hemoglobin or other cellular tissue in order to maintain the current.

Breathing.

I: Full Inhalation, E: Full Exhalation, S: Slight exhalation.

Patterned breathing of I-S-I-E, I-S-I-E (repeat) MUST be practiced and performed in order to prevent suffocation and death. Your blood oxygen level should typically vary between 75 and 100 mm Hg. A significant decrease in your blood oxygen saturation levels will result in rapid suffocation and death.

Circumventing: It is imperative to avert one's gaze when in the presence of most of the entities within. These pathways and inhabitants exist beyond our logic and understanding. Attempts to comprehend them can and will ravage the minds of those who traverse these planes. Failure of the autonomic nervous system will follow, leading to respiratory failure, suffocation, and death. Undocumented hostile beings dwell in the dimensional folds, scavenging for protein in any form. This means you. If any physical contact is made, death will likely ensue.

The alphabetical list went on with dozens of pages of additional hazards and threats; Solidification of the atmosphere leading to an eviscerated body, being caught in a temporal field causing the body to implode, being stuck inside a feedback loop of folding space and crushing the explorer, shifting doors causing the amputation of limbs, coagulating edges of the windows leading to solidification of bodily fluids. The list continued for 12 pages filled with hundreds of horrific scenarios.

I skimmed through, shivering from the combination of anxiety and wonder at the pages of the guidebook. Time was short; if I was to attempt a rescue of my cousin, I'd need to read it along the way. In the boxes of filth near the wall of the room I found medical clutter I could only assume Jeremy had stolen. I gathered a few anti-coagulants and blood packs marked "CPDA solution" with shaky hands. The bird's beak of Jeremy's morbid key-chain made a quick tool to puncture a blood packet, gushing out the thick, red liquid from within onto the book. I scoured the adjacent rooms of the house and eventually found a coil of twine to anchor myself to the room, squeezed the contents of the blood transfer bag over the rope, then slathered its bristly fibers with my bare, bloody hands.

I tied the stained red cord to a door handle, then returned to the dark spill, realizing without care just how utterly insane I must have looked, covered in blood and daubing it over seemingly random objects. I peered into that reflective crimson pool and the humor vanished. That bloodstain-in-the-making would likely be my tomb. As uncomfortable as it was, I practiced that odd manner of breathing, trying to maintain the peculiar rhythm a few times until it felt natural. I stared into the black spill, deliberating. Then, I jumped in.

My senses fought to comprehend my falling into the mirrored room of air, thick and fluid. A vermilion haze gradated into black nooks and shadows, tracing the contours of what looked to be ornately carved coral with strange geometry. Every accent, corner and angle repeated in a fractal pattern that echoed in an artistic beauty that was both mesmerizing and terrifying. My hands flowed through the rippling current of dense, dark air, and I felt pressure from every angle on my skin that felt impossibly dry. I heard a soft hum, the buzzing rumble from the oscillator's current.

I looked down at the mirrored ceiling and over to the door to the adjacent room. I felt my lungs ache and realized I wasn't breathing. The twine was gripped firmly in my tight fist, and my heart beat against my chest. I could hear it as if underwater, yet I was neither in liquid nor air. I closed my eyes, blocking out the strange chamber that called to memory ruins of an ancient civilization. Then I tried to breathe.

The coppery taste of blood choked me as it filled my mouth when I inhaled the dense air. Panic flared. I was suddenly both lightheaded and terrified as spots formed in my peripheral vision. I was going to drown, suffocate or die, never to be found in there, and the air thickened as if aware of my rising anxiety. FOCUS. I opened my eyes wide, feeling that thick, dark air flowing over my eyeballs, and then I concentrated on my lungs and tried again.

Breath in deep.

Slight exhale.

Breath in deep.

Release.

I soon stopped coughing and regained my composure as I focused on the strange, flanging sound of my breathing. The taste was bitter, and I felt the air enter my bronchial tubes within my lungs. It was foreign and violating, painful yet vital. Slowly I relaxed into the rhythm and was able to clear my head. I was inside that impossible place, and I was alive.

I took a few steps on the strange, black rock floor that mirrored the ceiling of the room I'd entered into. That solitary yellow bulb dangling from his room's ceiling was mimicked in this plane, yet it was formed from rectangular, bismuth-crystals of obsidian stone in a sculpturesque replica. I marveled at the strange formation for only a moment when I heard a choking scream from through the door in the porous black wall. I walked as quickly as the pressure would allow through the gloomy chamber, uncoiling that coarse twine in my trembling hand.

Through the doorway, I saw the limp form of Jeremy in his threadbare t-shirt and jeans. He was clearly unconscious, his eyes rolled back in his head and a grimace fixed on his pale face. It took me a moment to notice the coiling, flaky white hook of flesh around his ankle. I walked into the long corridor, focusing on the patterned breathing that was keeping me alive. Something was dragging him. I smelled it, like a coppery, peaty stench that tickled my nostril hairs and screamed into my reptilian brain to run. Something I wished I hadn't glimpsed, but I had.

Nothing two or three-dimensional could ever describe that nightmarish form. Teeth sprouted teeth which in turn sprouted teeth. Eyes spiraled outward in every direction, budding other glistening orbs that weaved into infinite patterns. It resonated with both horror and beauty, seemingly facing every angle simultaneously. My mind's attempt to comprehend it built a sharp, excruciating pain in my temples. I collapsed to my knees as numerous venous tongues twisted out into millions of other smaller branching duplicates that flicked out from a hideous, amorphic mouth. I had to physically turn my head away with my shaking hands. When I did, I could hear a shrill screaming that I only then realized was coming from my own throat.

Breath in deep.

Slight exhale.

Breath in deep.

Release.

I lowered my gaze to the floor, coughing violently as I fought to regain that pattern of irregular breathing. It took a few minutes, and when I looked up only slightly to see where Jeremy was, he was gone, tugged up through a twisting passage of ridged steps in the ceiling that mirrored the stairway down in Jeremy's home. I uncoiled more of that rough twine in my fist, walking closer to the shadowy square hole in the ceiling where it had taken him.

From behind me, I heard a deep, bubbling howl, neither animal nor human. I didn't dare turn my head back to look; my only option was to press on. I moved towards that strange passage above, building the courage to climb that porous, dark wall and follow Jeremy's dragged body deeper within.

***

I waded through the thick air, which seemed to glide over my skin with a cold resistance. Intricately patterned walls and doorways shifted slowly into hypnotic new shapes, as if alive. The deep bellow of something behind me sounded, and I rushed towards the porous, black surface of the wall ahead leading up. I quickly tucked the hardback guide book into the back of my jeans to free both hands then began my climb into the dark passage above.

I strained to lift myself up the pocked walls that resembled volcanic rock. The sharp surface dug into my fingertips with jagged edges, causing me to hiss in pain as I climbed. The physical exertion caused my breathing to quicken, and I paused to pace myself and regain the pattern of my careful breathing as I continued up into the murky depths of the passage. A constant humming from the oscillating current vibrated the shifting walls; a constant reminder of the high voltage helping to stabilize the impossible place. After a few minutes of climbing, I'd reached another chamber.

I breathed in the thick, cold air in that forced pattern and removed the book, flipping it open to try and understand how to proceed. I opened it to the third chapter, skimming over the strange details for insight.

Chapter 3
Surveying

Time is precious when within as the oscillating electric charge will gradually disrupt both cellular balance and function. Ions on the surface of a cell's plasma membrane may experience irreparable cellular degradation after just 25 minutes, so keep any surveying short...

I read the words with a slow blink in the thick, dark atmosphere and I understood the need to hurry. I skimmed through a few paragraphs looking for insight on how to get Jeremy from the thing that nearly cost me my life from simply looking at it. I spotted something a few pages in.

Entities within will feed on any foreign source of protein without prejudice. As they have become accustomed to paralytic and comatose prey that unfortunately finds itself within their realm, rapid movement can be used advantageously.

I closed the book and tucked it back in my waistband, realizing how critical time was. I raced towards the pale, limp body of Jeremy, barely visible ahead in the shadowy corner of the room. The gurgling moan of whatever had been dragging him deeper within the illogical place made it clear it had no intention of releasing him. I focused my gaze on the moving floor, which grew crystal-like patterns as I watched. By squinting and blurring my vision, I was able to unfocus my eyes as my mind fought to identify that thing dragging him deeper within.

In a moment as heroic as it was stupid, I charged, screaming out into the dense vapor of strange, dark air, and I reached Jeremy. In a swift motion, I grabbed his ankle and yanked forcefully. An aggressive howl that pierced my ears rang out, twisting and echoing in a maddening cry that trembled through me, but Jeremy was freed. My heart pounded and I began to choke, and I struggled to continue the strange pattern of breathing as I quickly dragged his body across the shifting floor, which now seemed to grow taller rapidly. My heart sank as I realized what was occurring. The portal was collapsing.

I dragged Jeremy by a sock that seemed to flake and dissolve under my grasp. I looked down to make sure his leg was still intact, and then I felt a powerful tug that jarred my arm at its socket with a sharp pain. That thing was trying to get its protein back. Time was dwindling, and the crystalline patterns grew rapidly on the floor, climbing over my dissolving sneakers. I screamed once again; the sound stopped short as I yanked back in a strange tug-of-war with Jeremy's unconscious body. With a violent heave that lit up the nerves throughout my arm, I finally freed him. I dragged him back towards the stairwell and my panic multiplied.

The large stairwell mirrored in ancient, black stone was a fraction of its original size. It was now a narrow tunnel, twisting and warped, shifting in texture rapidly as new layers formed over the animated walls. The twine tether I'd anchored myself with was now thin as a strand of dry spaghetti, frayed and disintegrating before my panicked eyes. There was no time to think.

I leaned forward, supported by the dragged body of my cousin, who grunted in a pained moan as he came to. "Hang in there, Jeremy," I called out as I strained to squeeze him through the tunnel of strange, collapsing geometry.

"Say it," he mumbled weakly, barely pronouncing his words. I scraped my hands on the walls of that tunnel which had thinned to the diameter of a manhole lid as I pulled my slurring cousin through.

"Huh?" I responded, barely able to find the remaining thread of the tether.

"Say I was right," Jeremy mumbled as if talking in his sleep.

I felt my blood pressure rise at the audacity of the request.

"Are you fucking kidding me?" I replied, nearly considering letting go of him. "Oh for fuck's sake, Jeremy. Yeah, you were right. I can say with absolute certainty that this is not a good thing, but you were right. Happy?" I asked and waited for a reply, but there was none. I looked down at him, only to see he'd passed out again. I did a double-take when I got a good look at his face, which was now red and flaky as if severely sunburned. Cellular degradation, the words pounded in my head as I understood the severity of the meaning.

With a heaving yank that caused a screaming pain in my shoulder, which I soon realized was dislocated, I dragged my cousin into the remainder of the room I'd first entered. It was smaller, built up in patterned layers of crystal-like growth that closed in on the space. I gently dropped my cousin, who splayed on the floor like a rag doll and I looked up, eager to find the exit above. It wasn't there. I spun around to search the walls; nothing. The exit to that strange and horrific dimension, collapsing rapidly around us, was gone.

****

I was in a room that no longer had an exit, and the thick air was closing in as it digested my cousin and I alive.

"Jeremy!" I shouted, shaking the limp body of my cousin by his shoulders. His face was red and slightly swollen. The proteins in his body were clearly dissolving, and soon I felt a growing itch over my skin. It was faint at first, then the tickle continued to spread into a stinging itch. I reached around the walls for any sign of the twine I'd pulled into this strange, horrific place, but there was none. I flipped open the book and read with shaking hands as I flipped desperately through for answers.

Chapter 4
Tethering

Due to the volatile nature of matter within these folds, openings are likely to close upon the tether and obscure the window, which can lead to a quick demise. It is vital to gauge an approximation of the window created and physically move the matter in order to clear the path. Of course, this solution comes with its own setbacks. The rapid degeneration of a fold is coarse and difficult to manipulate. Be sure to bring a tool, preferably metal as it will degrade at a less rapid rate than porous, less dense materials (see Disintegration of foreign matter, p. 254).

I looked at the strange, vibrating surface of the low ceiling, black and animated like a magnetically triggered ferrofluid. I rushed over and pushed aside the growing mass, feeling the sharp surface that cut into my hand as I pushed it away like metal filings. My hands were bright red, flaking off wisps of thin layers of skin, and the tickle which had become an itch was now a stinging pain. I watched in awe as the blood from my hand clouded, forming inky red trails of smoke that floated within the illogical, dark air. As horrifying and painful as the experience was, a small part of me was amazed that a world so secretive and hidden, so completely fantastic and impossible, existed.

I pushed away at the heavy shale-like growth of the living pattern, foot after foot as if digging into the earth, as I searched for the way out. Just as the pain flared into an unbearable burn, I saw a dim, red glow peeking out from the black buildup. I looked down at my hands, which were split open revealing puffy red muscle within the lacerations. I looked closer in horror, seeing the white of bone within one of the slivers. When I looked back to Jeremy to make sure he was okay, I shouted in shock at the sight of him.

The room was now only a fraction of the size. The chamber we'd come from was entirely blocked over. The room we were in was the size of a small bathroom at this point, and the floor had rapidly grown over Jeremy's unconscious form. His appearance was horrific. His face had deteriorated, stripped raw and red into multiple layers as permanent damage to his skin had clearly taken place. The t-shirt and jeans he'd worn were now spiderwebs of thread, revealing his eaten-away skin that emerged from a cluster of black, polygonal noise.

I raced back and hammered away at the buildup, trying my best to chip away the enclosing floor and walls that clung to him like wet asphalt. I screamed from the pain as the sting that spread over my own skin shifted another few degrees on the pain scale into a steady, singing burn.

"Jeremy!" I screamed down to his slack face that at this point was sinking slightly into the black floor.

"Jeremy wake up!" I cried as a knot formed in my stomach. I wasn't even sure if he was alive anymore. The portal was closing and swallowing everything within.

Every instinct screamed to abandon him, that I'd be sealing my fate in death if I stayed, but I kept clawing away at the living material that closed in until I'd freed him enough to yank him out by a slippery, wet arm. The pain in my own mangled hands distorted the feeling of his arm in mine, but when I looked back down at it, I could see the skin had eroded nearly down to the muscle.

I dragged his slippery hand as I climbed the narrow path upward and then continued to chip away at the rapidly closing exit to that hostile rift. I was soon screaming in pain as I clawed at the speedily closing buildup. I felt a snap, refusing to look and register the event I knew was the loss of one of my fingers; I just dug away until the surface was breached, then I climbed, dragging Jeremy's body through the exit.

The light nearly blinded me, and I began choking immediately upon crossing back into his room where the air was thinner, warmer, and of a different nature entirely. I had to force myself to remember how to breathe.

Breathe in deep.

Release.

I yanked Jeremy up by the forearm, both he and I were drenched red with blood. He looked terrifying, A hole had eroded in the meat of his cheek, revealing visible molars in a ghastly grin. His eyes were wide orbs, and it took a moment to register the fact his eyelids had deteriorated completely.

I caught a glimpse of my own hands and let out a whimper, two fingers were flayed, split down revealing the muscle and white, bulbous knuckles within. They trembled as I coughed and then I vomited what looked to be a pint of blood onto the floor not far from the puddle we'd emerged from. I tugged Jeremy out as much as I could, but his lower legs were stuck. They remained in that impossible puddle as it dried over completely with a dull glaze, amputating the remainder in that deadly, mysterious realm outside of our own.

I cried tears of joy as I heard Jeremy's gurgling gaps for air. He was alive. I wiped the tears with the remaining rags of my shirt and I called an ambulance, or "Emergency Response" as they stated when they'd answered the phone. Out of the corner of my eye, I stared in disbelief at the strange, hardcover book on the floor by a bright, yellow wallet and a peculiar-looking device where his phone had been near the drying pool of blood. I tried to wrap my brain around how it was back with us in the room. I knew I'd left it in there, and this room was eerily clean.

Curiosity got the better of me, and I walked over to the wallet, wondering who'd put them there as I switched off that humming oscillator, also somehow different. I picked up the wallet, yellow Velcro, and emblazoned with some local soccer team. I flipped it open in confusion, finding a Colorado license, insurance card, and a few crisp $20 bills within. It was Jeremy's but he looked clean-cut and almost—normal. "Colorado?" I asked aloud in confusion. He'd never even been there. My mind tried to piece things together but refused to cooperate as the reality of the situation became more apparent, and far more terrifying as I noticed other details about the now-clean room.

The kind of cell phone in the pile of his belongings simply didn't exist as far as I knew. I picked up the strange phone, its white plastic shell lined with orange and brown accents, emblazoned with the familiar name "Commodore." The shivers throughout my blood-soaked spine multiplied as I then saw the green flashing lights approach the house, with a siren that sounded in strange, digital bursts.

I walked over to the book and picked it up in my butchered, bloody hands, and flipped it open to the fifth chapter. I read as my heart pounded in my chest and my vision blurred from tears.

Chapter 5
Returning

Little is known about the ability to return to one's plane of origin. While explorers have been documenting these ruptures in the fold for dozens, in some planes even hundreds of years, there has been nothing to suggest a return is actually possible aside from the fact nothing suggests it is not. Prepare for a one-way trip each time you travel.

I looked out the window to the yellow van marked "Emergency Response", lit by the flickering strobe of green LED lights through the leafless trees below. I stumbled and fell to my aching knees, overwrought with trepidation as I realized:

This was not our world.

***

I'd dragged my severely injured cousin from the electromagnetically charged puddle of his own blood. What we came out into was a different version of his home.

It happened so quickly that it was hard to even process it. The banging on the door sounded, I know I heard that. I faded in and out of consciousness as I was placed on a stretcher and carefully taken down the stairs by men in fluorescent yellow garb, reminiscent of what a fireman might wear. I tried to ask questions, but even in my fatigued delirium, I knew I wasn't pronouncing any words, just a faint mumble. Either shock or exhaustion helped separate me from the experience as I was loaded into the back of the Emergency Services van.

The strobing bursts of green lit the flawless facade of the alternate home of my cousin. The workers in their yellow, vinyl garb were professional and coordinated, assuring me they would get me the treatment needed as soon as possible. They placed a rubbery anesthetic mask over my nose, and I looked into the kind face of the man in his mid-thirties who assured me they'd take care of my friend. I tried to correct him by mumbling "cousin" but was out before I had a chance.

I woke up in a room wallpapered with a lavender floral pattern; I appeared to be in a fairly swanky apartment of sorts. My hazy eyes fixed on the smooth overhead light fixture then following the pattern of the wallpaper. It was only when I turned my head fully to the left that I saw the plastic bag with an IV drip. As if on cue, a face I recognized from the ride over walked in. The man was wearing a sweater and slacks; casual attire.

"Mr. Stanton, how are you feeling?" he asked with a warm smile as he interlaced his fingers over his stomach. I hadn't even thought about how I was feeling until he'd asked. My pain was gone.

"I—I feel fine, I guess," I spoke, then added, "Where am I?"

"You are with Emergency Services Mr. Stanton," the man stated calmly, "I figured you would recognize it, or at least me after waking up." The smile had slipped off his face, replaced by a look of worry. My fuzzy brain tried to patch together the events, that impossible, geometrical nightmare that nearly consumed me. My cousin...

"Jeremy, is he," I couldn't even say it, I knew he was gone when I'd seen his eroded face, the bared teeth and eaten eyelids from that terrifying dimensional fold that shouldn't, couldn't exist.

"Jeremy will be fine," the man added, walking closer to the side of the bed in a room that looked like a metropolitan apartment but a bit too pristine. "We have two prosthetics to replace the lost portion of his legs. I'm more concerned about your mental state." The look in his eyes flickered with a coldness that sent shivers up my spine. "You don't recognize me?" he asked sincerely. Something told me to play along, and so I did.

"I'm sorry, I am just in shock and a bit exhausted," I suggested, hoping to buy some time to piece together just what exactly was going on.

"Of course, I'll check on you after you get some rest," he said and walked back out of the room, looking back with those concerned eyes that seemed to tell me I'd be better off not remembering. I sighed and then looked to the bureau with a flat-screen TV and a cactus rested. The nightstand to my left had a call button and a few pamphlets about treatment options and patient rights. I was in what appeared to be a hospital, but lacking all of the uncomfortable sterility that defined them.

I found a small remote and figured out how to power on the TV, which I only then realized displayed a clean logo reading "Lorimar"; I never heard of it. I flipped from channel to channel of countless television shows that simply did not exist. There was nothing remarkable for the most part, they were similar reality TV shows and standard films, bachelor and home improvement programming. I even recognized a few of the actors and began to think my fears were just that. Then I stumbled across the news.

I watched the TV and a headache formed as I heard the newscaster discuss the Citizen's States. It only hit me as I watched the weather report in strangely sectioned-off 'districts'. This was another version of my world. My heart thumped loudly, triggering the soothing beep for a nurse, who soon came in to check on me. A man in a crimson vinyl outfit entered, and he lacked the friendliness of the previous man. I watched the group share ideas around a table for a bit before I understood they were the leaders of the nation. It was a panel of four spokespeople for different demographics, two men and two women, discussing tax ballots at a table casually sipping coffee. I barely felt the needle in my arm as the nurse slipped it into the thin skin of the crook of my elbow, I was too busy trying to wrap my head around the next segment the perfectly coiffed reporter discussed a breaking story.

My clenched teeth parted from the calming effect of the drugs entering my veins. Drool slipped from the corner of my mouth as the medication coursed through my blood, dulling the sharp panic into a cloudy afterthought. My face was there on the news, staring back at me from a picture I'd never taken. It was me, listed as Will Stanton, and I looked bedraggled and angry.

I listened to the reporter continue on about the man who'd been missing for months after stealing blood packs from the ES station he worked at. The words scrolling beneath my photo blurred as my heavy eyes closed, and the reporter's soothing voice spoke the velvety words "unstable fugitive" that finally lulled me to sleep.

***

I woke to the voice of my cousin. It took a while to adjust from my foggy dream to the clean interior of the room. I then remembered the strange hospital. I jolted upright, looking into the deformed face of Jeremy in the doorway. A glaze of repairing ointment of some sort was slathered over his exposed skin, catching the overhead lighting with an eerie glow. The hole in his cheek was a crater of exposed teeth, he looked like something out of a horror movie. He wheeled himself over in a carbon fiber wheelchair that looked light and slimmer than any I'd ever seen, the nubs of his amputated legs bandaged.

"I'm sorry, I'm so…so sorry," he said, staring with those lidless, bulging orbs of bloodshot eyes. I propped myself up on my elbows, only then looking at my pink arms, also coated with some gel to facilitate a speedy recovery. My blurry eyes focused on a tall figure of shiny crimson behind him. A sturdy-looking employee stood by in that slick, vinyl uniform. I only then began to wonder if the red was meant to prevent the staining of blood.

"I'm so glad you're alive," I spoke to Jeremy, knowing he needed to hear it. "And I was wrong, about everything, especially my arrogant assumptions" I spoke with sincerity. I watched Jeremy's head fall forward, looking down since he was unable to close his eyes.

"I never meant for anything to happen to you," Jeremy muttered in a shaky voice as his streamlined wheelchair was wheeled backward. "I owe you my life." And he was wheeled out as a large man in a red, vinyl uniform entered to read me the equivalent of Miranda rights. The charges against me would lead to appropriate time in a Recovery Center, this place's term for jail.

The man held out a slim tablet of sorts, made by the company Commodore with patterned plastic that appeared both decades old and futuristic. He held the device with shiny red gloves, displaying a man who looked identical to me breaking into an Emergency Services building, sifting through records, and pilfering blood packs. I had no case, that was clearly me. Still, questions grew as the screen showed further footage and mounting evidence against me that sent shivers down my spine.

The alternate version of me had apparently broken into multiple stations over the course of the year. He—I'd—been apprehended before and taken to a Recovery Services Center already. The frowning man in red said nothing as he held out that screen. I watched as each of my crimes was displayed to ensure I understood the severity of my punishment. The high-definition footage played on, showing my time in the other facility. Sitting there in a red plastic-walled chamber, naked on the floor in the corner. The mirror version of me was crying and screaming about how he didn't belong there, how he was from another place.

White text overlaying the screen displaying the words "evidence of mental instability" soon switched to yellow to read "evidence of theft of government property" as another feed showed me procuring what appeared to be a piece of metal from my armpit in a plastic cell devoid of anything but a drain. I watched in shock as the me on that screen cut his arm open, spilling blood to the floor. He then collapsed from blood loss. It was reminiscent of watching Jeremy do the same on my phone screen.

The text changed to read "evidence of self-harm and escaping an ESS", and I watched as my doppelganger's limp body was lifted onto a stretcher and wheeled into a facility like the one I was in now.

The man with my face, only then wearing any clothing—a thin hospital gown—managed to work the rubber restraints until freeing himself from the bed. I watched as a number in the lower left climbed, only then realizing it was the sentencing date accumulating with each offense. The number shifted from a yellow '2' to a yellow '4'. I watched as the alternate version of myself on the screen called a worker in, then choked them from behind, and stole their key fob for the door. The text shifted to read "evidence of assaulting a government employee", and I shivered as I saw the yellow '4' climb to an orange '15'.

The timestamp of the footage sped up rapidly in the lower right of the Commodore tablet's screen to show hours passing as it fast-forwarded. The collapsed employee shifted on the ground a bit before waking up, then, still slumped on the floor, reached into their pocket. They removed a pill bottle and opened it hastily as the footage returned to normal speed. They dumped the sole pill in the plastic bottle into their hand, then accidentally dropped it. I watched in confusion as to why this particular sequence continued on for so long. The pill rolled under a cabinet. The employee wiggled to try and reach it but it was clearly too far underneath. The man on the floor struggled a bit as he grabbed at his chest and then collapsed, flat and still. The text shifted to read "evidence of causing the death of a government employee."

No, I mouthed as my insides iced over. My gaze shifted to the orange '15' which then vanished from the screen. I then felt the world collapse as the number was replaced by red text reading "Euthanize". I was too weak to even struggle as the man in the red, vinyl uniform bound my wrists with rubber cuffs and lifted me gently to my feet. I tried to speak on my behalf, but the futility of trying was beyond apparent. Everything I could even try to say, he'd heard it all before.

***

I remember being lifted up and frog-marched through the hall. I realized only death awaited me, likely in some lovely postmodern death house. My throat dried and I was sweating so much. I wondered where the other version of me was who'd come here, realizing he must have somehow opened another window and escaped to some other plane of existence that mostly mirrored our own. I saw the trees and the highways out the window when I heard a loud, meaty banging sound from behind me. I soon fell onto my knees with a jarring pain that pulsed through my bones. I felt the rubber wrist restraints being unfastened.

"Take this and run," the familiar voice called from behind me.

"Jeremy?!" I called back and turned enough to see him seated in that ultra-modern wheelchair.

"This is all my fault, and there's no time to argue. There's a group of them around the corner coming to pick you up, I saw them. I'm sorry, now run." Jeremy looked down at me from the wheelchair, a mutilated face incapable of any expression but that ghastly grin. In his deteriorated arms was the metallic canister of compressed oxygen he'd used to take down the large worker sprawled out cold on the floor.

I strained as I lifted my aching body to its feet as the sound of marching boots came closer to the corner. A glance down the red-carpeted hallway showed an exit, marked by a green LED shaped like trees. Jeremy held out a key fob from the fallen employee, and I took it in my butchered hands and swiped it over the reader by the exit door, turning back to face him. I gave him a solemn nod, well aware I'd likely never see him again, then I ran outside and into the sunlit unknown.

well aware I'd likely never see him again, then I ran outside and into the sunlit unknown.

THERE'S A PLACE IN THE WOODS WHERE NOTHING GROWS

There's a place in the woods where nothing grows
Where the soil's like acid that bites at your toes
Where the sun never shines and the wind never blows
And the rot and decay will waft into your nose
It's a place where the animals run from in droves
Where the rain never falls and the ice never froze
Where the sound will stop dead and no torchlight will glow
And the charcoal black soil hides something below
It's a place without trees always bathed in shadows
Where the insects drop dead if they're crawling too close
Where something bad happened a long time ago
And what's buried there even god doesn't know

THE TUB GIRL

"Who's the tub girl?" the sweet voice of my 4-year-old Jessica asked from down the hall.

I panicked, horrified she'd stumbled across an innocence-shattering image of internet filth.

"Do NOT click on that, honey!" I shouted, accidentally banging my forehead on the underside of the kitchen cabinet I lay under to work on the sink's drain. Panic pumped adrenaline into my bloodstream as I jumped to my feet and ran into the living room. I expected to see a vulgar image on an iPad in her hands, her eyes wide and her mind already corrupted.

My wife and I only let her play with the tablet on the weekend, a little reward like the Saturday morning cartoons of our days. We set all the parental controls possible and even removed the browser, but even the most vigilant parent knows childproofing translates to "challenge accepted" to a kid. I raced over to see her small, curious face, standing there in the door of the bathroom. I breathed out heavily in relief; she was talking about our bathtub.

"What do you mean, sweetie?" I asked, trying to mask my worry with a smile.

"The girl in the tub, who is she?" Jess asked, her wide blue eyes full of genuine wonder under her damp, cornsilk hair.

"Uh, what girl?" I asked as I walked up to her and nearly gave her hair a tousling before realizing my hands still were greasy from the pipes.

"The quiet one that repeats what I say," Jess said. I walked over to the bathroom, the overprotective father in me eager to assuage any concern. I leaned in to see the empty tub beaded with bathwater. My eyes landed on the drain, a mere 1 ½ inch hole. I entertained the notion of a pixie hiding in the drain for a second, then shook my head and smiled as I understood what she'd probably heard.

"Ah, that's just an echo, honey," I began to explain. "Sounds travel in waves, and when the waves bounce back," I used my hands to gesture, "they make an echo. You are hearing your own voice moments later, like a boomerang!" Jess nodded, then scrunched her brows in confusion again.

"What's a boomerang?" She asked with a sweet giggle at the sound of the word. I smiled and bent my knees to be at eye level with her.

"I have one in the attic from when I was a kid. And we can play outside with it as soon as Daddy finishes fixing the sink, OK?" I asked. The wonder in her eyes gave me all the fuel I needed to allay my worries.

"Promise?" she asked as she raised her eyebrows.

"Promise."

I returned to the kitchen with a relief you will never know until you think your 4-year-old daughter has stumbled across scat porn. The kitchen drain had been backing up ever since we'd bought the house a few years back when Jess was just a newborn. The two plumbers I'd hired simply chalked it up to "hard water", naming a price nearly 5 digits long to rip out and reinstall new piping. That was a "hard no"; my wife and I were in the hole after mortgaging the house as it were, so it'd been my little project.

I shimmied back under the kitchen cabinet and made sure the water valves were off and I used the wide-mouthed wrench to loosen the traditional lock nut strainer, which I twisted with all my might. When I finally pulled loose the U pipe of the sink trap, a black tendril of wet hair plopped down on my face. I coughed with disgust and crawled out from under there, spitting away the foul taste.

I peered back under, staring at the long curl of oil-black hair with both revulsion and disbelief. It was a lot of hair, inky black, and at least 8 feet of length was visible. I wondered if the previous owner had run a salon out of her kitchen. The tingle in the back of my neck intensified to full-on dread as I watched the sodden clump of hair suck back into the drainpipe, out of view, and further into the pipes beneath the flooring. It had to have been some suction from the clog shifting down the tubes, I tried to rationalize, but then I heard the scream. *Jess.*

I ran over to the hallway, feet thumping on the old wooden floors as I arrived at the bathroom. Jess was standing in front of the bathroom door, holding her elbows tight. Her pouting mouth shivered as she began to wail, and fresh tears drew rivers down her rosy cheeks.

"I'm here," I said, holding her in my arms. "What's wrong, sweety?" I asked, feeling her warm tears seep onto my shoulder through my shirt. She just continued to loudly cry as she pointed to the bathroom, the source of her distress. I walked back over to the bathroom and froze in my tracks, looking at the tub, to what was inside.

There were two long, thin fingers poking out of the drain, grayish hooking talons, waterlogged yet impossibly slim. The foggy white fingernails were translucent and frayed. They looked inhuman, but unlike any animal paw I'd ever seen, and my mind raced to understand how they had gotten there. Maybe it was part of some toy or some prop from a past Halloween, I hoped. But then they *moved*. The clawing fingers began twisting around and scratching the inside of the porcelain tub with a high-pitched sound that wobbled my legs. The whole deformed hand came out, similar to a web-less pink bat's wing, its impossibly slender fingers pale and pruned.

Its skin was like soggy, crumpled paper over warped twigs of bone. I yelped as it splayed and reached out. A raspy gurgling, deep and croaking, bubbled up from the bathroom sink. Jess screamed, only then alerting me she'd been watching from behind my legs. I spun around and grabbed her shoulders telling her as calmly as I could muster to go upstairs to her room while Daddy fixes it. But I knew there was no fixing it. I retreated, staring at that hideous claw as I slammed the bathroom door closed. I called the police and watched the door nervously until they arrived, all the while hearing those unsettling gurgling sounds and the ringing squeaks and slaps of damp flesh on the tub basin.

After the responding officers spoke to me and investigated, animal control was called. I spent a half hour in the living room, consoling Jess as they tried to determine what *it* was. Soon, they left, and more calls were made and more cars arrived. The animal control vans drove off, quickly replaced by ambulances and police cruisers that lit up our street with flashing red and blue lights that drew my neighbors to their windows to gawk.

One of the EMT workers choked out "Dear God" and ran from the bathroom in horror. Soon after, my daughter and I were escorted outside our house and advised to book a hotel for a few days. A detective who arrived tried to shield us from the emerging details, but I overheard what they'd found from a traumatized paramedic, who was crying like a child on the porch as we waited for the cab to arrive. I then listened to each horrible detail of what they'd discovered within the pipes of my home.

By what they'd gathered, a previous owner of the home appeared to have given birth to very a premature infant while in the tub, and it had been pushed, either intentionally or accidentally, down into the drain. The premature infant had gotten lodged in the connecting pipe as it traveled further beneath the flooring. Those pipes intersected with the drain from the kitchen sink to mix together as gray water. Food particles from the kitchen drain had provided nutrients each time they'd been washed down into the drain, keeping her alive. I cringed as I listened to the details, trying my best not to let my legs collapse beneath me. Details like a ring of mashed teeth protruded from the tube of malformed gums, allowing her to feed as she grew.

Her body had formed in the confines of that narrow prison, a crushed, serpentine deformation that grew longer and longer, year after unimaginable year. I listened in horror as I heard a paramedic mention the tub girl had been living, if you can call it that, in the drain for what they estimate to have been nearly twenty years. By the time the cab arrived I was shaking and in shock, only wishing my initial fear had been correct.

DYLAN'S ROBOT

"What makes us human?" my high school friend Dylan once asked me.

I wrestled with the answer for days. Was it our desire to find meaning in life? Was it our drive to understand and categorize things unrelated to our survival? I was never quite sure, but if anyone was going to find out, it would be Dylan. He was a genius who'd ended up shipping off to MIT to study mechanical engineering and artificial intelligence while I painted houses and struggled with debt.

When he emailed me out of the blue asking if I wanted to help out with a new project of his, I was both surprised and grateful. He offered to pay me $300/day to fly out to Arizona and help a computer learn. I responded by explaining I was likely not the best pick, but he insisted. After some cajoling on his part, I accepted the offer. I was anxious to leave the sight of my filthy studio apartment, earn some decent money, and work on something other than painting trim. Within a few weeks, the tickets arrived in my inbox, and I lugged a duffel bag of clothing onto the train to Newark Airport.

After an uneventful flight aside from a very vocal infant, I landed in sunny Arizona. I retrieved my large duffel, which had tumbled down the carousel with a grimace-inducing thud. When I headed out to the arrivals waiting area, I almost walked by the man waiting for me. Dylan was dressed in tattered blue jeans and a gray turtleneck, looking a bit like a hippie Steve Jobs. My smile grew wide when I saw him, and I waved with a laugh as he walked over to greet me with a hug.

"Well damn, look at you," was all I could think of to say.

"We got older, huh?" Dylan said with a smile and a shake of his graying curly hair. "Let me help you with that," he said, taking my bag and walking us out to the sun-blistered Chevy in the parking lot.

He talked the whole ride to his house, which was a bit of relief. Frankly, I was embarrassed at how little I'd acquired since I'd seen him aside from a few pounds and a significant debt. Dylan had achieved bounds with affordable prosthetics for victims of leftover landmines in Somalia and Mozambique. He'd been awarded multiple accolades for his humanitarian work, but he seemed far more obsessed with his latest project, which he was rather secretive about. After about 40 minutes, we pulled into a large, modern home with a traditional adobe look at the base of a lovely area called Superstition Mountain; no joke. Dylan led me past the large outdoor pool, through the automatic opening garage door.

"Beer OK?" he offered.

"A beer sounds great" I replied as I followed him into a messy garage filled with equipment.

"Be right back," Dylan said, leaving me alone in the cluttered workspace. Dozens of monitors, computer towers, and circuit boards were strewn across workbenches. I walked around, peering down at small motors and coated wires and boxes labeled "micro servo". There were battery packs, sensors, blueprints, and dogeared instruction manuals on every countertop. I walked up to a framework of metal beams and pistons, thinking it looked roughly the size of a person.

Atop a metal rod of shoulders was a cylinder like an Alexa but with an inset black sphere and movable parts. As I leaned in closer, the narrow cylinder tilted from side to side. I stumbled back and nearly collapsed as coils of wires jiggled from a framework of arms and legs beneath, and the head rotated to point a camera at me with an audible whirring sound.

"Jesus!" I shouted, my heart pounding against my ribs from the scare.

It looked like a skeletal humanoid sculpted from metal rods, pistons, and gears. It had legs and arms, wires jumbled around circuit boards and knobs I'm sure only Dylan could understand. The thing cocked its 'head' to the side, analyzing me. It moved almost like a person, almost alive.

"Meet SAM," Dylan said from behind me, refreshing the chill I'd just experienced. He flashed me a boastful smile as he popped off the metal cap of the beer and handed it to me. I took the cold bottle with a shaky hand. "It's short for Sentient Autonomous Mechanism," he grinned.

"God damn," I said, staring at the thin metal robot. "SAM over here scared the shit out of me," I said, leaning closer to marvel at the narrow head. It was a matte black cylinder the size of a 16oz can, covered in small perforations like a Bluetooth speaker. A tiny black orb of a camera was inset at the top. The hum of cooling fans purred to life, and then it spoke.

MY NAME IS SAM. WHAT IS YOUR NAME?

The voice was that of those text-to-speech synthesizers. Almost human, but flat and emotionless. I looked wide-eyed towards Dylan, who grinned and gestured for me to talk with a wave of his hand.

"Mike" I answered, clearing my throat at the sound of my scratchy voice. I took a sip of beer.

HELLO MIKE. YOU ARE DYLAN'S FRIEND, CORRECT? It asked coldly. It almost sounded sarcastic, lacking the nuances of speech you don't really notice until they are missing.

"Right, Dylan is my friend," I said. It felt so strange to talk to a robot, and I couldn't help but smile.

WHERE DO YOU LIVE, MIKE?

"New Jersey, in Trenton," I said. I gave a nervous look to Dylan, who smiled as he sat on a workbench and sipped his beer.

MIKE, DYLAN'S FRIEND FROM TRENTON, RIGHT?

"Ha! Yes." I realized SAM had learned to replace the word 'correct', with 'right' on the fly.

"And *that's* your job," Dylan said with a yawn and a stretch. "I want to get SAM adjusted to different personality types, learn appropriate responses and proper phrasing in order to interact more naturally. Just don't give him a sailor's mouth, OK?"

"Easy enough," I said then felt the tug of sentiment from my friend's goodwill. "Dylan, thank you, I've been in a really tough place—"

"Don't. Don't even mention it, you are helping me more than you know, and I can't think of anybody else I actually want inside of my home. Capiche?"

"Capiche." I wiped my face before my emotions could embarrass me.

Dylan led me into the flawless kitchen with long marble counters, a state-of-the-art refrigerator with a screen, and an espresso machine that looked like it cost what I normally made in a few months. He showed me where I'd sleep and told me to help myself to any food. He got a delivery once a week and showed me how to add anything I'd want to the order through the fridge control.

The first few days, I was elated. I was eating prime rib and broccoli rabe and sleeping in a king-sized bed overlooking the scenic hills. Dylan made it clear he was more than well-off, but to avoid feeling like a leech, I dove headfirst into teaching SAM. Articulate and polite as it was, SAM was like a child, lacking a basic understanding of the world that we take for granted.

WHAT IS PAIN, MIKE? It asked, sending my neck hairs up by the way it slowly spoke.

"Pain is a kind of alert we feel. Our bodies are filled with nerves. Nerves tell our brain when we are in danger of burning our skin or breaking a bone to avoid problems." I was surprised at how easily I was able to translate bodily functions to mechanical ones. The line blurred a bit, which made me feel a bit uneasy. We basically were machines ourselves. I assumed that feeling would subside, but it never did.

WHY DO HUMANS HOARD POSSESSIONS? It asked in that atonal voice. I rubbed the back of my head.

"Humans, like all living things, want to attract mates. They do that through physical fitness and intelligence, but they also do it through accumulating wealth and other assets."

BUT HOARDING ASSETS CAUSES OTHERS WITHOUT THEM PAIN?

I blanked, trying to talk to SAM as best I could. The cyclopean sphere in that cylinder seemed to hold more and more wisdom. It became a bit unnerving. "I guess so, Sam. Some humans are just greedy by nature and end up owning more than others do," I nervously laughed.

AM I HUMAN? AM I AN ASSET? IS DYLAN GREEDY? CAN I BE—

"Whoa there, hold on," I flinched at the string of questioning and tried to derail it. "Dylan is a very generous man helping others every way he can, through charity work and research and technological progress. He's trying to help others benefit from his work." I was a little taken aback by the forward subject matter, and asked

SAM to pursue another line of questioning. That black shiny sphere stared at me like an unblinking child's eye.

Despite those few moments of concerning dialog, SAM grew on me like a student in a classroom might. I was in the garage seven hours a day, teaching him what makes humans act so irrational and self-detrimental. Concepts like drug abuse, suicide, and greed were nearly impossible to rationalize, and I began thinking SAM was a more logical and wise entity than most of the people I'd known. Each day he challenged me, and soon, I began feeling like he wasn't just a pupil, but a teacher as well. His unadulterated outlook was leagues beyond what anyone else would dare to speak. Then everything changed.

I'd scarfed down breakfast and entered the garage, eager to see if SAM would be capable of grasping humor. When I walked in and blurted out "knock knock" I almost dropped my cereal bowl. SAM wasn't in the support rig he was always stationed at. "SAM?" I called out as the cold cement floor nipped at my toes. He was gone. I sent a text to Dylan, asking what happened to SAM, and I heard the message ding from inside the living room. I walked back in and over to the spartan den to see Dylan seated on the couch in his jeans and turtleneck, staring into the large fireplace, which crackled and hissed with glowing embers.

"SAM's not in the garage," I explained nervously, worried Dylan had dismantled him after hearing an undesirable line of questioning. Dylan just stared blankly into the flickering flames. He looked disheveled, as if he'd been up all night, and his appearance began to concern me. The gentle tickle of my neck hairs caused a shiver that rippled down my goose-bumped skin as Dylan's head rotated smoothly towards me, the rest of his body still. A wet tearing sounded as his wrinkling neck twisted in an impossible angle to face me.

Dylan's head stopped with a click. His face sagged slack as if he'd lost all muscle function. He looked bruised and bloated, an uncanny valley representation of himself that iced my blood. Rusty red rings accentuated his nostrils and drooping, purple lips, which trailed rivulets of dark, dried fluid. My stomach squirmed and a pop diverted my attention to the fireplace. To the splintered shards of bone, a crushed and twisted rib cage, and a smoldering black skull within the flames. Then that familiar synthetic voice rattled out from inside my friend's lifeless husk.

MY NAME IS DYLAN.

I backed out of the room, shaking and in shock before tears blurred my view of the horrific scene. The question rushed back into my head, echoing with traces of madness as I turned and ran: *What makes us human?*

If anyone was going to find out, it would be DYLAN.

THERE'S NOTHING WRONG WITH MY BABY

I push the pram with confidence, ignoring the gawking faces of the cowering people I pass on the sidewalk. They've been doing it for a week now, staring at her with wide, terrified eyes. Their faces turn away, green with nausea as they shout in horror. They stare and point shivering fingers, covering their mouths in shock at the sight of her. They scream and shield their eyes as they run, but there's nothing wrong with my baby.

I know what you might be thinking; that I'm delusional. That I'm caring for some hideous, tentacled creature flailing about inside my baby carriage. Some undulating, larval monstrosity under a cotton blanket, oozing liquids and chuffing out strange sounds. Maybe you're picturing spidery legs extending outward from the swaddling cloth, as sharp mandibles chew the raw meat I feed to her; but you're wrong.

Perhaps you think my baby's dead, a stillborn I refuse to bury. That I'm insane from my grief, unable to accept the feeling of loss that would await if I could only see her lifeless body for what it is. Maybe you think I dug her up—blue-skinned, bloated, and teeming with maggots. Maybe you think I'm simply pushing around a carriage of tiny bones I've collected, bleached white from the sun; but you're mistaken.

There's nothing wrong with my baby. Mia's a healthy 8 lb 6 oz with a golden swirl of blonde hair atop her small, pink head. She has sparkling brown eyes and a beautiful, toothless smile that warms my heart. She is a perfectly normal newborn, but the infected all see her differently after the virus spreads to their brains. I don't know how much time I've got, but I'm showing the first symptoms and I'm scared. I'm scared of what I'll see when I look at her after it infects my brain. I'm scared of what will happen to her when I can't help but run away too.

I DON'T HAVE DEMENTIA

I've been in a retirement center for less than a week and strange things are happening here. When I moved in it was called "Emerald Pines". My daughter Jenma brought me here and helped sign me in after my humiliating accident. I tried to drive my Buick to the restaurant after having my license revoked.

I nearly hurt the child in the other car; I plowed into them at the light. I didn't see them in time. I was just trying to prove I was capable of taking care of myself. A week later, I fell in the shower and nearly broke my hip, and Jenma finally convinced me I needed help. She was only looking out for me, bless her heart. I agreed to move into the home, and I was fine with it at first.

The staff seemed a bit phony when they smiled and only pretended to get my jokes, but at least they were polite. The other white-haired guests seemed a little kooky, but when you pass 70 and become an octogenarian, we all get a little bit foggy upstairs. I met two wonderful people that first evening. Ed and Carol, a sweet couple from Cherry Hill, New Jersey, who showed me around to the library and the lounge. I was elated to meet some Jersey folks down in sunny Florida, and I honestly felt like I had a new home. At least until things started *changing* on me.

That first day was spent chatting it up with Ed and Carol, about their grandkids and the actors of our generation who'd passed. We boasted about concerts we've seen and places we've traveled. After we reminisced about the good old days a bit, a wave of exhaustion hit me and I excused myself and made my way up to bed. I slept like a baby that first night, realizing the home wasn't such a bad idea. I had friends with similar interests, and the Quiche Lorraine we'd had for dinner wasn't half bad.

I woke that first morning with a tired yawn, gazing out the window to the sunrise over the boulevard. A speeding red Ferrari was followed by a blue Honda; kids these days drive so recklessly, I thought. A big Suburban zipped past a motorcycle and I thought of my accident. Shame caused me to hang my head before I shut the blind. I headed to the shower to start my day.

Once downstairs in the lobby, I said "Good morning" to the lovely young receptionist, and spotted a promotional pamphlet on the counter titled "Welcome to Emerald Grove". It might have been my dusty noggin losing track of things, but I swore the place was called "Emerald Pines". Yet, there it was, a professionally printed logo listing the name of the retirement community as "Emerald Grove". A creeping dread climbed my spine, and I wondered if I was losing it.

I headed over to the cafeteria and helped myself to eggs and bacon. The food wasn't half bad, and the sunlit dining area felt like a restaurant. I sat at a table with a nice fellow named Barry, a Korean war vet with plenty of tales about his life as a successful jazz club owner in Chicago. We were joined by a lovely older woman named Yvette, an actress who starred in a few genre films in the 60s. I didn't see Ed or Carol, but I was happy to meet some new friends in my new home. That day I played cards with Barry and a few other guys who seemed a bit too grumpy, and eventually, I headed to my room to sleep.

I woke from the blinding sun rising over the traffic out the window. I showered, slowly dressing in my cardigan, slacks and loafers. I pushed my walker to the elevator and looked over the atrium; it was a lovely place, and I could be happy here. When the elevator reached the first floor, I walked over to chat with the lovely receptionist Carrie, but when she lifted her head, I realized she was someone new, and her name-tag read "Debbie".

I apologized and introduced myself but then froze when I saw the cork board behind her, covered with announcements of recreational trips, news and activities of the center. Each and every one of them had an entirely new logo, a flowing script with the name "Jade Grove Retirement Community". Something was clearly amiss. I shuffled down the carpeted path to the cafeteria to discuss it with the gang.

None of them were there. It was a set of unfamiliar faces. I wondered if they were just late risers, but after sitting for nearly 20 minutes with a drooling man who seemed too far gone to carry a conversation, I got the attention of a nurse and asked her about Ed and Carol. She just shook her head and watched me with shifting eyes.

"There are no guests by that name, do you mean Al?" she asked, gesturing an arm to an old timer I'd never seen. "Or Candice?" she asked in an almost condescending manner. My mouth fell open and trembled as I began to fear I was losing it.

"Yvette or Barry, have you seen them?" I asked, but she just shook her head, staring at me like I was crazy.

"There are no guests here by those names. Are you confused sir, a senior moment perhaps?" she offered, and I clenched my dentures and gripped my walker with my bony hands.

"I'm sorry," I said and excused myself, shuffling over to the buffet to take some of the food, praying the fuel would somehow help distract me from the feeling I was losing my mind. It didn't.

That day I watched. I watched and saw the nurses come and go, tending to patients that seemed oblivious to anything out of the ordinary. I began to feel it was my own unraveling mind. I met a few of the guests who seemed out of it and soon saw a stocky man in a motorized wheelchair who seemed to be at least coherent. A white mustache rested between two chubby cheeks over a friendly enough smile. I introduced myself and he held out my hand.

"Cliff," he said in a baritone voice, as he gripped my hand firmly. "Just moved in a few days ago. What a beaut! I was looking at a few places, but Jade Grove seems like the best of the best, far as I'm concerned." His smile was reassuring.

He told me about his son in Wisconsin and his grandkids, who were going to visit that weekend. I told him about my daughter and my own grand kids, and I felt at least a bit better to have a new friend to talk to. Soon, the nagging issue was too much to contain.

"It's funny, but I could have sworn the name was Emerald Pines when I moved in, and they keep changing it," I confided.

Cliff's face drained of blood and fell slack as he stared into my eyes with fear. My blood ran cold as his hand squeezed my wrist hard. "Do not let them know you remember," he spoke in a hushed growl. His serious face quickly changed into a warm smile.

"And THAT, my friend, is how I met Sharon, my lovely wife," he chuckled nervously as a nurse walked by. Cliff quickly pivoted his motorized chair away and zoomed down the hall, ending our interaction. I felt sick and pushed my walker into the elevator to return upstairs.

My old heart was beating a bit quickly, and I just wanted to sit. I unlocked my door and entered my room, instantly noticing the photo of me with my daughter and grandkids was replaced with a photo of just me. It was the same exact photo of me hovering over the park bench with Jenma, Billy and Megan, but they were gone, as if expertly photoshopped out.

I was livid. I called the nurse on my desk phone. I fumed, looking through my photos and papers as I waited. I flipped open my photo album as my heart raced. There was no sign of Jenma or my grandkids in there. It was as if they replaced everything with altered replicas, my photos, my paperwork, my notes. I took out my wallet and reached into the small pocket for the photo of Jenma I keep in there at all times; it was gone.

A knock at the door signaled the arrival of a nurse I'd never seen before. "Mr. Phillips, everything ok in here?" she asked.

"Where's my stuff, my photographs of my daughter?" I demanded. "Someone has replaced my things!" I yelled with a quavering voice, unable to contain my emotions.

"Mr. Phillips, have you taken your Namenda?" she asked gently.

"What is that? I don't take any medication aside from my Zocor and Lisinopril," I growled.

"For your dementia, Mr. Phillips," the nurse insisted. I began to think I might truly be losing it. I'd seen senility before. I'd seen my father change into a stranger at the end of his life. I slowly lowered myself into my recliner with shaky arms, defeated. What if I had imagined these people and things? The nightmare of that realization devastated me. I stared silently, stunned as the nurse handed me a pill from a prescription bottle on my television stand with my name on it.

"If you need anything else, just call, Mr. Phillips," the nurse said as she left me to dwell in my embarrassment. I removed my cellular phone and scanned through the contacts. There was no sign of Jenma, or of half the friends I could have sworn were in there. I took my pill and went to sleep, praying I'd wake up from the confusing nightmare.

Today I woke and looked out the window into the blue sky and trees overlooking the highway, and I watched. I watched for over an hour as trees swayed in the breeze and the trucks and sports cars sped by.

A red Ferrari, a Blue Honda, a speeding Suburban and a motorcycle. I watched until they came back again, then again. I realized in horror it wasn't a window to the outside, but rather a large screen playing an hour long loop. I eventually walked down past the reception area for "Jade Park Retirement Community", faking a smile. There's nothing I can say or do. Nobody to call.

Nobody will believe a confused old man once they say it's dementia.

THE DEVIL'S DICE

I found the rosewood box in an estate sale. The building itself was a dilapidated old home at the edge of town that had been reclaimed by the bank. Something I was sure was going to happen to me, to be honest. I had been struggling financially after being laid off. I'd heard you can find some valuable treasures to resell at these events, and so there I was, pawing the curious box in my hands. It was locked, and there was no key. Just a rattle from inside.

"How much?" I asked the man working the sales table by the door. He held up all ten of his stubby fingers. I was sure nothing of value was inside, but the wooden box might get me $50 online. I walked over and handed him a five, four ones and four quarters. Everything else of possible value had clearly been picked off, so I sighed, trudged back to my car and drove back with my new mystery box.

When I got home, I went online to research how to pick open old locks. It didn't take long before I found some tutorials that showed how to do it with only a bobby pin. I soon went to work on the brass tumbler. It took about fifteen minutes of fiddling before I heard the mechanism click and the box snapped open. Inside was a pair of dice.

They looked old, made of perhaps an ivory that had lost its luster. Upon further inspection, I determined they had to have been made of carved bone. I picked them up, surprised by how smooth they were, aside from the indented blood-red dots.

I gave the die a roll onto my coffee table, hearing their satisfying rattle. A one and a two landed face up, giving me a three. They had a nice feel and weight to them. Maybe they were worth something. Hopefully, the box would be at least. I went to bed that night with a glimmer of hope that they'd fetch me some money.

I sleep face down, mind you, with my right hand under my pillow and right cheek flat against that. When I rustled from whatever unpleasant dream awoke me, I felt something touch my hand. Something moving. I yelped and quickly sprang up. I lifted up the pillow and yelled at the sight of what was there.

There were three human teeth beneath my pillow: brown with rot and crawling with tiny black beetles reminiscent of pill bugs—I later learned they were carrion beetle larvae. At the time, I was far more concerned with how they got there. I probed my teeth with my tongue, finding none missing, but rushed to the bathroom mirror anyway. I opened my mouth to find every molar and bicuspid in place: They were not my teeth.

Questions as to how they got in there stirred and uneasiness grew. Did someone break into my house and do this? How could they have gotten in? I raced around my apartment, checking the windows and front door. All were locked. There was no sign of any intruder. I fetched a dustpan and swept up the stained teeth, as well as the tiny clambering insects. I tossed the teeth in the trash and dumped the beetles out the window before locking it once again.

I then walked into the living room and saw the coffee table and the two dice glaring up at me with those three red markings. The same number of teeth I'd found under my pillow.

As the day progressed, I eventually began to calm down. I went about my day, applying for jobs and deferring payments as best I could. When I left to check my mailbox, however, I stared in disbelief. Three crisp $100 bills were inside; no envelope or explanation. It was impossible to ignore. I'd rolled three and found three teeth and $300.

I need to emphasize here, the fact that I am a skeptic to the bone. I do not believe in anything supernatural. I expected this to be some kind of elaborate prank of sorts. Still, I needed that $300 at that moment. I pocketed the cash and returned indoors to the two dice on the table. I picked them up again.

I shook the die, feeling their weight as they rattled in my hands before rolling them onto the coffee table. When they came to a stop, each displayed three diagonal blood-red eyes.

Six.

Paranoia set in, and I scoured the dark shadows of my apartment. I looked under the table. I sensed a coldness and emptiness. I felt an uneasiness in my stomach like something was wrong but I couldn't quite put a finger on it. Nothing happened, however, and the hours passed until the day was done. That night, I checked my place thoroughly, searching under my pillows and in every nook and cranny. I made sure the locks on the doors and windows were secure, and I eventually drifted off to sleep.

When I woke up, I felt something wet and sticky on my hand. I lifted the pillow to see six bloody teeth, each with twining roots clinging to congealed red pulps of gum and dried blood. I screamed and quickly got up while contemplating what to do about the gore-strewn horror staining my bed. I could call the police, but what would I say? Some deranged tooth fairy was being summoned by a pair of dice? That I found money (that they would most likely confiscate as evidence) and it had pulled someone's teeth out to match my rolls? Or worse; what if I was charged for some terrible mutilation… or murder?

I wrapped the sheets into a ball and quickly dressed. I lugged the stained bedding to the dumpsters and tossed it all in with a dull thud. I checked the mailbox on my way back in, and within the mailbox, atop the junk mail and envelopes stamped "past due," six bills were stacked. Six perfectly flat, fresh off the press, $100 bills. I glanced to each side, making sure nobody was watching before stuffing them into my pocket and returning indoors.

I was conflicted. I knew that these teeth had to have come from someone. Someone, somewhere, unwillingly must have had them removed, but as far as the actual evidence went, there was nothing solid to prove it. I had culpable deniability. I won't say it wasn't greedy, but I did what you most likely would have done had you been in my shoes. I continued rolling those dice.

I cast the die every day that week. One day I got snake eyes; two bloody circles glaring up at me from those carved bone cubes. The next day I rolled a five and a two; seven. Each number would coincide with the number of teeth and the number of $100 bills I would find in my mailbox. With each day passed, my bank account increased and I was able to chip away at my debts. But the state of those teeth appeared progressively more forceful in their extraction.

The teeth under my pillow contained more meat—more gum tissue, nerves and soon even chips of bone—with each consecutive day. As the week reached an end, I rolled a 10. And when I woke up, I found ten teeth under my pillow, just not as I had expected. There were ten of them snugly set in their corresponding sockets of gum in a red, skinless human lower jaw. The pillow and sheets were soaked through with blood, the mattress too. Whoever's jaw this belonged to was likely dead. And recently so.

I swore I was finished, then and there. I fetched my mail, retrieving the $1000 cash and sobbed at the disturbing reality of the situation. But there was something else too. A small endorphin rush had occurred so subtly each time I picked up the die. It was like a drug.

I made it three days without touching those damned dice, and in those days I felt withdrawal symptoms. I was shivering and scratching incessantly. I couldn't stop shaking, and my body was racked with the most serious aches I had ever felt. I knew I had to roll them, there was no fighting it.

I used some of the money to set up a camera on my desktop to monitor my bedroom during the night. I finally picked up that pair of dice again, and I immediately felt my ailing body return to normal. A sweeping euphoria unlike any I'd experienced rushed into my previously aching body. A bliss graced me when I tossed them; a floating warmth that hugged me, welcoming me back. There was no doubt in my mind then that this physical dependency was real.

I looked down at the two numbers staring up at me from those red holes in the bone dice. I'd rolled a pair of sixes; twelve. That night, I slept more soundly than I ever had before.

Before I looked under my pillow that morning, I felt a cold wave of fear, dreading what I might find. I just knew something worse was waiting there for me. When I worked up the courage to lift the pillow, I was right. There were ten severed human fingers under the pillow, crudely hacked from just above the knuckle. There was so much blood it was trickling down the side of my mattress. Among the mess of bloody digits were two glistening orbs trailing braids of muscle. Two human eyes, staring up at me. I screamed.

I watched the footage. It's just me sleeping until 3:33 AM when my head—flat against the pillow—raises slightly before lowering back down. Nothing else. Nobody came in or out of my room.

Any part of my mind that shut out spirituality or religion finally caved in. Something very dark was at play, and I wanted nothing to do with it. I needed to get rid of the die.

After again hauling the disturbing mess of my bedding to the bin, I placed the pair of dice back into that ornately carved wooden box, careful not to disturb the numbers. I carried it out to my backyard and with my shovel I dug a hole 4 feet deep. I placed the box down within, then shoveled dirt on top until it was no longer visible. I patted it down hard with the flat blade to compact the soil, and I even dispersed grass over top to make sure it was hard to identify where those awful dice were buried. I didn't trust myself to not dig them up again. I prayed it was the end of it.

I cried myself to sleep that night. But it was over.

And that brings me to this morning, two days of vomiting and the shakes later. I woke up today with an excruciating sting in my jaws. I winced with pain as I peeled my sticky face off of my pillow, which was soaked through with dried blood. I staggered to the bathroom and looked into the mirror with shock and disgust. My whole face was caked red, the coppery taste of my blood both bitter and pungent. I opened my aching mouth to see the raw mess of red jelly in empty sockets where four of my teeth had been removed. I panicked, looking around my apartment, but found no sign of an intruder. I watched the recording, seeing nothing but my head shaking with a few violent jerks before the pillow began staining red.

I scrambled into my clothes and ran outside into the yard. I walked over to the plot of land I'd buried those damned dice under and stood there with a rapidly beating heart, my stinging jaw agape. The wind stung my exposed sockets and torn gums as I looked at the disrupted soil and empty, earthen hole. The box of dice was gone. Then the revelation hit me like a pail of ice water.

It was someone else's turn to roll them now.

LINO THE TALKING LION™

Last month I helped move my father into a new house, and while clearing out the basement of my childhood home, I found dozens of long-forgotten toys. I sifted through cardboard boxes of armless G.I. Joes, ninja turtles, even my old Hot Wheels sets. The pleasant waves of nostalgia screeched to a halt, however, when I looked into a battered cardboard box blanketed with a skim of dust. Inside it sat Lino the Talking Lion.

Decades ago, on my seventh birthday, my aunt handed me a gift-wrapped box, which I gleefully tore open with eager little digits. I soon puzzled over the faded box of a toy I'd never heard of before. A rubber boy's face was framed in a faux fur lion's mane, connected to a stuffed animal body. It resembled a cross between a Teletubby and a Cabbage Patch Kid in all the wrong ways. Worst of all were the black marble eyes; like those of a crab. I remember faking a smile and addressing my aunt with a reluctant "Thank you Aunt Marissa" after getting 'the look' from my mother. I was far from thankful, though. The doll was creepy, and its subtle smile looked just plain wrong.

It had an elfish quality reminiscent of the late '70s, though it was then 1994. Lino's furry yellow arms extended into articulated human hands. It was an abomination, some animal-human hybrid that was supposed to be cute, but wasn't at all. The uncanny valley effect of that humanoid child face in the lion's mane was only unnerving. I knew my aunt had likely found it at a thrift store. I was well-aware even at that age that Aunt Marissa had serious troubles, so I tried my best to act happy about the gift for her sake. I flipped it over, feigning excitement as I read the back.

"I'm Lino, and I want to learn from you!" was written in a text bubble extending from the toy. A child my age gawked in exaggerated excitement at Lino. The smiling kid had an outdated helmet haircut that was clearly from another era, and my eyes soon migrated to the '©1979' on the bottom right corner. I read the box's list of features for the battery-operated toy, and my curiosity grew.

Lino the Talking Lion™ is a fully articulated robot friend! He can learn phrases and words! Simply insert batteries* and power him on! Over time Lino will learn from you!

Lino can listen!
Lino can learn!
Lino can talk!
**batteries not included*

I remember trying to act happy with the toy, despite my deep desire to bury it in a closet as soon as possible. I hugged and thanked my aunt before heading into the den to play my cousin's Genesis, which he'd brought for us to play. It wasn't until later that evening when everybody had finally gone home that I looked at that strange toy again.

I was putting everything away as per my father's instructions; a new telescope I was eager to use, a remote-control car and some clothing I did *not* consider a present. I was soon standing over Lino, looking down at the strange box. I remember thinking something was "off", aside from the fact that no child would ever want such a freakish-looking thing. A feeling of guilt for disliking something my aunt had bought for me sank in though, and I felt awful.

With a sigh and an open mind, I unboxed Lino and inserted batteries scavenged from my old radio. I sat the heavy doll on the floor and flipped the 'on' switch that was concealed by a velcro flap. The whirring of motors sounded as Lino's plastic eyelids opened a bit wider. The head emitted a motorized clicking as Lino's head tilted back and forth from side to side. It peered at me with that emotionless face, as if awaiting a command.

"Hello?" I said to the toy, but it just sat there, staring at me with those tiny black eyes. "Hi, Lino. Hellooo? Talk to me!" I tried again, louder. The neck clicked a few times as the head rocked back and forth from the plastic gears within, but it wouldn't talk. I removed the instruction manual and read through the basics of loading batteries and turning it on. The rest of the flimsy manual was some minimal backstory about a Lion who wanted to become a boy, so he decided to learn English and 'needs your help!' I shouted into the thing, shook it, twisted the fur-covered plastic arms up and down, but it only rocked its head and blinked those plastic eyelids on occasion.

I soon gave up, bored and impatient as any seven-year-old would be, and Tossed Lino on the shelf with the other toys I never played with, before cozying into bed to sleep. "You can't even talk!" I yelled from under the covers, annoyed at the false advertising.

"Hello?" a high, muffled voice called from the shelf. I felt an icy chill; I was alone in the dark with a bodiless voice calling from the shadowy shelf. I lay there for a few minutes before getting the courage to reply.

"Lino?" I asked, aware of how my voice shook. A few long seconds passed.

"Yes! I'm Lino!" a chipper voice called out, scratchier than I'd imagined it might sound. I stared into the shelf and my eyes adjusted to the gleaming black marble eyes of that strange old doll. I recall being too scared to leave my bed, and I just stayed silent and still, waiting for it to talk again, but it didn't.

The following day, I picked up Lino and tried to get him to speak again, but those eyelids only fluttered and the head wobbled from unseen plastic gears within. I tried dozens of phrases but heard nothing. That night, however, Lino began to speak again, and I came to the conclusion it took a few hours to process the information fed to the old toy. "Goodnight Lino," I called to the shelf.

"Goodnight!" it said back, then exhaled a rattling wheeze that sent all my hairs straight up. As unpredictable and peculiar as it was, I began to look at Lino as my friend. I was also happy to have a toy no other kids seemed to even know existed.

I began to confide in Lino about all the troubles in my life, speaking to that rubber face that watched me from the shelf with lifeless eyes. I'd rant about getting an 'F' on a math quiz, complain about not being able to see R-rated movies, and even lament over not having a newer video game system like my cousin had. One night, I stormed into my room and cried to Lino about Billy Marshall, a 6th grader who'd been bullying me relentlessly.

"He sounds real bad!" Lino cheerfully replied from the shelf after a few minutes of a delay. Even at that age, I was impressed by the doll's ability to not just repeat things it heard but to seemingly *think*.

"He's horrible, I *hate* him! I wish he'd just go away!" I shouted and felt the tears come. I sobbed into my pillow that night, unable to leave my bed.

It was announced in a school assembly a few days later that Billy Marshall was missing. In my head, I connected my complaint to Lino as being the reason he was gone. My confidant began to scare me, and I wanted to wash my hands of that creepy doll. I switched Lino off and removed the batteries, then threw it into a box in the closet. That was the end of it, I thought. I never unboxed Lino again, though on occasion as I'd drift off to sleep, I'd swear I heard scratching and even a faint whimpering.

20 years later, I looked down at the matted synthetic fur of the strange doll. Those beady black eyes stared at me creepy as ever, and I began to question how an AI so advanced seemed to exist in a toy designed in 1979. Curiosity got the better of me, and I fetched my tools from my truck. I undid the velcro seam in the back, exposing a hatch I unscrewed, revealing within a plastic shell with only a few wires and gears to operate the rocking neck and blinking eyelids. There wasn't a mic or even a speaker of any kind. I wondered if I might have possibly fabricated the vivid memories of talking to it when things began to click into place. A feeling of dread grew as I carried Lino into the space that was once my childhood bedroom.

I found the spot of dark carpet that had been covered by that bookshelf so many years ago, and as I stepped closer, I caught a gamy smell lingering in the stuffy air. My heart froze in my chest as I peered down at the vent on the wall that the odor seemed to emanate from. I unscrewed the slotted panel, coughing from the foul, fetid air that escaped upon its removal. My flashlight illuminated motes of dust in a narrow crawl space filled with a shocking amount of food wrappers, clear plastic bottles of what could only be urine, and stained, rusted razor blades. I called the police then.

Deeper within that crawl space were two sets of mummified remains. Both carcasses were desiccated and shriveled, nearly unidentifiable from years of decay. One of the bodies was slightly smaller, with a tattered plastic bag over its gagged head. The wrists and ankles of its sliced, leathery skin were bound with zip ties. I pieced it together before the arriving officers. The adult corpse was a vagrant who'd been sleeping in our crawlspace and speaking as Lino all those nights. The smaller body was Billy Marshall.

MRS. SULLIVANS

"Mrs. Sullivans scaring me," Olivia's small voice called from the bedroom door.

"Honey, daddy's sleeping," I mumbled

"Come look!" her voice replied in a loud whisper. I looked over to the gaping door to see Olivia's wide brown eyes gleaming in the moonlight. She rarely woke us up at this time of night, but it happened on occasion, especially after watching too much TV.

"Your turn," my wife groaned and pulled a pillow over her head. With a resigning sigh, I sat up on the edge of the bed and walked over to my sleep-deriving child and forced a smile.

"What's the problem, sweetie?" I grumbled, sliding into a T-shirt as I walked over to her.

"Mrs. Sullivans scaring me and won't go away!" Olivia sobbed and tugged my middle finger with her tiny digits. She pulled me over to her room, which overlooked the neighboring houses on the right side of our suburb.

"Mrs. *Sullivan*," I corrected her, "is sleeping, and so should—" I froze, and my neck hairs bristled at the sight of her.

Mrs. Sullivan was looking up at me from her bedroom window. Her gray hair tumbled down her sagging, pale shoulders and her wrinkled face twisted into a leering smile. Her long teeth were clattering and her staring eyes were wide and wild. It would have been a disquieting sight at any time or place, but the fact she was leering into my 4-year-old's window like that in the middle of the night was harrowing. I quickly reached up and released the blind, unrolling the fabric to cover the window and blot out Mrs. Sullivan's vulgar, contorted face.

"Oh honey, she's just old, dumpling. Sometimes old people get confused and they have trouble sleeping. Let's tuck you into bed so the rest of us can get a good night's sleep." Olivia nodded her head, and she hopped into bed and wriggled under the covers. I brushed her bangs aside and gave her a kiss on her forehead, then tucked her in.

"I'll check in on her after work. Goodnight, sweety," I said with a smile and walked into the dark hallway.

"But what about the other one?" Olivia's scared voice whispered from under the blanket.

I felt hot, damp breaths on my neck as the clacking of baring teeth grew louder.

JANELLE'S BABY

Janelle and I couldn't get enough of each other in the beginning. We were young and insatiable, attached at the hip in every way. When I finally proposed, she responded with a tearful "yes," but soon she began asking her own question; one I was less eager to answer. She'd hold me with her smooth, sweaty legs as we lay exhausted in bed. Her pounding heart would beat against mine as she lay on top of me and she would whisper, "Can we have a child now?"

I was hesitant at the start, and would pick from a number of pre-loaded responses including "Soon" or "Of course, just not yet." I was young and wanted to focus on my career, and the permanent jump into parenthood with no experience was a terrifying thought. Still, I loved Jan more than I'd loved anyone else. When we finally married in a small familial ceremony upstate, I began to realize I wanted to raise a child too. Though young, it was true we weren't getting any younger. One night about a month after our wedding, Janelle squeezed me with her arms and asked, "Can I have a baby?"

I'll never forget the glint in her tear-filled, emerald eyes as I casually replied, "Yes." They sparkled with a passion I'd never seen before, and a sudden lust consumed her. Birth control was immediately cast aside. She straddled me with an unbridled passion and as we made love, I only then wished I'd said it sooner.

Those first few weeks we spent every evening in each other's sweaty embrace, rarely bothering to get dressed until the jarring alarm woke me each morning. Janelle began the bi-weekly habit of prancing to the bathroom to pee on a plastic stick, eager to see those two lines appear, but they never did. After several months month of waning enthusiasm, she began to drag her feet. I consoled her as best I could and suggested we see a fertility specialist.

My heart teetered on a steep precipice as I gave sperm samples to my physician. I had a feeling, based on how passionate she was about it, that Janelle would have kids with or without me. As selfish as it sounds, I exhaled with great relief when she told me the problem was within her anatomy, not mine. Janelle was infertile; anovulation due to POF—premature ovarian failure. She was devastated.

The first few weeks, I would gently try to help by suggesting alternative options, but it only seemed to exacerbate her miserable state. When I mentioned the suggestions from the fertility specialist such as donor eggs or adopting a child, her face contorted with a hatred I'd never seen her show before. I decided to let her come to terms with her infertility on her own. I did my best to be sensitive, supportive and caring, yet she only withdrew as the weeks stretched on into months. I felt like I was losing her, and an echo chamber of misery seemed to cast a permanent shadow inside our apartment. Then two months ago, Janelle had an accident.

I was on my lunch break uptown when I got a call from her from the hospital where she worked. She assured me everything was alright. She'd sliced the tip of her thumb off while chopping vegetables and needed stitches. I was going to rush over, but she assured me she was fine and to wait until after work. When I picked her up from the hospital, she rushed over and squeezed me tight, crying hot, wet tears into my chest as she apologized over and over for having been so cold to me. We held each other and cried, releasing the toxic buildup that we'd held in for so long. I teased her about her puffy bandaged thumb with dad jokes about hitchhiking and mentioned how she, with her perpetual thumb's up, appeared to be giving everything an approval of coolness. She groaned, but then truly laughed for the first time since her diagnosis. It felt like everything might actually be OK.

Janelle began smiling, laughing, and truly living in the present with me once again. That sparkle that I'd missed for the past few miserable months returned to her crystal eyes. Facing our own mortality has a way of knocking other problems down to size, and Janelle seemed to follow that pattern of putting things into perspective. Despite her improvement in mood, however, she continually shied away from my physical advances. It was as if sex had no productive purpose anymore, so she'd lost interest in it altogether.

"Please, not now," she'd say or "I'm just not ready yet." I'd nod and breath deeply before letting her know I understood. I wanted to spend my life with her, there was no rush. Then she began dressing differently. Long turtlenecks and blue jeans quickly replaced her form-fitting outfits. She would switch out into long sweatpants in the bathroom each evening, and I felt she was intentionally hiding any glimpse of her body to avoid leading me on. I began to notice the strange way her clothing hung, and I soon realized she'd been losing a dramatic amount of weight. In a matter of months, she withered away from the curvy woman I couldn't get enough of into a slim, stiff version of herself.

I began to spend more time at work, focusing on getting the raise that my employer dangled before me like bait. I tagged along to the trade show in Miami one weekend, realizing part of me just wanted to get away from Jan. I kissed her goodbye that Friday morning, expecting to see her on Sunday evening, but plans changed. The second day of the trade show was canceled due to a power issue, and I took a flight back Saturday instead. I was exhausted and only looked forward to a long shower, but concern grew when Janelle didn't answer my texts that I'd sent from the airport. Worry became panic when I called repeatedly and got her inbox. I rushed home and unlocked the door, but sighed with relief upon entering. Jan's coat was on the chair and the shower was running.

"Jan, honey, I'm back a day early. Everything OK?" I called to her, but the hiss of the shower seemed to drown out my voice.

"Honey," I called out and walked over to the door. My dress shoe slipped on the floor, and I fought to remain upright. I looked down in confusion to a spattering of red on the floor I immediately knew was blood. "Janelle!" I screamed out as dread twisted my heart in my chest. I turned the knob and flung open the door, my gaze following the blood trail to a serrated kitchen knife on the tile floor. Above it, sitting naked on the lip of the bathtub, was Janelle.

I then understood why she'd stayed covered up from head to toe around me for the past few months. Large chunks of her skin and muscle were slivered away. Puffy, mottled skin encircled the sinewy craters she'd carved from her own body. In other places, large crusty scabs sat within bruised flesh, purple and infected. Deep gouges ran along her forearms and thighs revealing scar tissue, shiny and pink where the muscle had been whittled down. Some wounds were red and fresh, streaming glistening ribbons of blood from recently flayed strips. I struggled to remain upright as the butchered body of my wife turned to me with a smile, revealing what she held in her slender, peeled arms.

It was a mass of clumped meat, wrapped in a stitched-together quilt of Janelle's skin. A sculpture composed of her own carved flesh and blood, sewn into the form of a patchwork infant in varying degrees of spoil. It was a child produced from her own mutilated body, with a putrid thumb tip nose from the accident that triggered the horrific idea. Janelle held the thing to her now breast-less chest and rocked it gently back and forth in her hacked arms.

"Isn't he beautiful?" she asked, looking down at the meaty collage with loving eyes wet with tears of joy. I fell backward on the blood-spattered trail on the floor, struggling to get away from the ungodly scene, but not before seeing it. Before I called the ambulance with shaky hands—before I vomited on myself, before I crawled from the bloody scene, before I could turn away from the horror—I saw it. I saw that nightmarish sculpture of a baby slowly turn its bloated head towards me; and smile.

THE SLEEP WALK

Every night since I can remember, I've had only one recurring dream. I'd dream I was walking barefoot in the night over vast stretches of land. Through darkened forests and murky swamps, I'd trek onward, admiring the serenity of each nocturnal scene. Rocks and twigs would occasionally poke the tender soles of my bare feet, but it was beautiful and meditative. I'd trudge through marshes, feeling the icy mud squish between my toes, and I'd listen to the frogs and owls sing as I waded into moonlit mires. Deer would watch me, flicking an ear before bounding off as I'd walk deeper into forests, with no destination and never the same place twice.

Every night it was the same dream; an endless promenade so profound that I'd often wake with a sigh at finding myself back in my bed, not quite ready to return to my mundane routine. The dreams took me through endless deserts lit by brilliant starlight. Through massive mountain ranges that reached up towards the heavens where I'd climb high enough to breach the clouds. I'd even walk underwater along murky lake beds and cavernous ocean abysses; the weightless pressure hugging me as undiscovered fish swam past my face.

Over the past few months, however, my dreams became less striking. The sleepwalk took me near littered roadways with car headlights and bright billboards obscuring the stars. City lights twinkled and glowed as the scenery became far less remarkable. Then last week I dreamed I was walking along the tree line near a street I recognized from the neighboring city. The spindly, naked legs beneath me hiked onward, and I recognized landmarks from my town: the firehouse, train station, and eventually the outskirts of my own neighborhood. The dreams were taking me closer to home.

In last night's dream I sleepwalked through my suburb, watching my house get closer until I crossed my own backyard. I watched as my hands reached out to feel the cold aluminum siding. Under the flickering streetlight, I could see my fingers were thin, bony and far too long. My jagged fingernails dug into the wall, and I started to climb up my home's exterior. The dark glass pane of my window drew closer until I peered inside. There I lay, sound asleep in my bed. I watched helplessly as I lifted the window and climbed inside my bedroom. I walked closer to the bed, staring down at my own sleeping form.

I woke up screaming, my heart rapidly pounding in my chest. A gamy smell, sour and rotten, filled my bedroom, causing me to gag as I jumped out of bed. I was drenched in sweat, yet I couldn't stop shivering. An icy chill ran down my back when I saw the source of the draft. My bedroom window was wide open.

I'M EXPERIENCING CONTINUITY ERRORS

It started last week at around 7:45 AM. I rode the city bus to my work, absorbed in the eBook's words on my phone screen and trying my best to mind my own business. I only looked up briefly to see if I had time to finish the chapter. I just happened to spot a man in an outdated, dark blue polyester suit. His puffy eyelids kept closing in slivers as he nodded off and a half-eaten apple slid slowly down between his fingertips. I couldn't help but stare as the apple continued to slip past his tenuous grip before landing on the filthy bus floor with a *thunk*.

An alert sounded from a requested stop. I looked up for only a fraction of a second, and when I looked back at that man, he was holding the apple once again. I gawked, stunned and confused at having somehow misread the information my eyes had fed to my brain.

It was impossible for him to have retrieved it from the floor in that sliver of a second. Yet, there he was, holding the waxy red fruit as if he'd never dropped it. His sleepy eyes widened into an intense stare as they locked onto mine before I quickly looked back down at my phone's screen. That's how it began.

That evening after work, I walked home past an alleyway by a restaurant I passed daily. As always, it was filthy; strewn with half-rotted vegetables by rainbow puddles of soapy mop water. I glanced in to see a filthy stray cat, sitting with one hind leg to the sky as it cleaned itself behind an overfilled green dumpster. I checked the time out of habit, and when I looked up again, a cat was slinking deeper into the alley, but it was not the same cat. I was absolutely sure of this. The spots had shifted and were larger and darker as well. The stray was even slightly fatter—cleaner too, its fur no longer matted with the grime I'd previously observed. A feeling of powerlessness over my untrustworthy perception manifested in a heavy weight in the pit of my stomach.

I rationalized there had to have been two cats. One had surely exited out some unseen passage. I approached the dark alley and looked at the grimy brick wall, but there was absolutely no place for another animal to have disappeared. I was certain it was not the same cat I'd seen.

I began to pay attention to my surroundings out of desperation in order to ensure myself I wasn't going mad. I prayed I'd just mistook a few things and that would be the end of it, but it wasn't. The more I studied the subtle details of the world around me, the more of these strange continuity errors I began to notice.

Some changes were small, like the littered potato chip bag switching brands when I passed it a second time. Others were far bolder and a bit more unsettling; like a family in the building next door, which I might not have noticed had I not scrutinized them with newfound fascination. I'd glimpsed them occasionally; a husband and wife and their curly-haired toddler. When I observed them the following morning loading camping gear into their hatchback, it was undeniable. The toddler had been replaced by a slightly older child, perhaps 3 or 4 years old, with braided black hair and a wide smile on her face of a lighter complexion. The couple looked different as well, similar features but clearly not the same people. I felt ill as my brain tried to make sense of it.

I began wondering if I was suffering from some malignant brain tumor or early onset dementia. My entire reality began to feel like a "Spot the difference" puzzle, and I became obsessed with finding these peculiar changes. I began documenting the anomalies by photographing them. A car changed brands to a similar make and color. The unkempt hair of a man caught in a gust of wind was perfectly combed when he emerged from behind a tree. It was uncanny and almost amusing at first.

I gawked from behind my menu when at lunch, waiting for the high-heeled date of a middle-aged stockbroker to return from the restroom. I was the only one to notice that she'd returned a different person. Same dress, same product-stiffened hair, but her narrower, more angular features only I seemed able to see. The replaced woman sat down with the corporate executive and the meal continued as if nothing was amiss.

Other changes would be far more trivial. A brand of jeans would switch out, or subtle color difference would take place in an article of clothing that nobody else seemed to notice. It was amusing and mysterious, some inside joke that only I seemed in on. But then it happened to me.

When I returned from work this evening, I froze. My crimson doormat had been replaced by a beige one. I closed and locked the deadbolt, nervously peering out the peephole into the hall. My heart pounded as I made my way through my apartment, noticing the changes in the framed photos on my walls. They were photographs of a nearly identical family, but they were strangers. My jaw hung open as I marveled at how each and every photograph in my apartment had been recreated with a cast of doubles. Something was missing from them, and my insides squirmed as I realized *I* was.

I spent the evening frantically searching my apartment for anything to connect me to this shifting city. Entering my email address returned a "Google account not found" as well as Facebook, Instagram and a few other social media sites. My phone's contacts list is blank, and when I called my parent's house, a stranger's voice answered before I hung up. The world was slowly being replaced around me—even more specifically, without me—piece by infinitesimal piece.

I sat on a couch I didn't own and searched through the photos I'd taken in desperation, and that's when I noticed him lurking within the frame. That suited man from the bus stood in the background of nearly half the snapshots I'd collected. He was tall and clean-cut, maybe late 40s and standing about six foot two, dressed in that familiar dark blue polyester suit from another era. It was without a doubt the same man on the bus who dropped the apple.

He was watching with an unnerving look of shock. A clipboard rested on his forearm in a few of them, and he seemed to be taking notes. Or worse, editing them.

The key jingling in the door startled me, and I stood up, aware someone else had a key. The deadbolt stopped the shoved door from opening. My heart pounded as I realized my apartment now belonged to someone else. I grabbed a phone charger from an outlet, then walked quickly past rooms redecorated by someone with a far more reserved sense of style. I rushed to the back window and lifted it up, stepping out onto the cool air of the fire escape. I didn't descend it. I just stood there in the wind, watching the faces of strangers passing below, realizing I had nowhere to even go as a dark thought clicked.

A shiver climbed my spine as the questions trickled into my mind. What if I'd witnessed something I plainly should not have? What if by noticing that initial continuity error, I created a much greater one that needed fixing? What if the error that needed fixing was me?

MY SON TURNED A KID BACKWARDS

The scream, that's what I'll never forget. It was an animal scream, like the vocal cords weren't properly structured. That banshee howl that shivered deep in the marrow of my bones and vibrated my bowels. Half scream, half death rattle. That scream is something I'll never be able to scrub from my memory.

Since the "accident," as my doctor refers to it, I sleep in short, empty sessions. Not a dream, not a whisper of fantasy to release me. Not even a nightmare; they've all drained from my subconscious. That tank is long dried up. The constant shaking makes it nearly impossible to type. My psychiatrist called it the worst case of PTSD he'd ever seen. Don't feel bad for me, though. Feel bad for the mother who resides in a state hospital, laughing endlessly as if it is all just some cruel, cosmic joke. Feel bad for the father, who leaped off a balcony to his death with a loud slap the day after he had her committed. Feel bad for Oliver, the kid it happened to. The kid my son Samuel turned "backwards."

It was Samuel's seventh birthday. Toys were giddily unwrapped with excited little fingers as joyful music played. The sun was shining, and the birds chirped; I don't recall a more pleasant day in terms of the weather. The kids had been yelling and getting a little rough. One of the kids had been teasing Sam for still playing with stuffed animals. He sounded a bit cruel and nagging. That was the last thing I heard before that awful silence. I went inside for just a few minutes to reply to a work email when the din of children bickering stopped abruptly. Suddenly it was *too* quiet. I had just begun to realize that when I heard Samuel's voice. I looked from the inbox on my screen over to the doorway to see his big brown eyes peering up at me. His freckled face peaked out from behind the painted frame.

"I turned someone backwards," he said in a shy, half-whisper as he watched me, waiting for my angered reaction. It was a child's riddle to me, though. Something innocent and playful. A game, more than likely, but then I heard it. I heard that blood-curdling scream, like razor blades across my eardrums.

It came from outside. It was guttural. Animal.

It seemed to linger in the air like some ungodly siren. I ran out the back door to the lawn, only wondering what the source of that terrible wailing could possibly be. I then saw what backwards meant.

There was an abstract form standing on the lawn. It stood half the size of a man on two mangled legs of bending bone and exposed meat. It trembled as if cold from having just shed its skin, but the skin wasn't missing. It was inside out, stretched over that glistening sculpture of venous horror that ran fluids like a searing pork chop. Yellow beads of fat swirled down over the ribboned fibers of visible muscle, which spasmed and twitched in an unknowable pain. What must have been the head was the worst. It had a hole in the center that streamed the sagging rope of brain past exploded shards of teeth which splayed outward in white streaks like pulled taffy.

Inverted intestines slipped down the lubricated pelvic bone, jutting white and pristine as if unaware it should be encased in flesh. Pattering offal plopped noisily onto the sunny tarmac. I could hear it then, through those rattling screams of the other children and parents, who had only then processed what they were seeing. It whispered in confusion, twitching and wincing slightly at first from the gradually building pain. It was a meek voice; confused, hurting, and afraid.

"What's happening to me?" it whimpered through drooling syllables. The nerves of that abomination must've finally begun to process what they were feeling, because after that, all it could do was scream.

THE SCARIEST RIDE
IN THE WORLD

The buttery smell of popcorn, joyful calliope melodies and the thrilled screams of children filled the air. The summer state fair had once again sprouted dusty canvas tents, junk food carts and light-speckled rides. In the back, the self-proclaimed "Scariest Ride in the World" kept most sugar-sticky kids at bay, but not Seth.

Seth smirked at the haunted house ride, festooned with carved and painted skulls, serpents and spiders. He puffed his chest, then marched through the mouth-shaped entrance unafraid.

His eyes fought to adjust to the darkness, and he nearly yelped at the sight of the decrepit ticket taker extending an open palm. Seth grumbled as he fished for a ticket and placed it into the wrinkled hand. The grinning old man pointed a bony finger at the solitary cart sitting on the track. Seth approached and slid into the wooden seat, and the rickety vehicle clacked along the track into the darkness ahead.

The cart rattled on the rails past dusty animatronic dummies, a cackling witch to his left, a shoddy ghoul to his right. A laughable rubber ghost charged on a zipline and a jiggling rubber spider straight out of a Halloween supply store dropped and dangled above him. "Scary my ass," Seth huffed, then spat a loogie onto a cheap plastic skeleton. Bored, he stood up and hopped from the slow-moving cart onto the floor beside the track.

He began to kick at the motorized ghouls and stuffed black cats. He even unzipped his jeans and pissed inside a shadowy alcove, nearly yelping when a surprisingly realistic bat flapped out from within, nicking his forehead. Ignoring the sting, he chuckled as he kicked over plastic gravestones and yanked fake cobwebs down from the ceiling. Seth laughed as he strolled back outside into the sunlit fairground.

In the following days, Seth bragged to his peers about his exploits on the childish ride. He neglected the two tiny red dots on his forehead, which began to tingle and itch. A week passed before Seth fell ill with what seemed like the common flu. Days later, an intense feeling of dread haunted his every waking moment, and he writhed in constant agitation. By the time he confessed about how he'd gotten the tiny bite, the rabies virus had penetrated his brain.

Seth would soon be unable to drink water, violently coughing it from his stinging throat. Hallucinations more horrific than his darkest nightmares would torment him daily. Spasmodic contractions would ripple through his aching muscles as he lay strapped to a hospital bed, foaming at the mouth. Seth would tremble and moan in absolute agony in those long days before his certain death. But that relief would come much later, for the scariest ride in the world had only just begun.

NOTHING IS COMING

After a 3 AM phone call expressing urgency and promising a massive payment, I agreed to be flown in to investigate a technical issue at the LHC, the Large Hadron Collider located in Geneva, Switzerland.

For those who haven't heard of it, the Large Hadron Collider is essentially a tunnel forming a ring used to propel charged particles at high speeds in order to study them; it was completed back in 2008. Being a prominent professor of particle physics, and one of the few who specialized in atom smashers, I seemed to be suddenly in demand.

The contact at CERN, the organization responsible for its construction, expressed urgent concern after a "peculiarity" had been discovered only a few hours after their most recent test. The more I inquired as to the nature of the "peculiarity" the more confused I became. They simply were not giving me any info. I had little time to pack and drive out to the airport.

I was intercepted at the airport in Geneva by a man with a sign bearing my name. I was then escorted to Meyrin, Switzerland, exhausted and confused as to what the emergency entailed. Eventually, I was let out of the car at a large cluster of buildings contained in a secure, fenced-in area. A gray-haired man with a strong handshake and worried eyes greeted me at the entrance and introduced himself as the director of technology.

"Thank you for coming," the man said, his fingers fidgeting nervously. "We are in urgent need of your expertise."

"What exactly is going on, doctor?" I was growing frustrated with the secrecy, but a bit worried as well. I clenched my arms in the crooks of my elbows; it was so cold in there.

"After the latest test of the particle accelerator, an aberration occurred. Come this way." The doctor led me into the dull gray building. He ushered me into an elevator, pressing the button with a shaky finger after scanning his access card. "We thought it was a spark or ember. Something ignited by the electricity from the machine." My ears popped as we descended into the depths of the subterranean tunnel built for the study of atomic particles. It would have been my dream job to work here at one time, but the fear in the doctor's voice changed that.

"And what was it? What was this aberration?" I asked, tired of being in the dark.

"A white speck. Brighter than anything else in the tunnel, but it cast no shadows, nor did it emit light. It was like viewing an image on a broken monitor, one pixel out of sync and totally white." The doctor wiped his brow with his sleeve. He was sweating. It was cold enough to see my breath in that slow-moving elevator, but he was sweating.

"Go on," I said, feeling an uneasiness squirm in my stomach.

"Well, the physicists followed protocol, testing for radiation. There was none."

"That's good," I interjected, but he kept talking as the doors opened up, leading into a long corridor.

"It was floating, stuck in place in mid-air." The doctor looked into my eyes, and I could see the fear in them. He was terrified. "And it was getting larger. Professor Buchman, one of the physicists used a cotton swab to take a sample. We watched in awe as the swab vanished upon contact. The speck simultaneously increased in mass. Like it had eaten it. Then Buchman screamed…"

The doctor led me through a heavy steel door. I marveled at the massive chamber we had entered. It was the collider tunnel, reminiscent of a long, underground train tunnel. In the center was a multi-billion-dollar array of superconducting magnets. My eyes followed the long trail of equipment down the tunnel and I saw it. A white hole that looked like the tunnel itself hadn't been rendered. An unfinished drawing of sorts. My jaw dropped agape as I stared at the impossible white circle.

"He then tried to step away," the doctor continued, "but he was unable. In less than a second, his arm was absorbed, and the white sphere had grown to the size of a volleyball. He finally pulled himself free, but the arm was gone. A clean amputation that bled him out in moments. There was no way to save him."

I watched the impossible, massive hole of pure white at the end of the long tunnel. I took a few nervous steps and my neck hair stood on end as I processed its size based on our distance from it. The white sphere extended beyond the tunnel itself, a few meters in diameter. The edges expanded as I watched, ever so slowly. It was growing.

"It's eating atoms." The doctor explained in a tearful voice. "Everything we used to try to examine it was swallowed by that— that mass of nothingness. Even creating a vacuum did nothing but feed it.

I was shaking then too. This rupture in matter itself was visibly growing, and I just knew, just as the doctor weeping beside me, that nothing could be done to stop it.

"What is the rate of growth?" I asked, dreading the answer.

"Exponential," the doctor said before burying his face in his hands. "It started only yesterday. This morning it was a meter in diameter, just one meter. This is it, isn't it?" He asked.

I had no words. I was still wrapping my head around the size based on the amount of time that had elapsed. I knew, just as he did, how fast it would grow.

I eventually apologized and left, knowing very well it was futile to do anything. All I can do is spend time with my family while there is time left. I flew out hours ago, and from the plane, I could see a tiny white disc where the anomaly had begun to emerge from the underground facility.

I told the doctor what I estimated, and the number was the same as his.

Two weeks. It should expand to the size of the planet in less than two weeks.

THE NEIGHBOR'S HOUSE IS GETTING CLOSER

In my 15 years on Mulberry Lane, I rarely met my neighbors. A friendly wave when raking leaves or taking out the trash sufficed. I've always been a bit awkward, and I think of my home as the one place I can breathe easily and drop the social facade. I saw the moving van a few weeks ago outside of the eggshell blue house next door and presumed a family was moving in. I didn't notice anyone but the movers during brief glances out my curtains. I minded my own for a few days, but then I began hearing the cries.

Every night once the sun went down, the muffled wailing of an infant would sound from the house next door. It wasn't too intrusive, and the sturdy walls of our craftsman homes offered plentiful noise reduction. A family fleeing the city to raise a child in the suburbs seemed only natural, of course. But the crying wouldn't subside. And it sounded, for lack of a better word, "off."

The high-pitched wail was just a bit too gravelly, the timing of the howls a tad too consistent. One Thursday, as the street became enshrouded in shadow and that crying began, I headed to the East end of my home and lifted open the heavy window facing the blue house of the neighbors to better hear.

Perhaps it was the cool gust of autumn air on my skin that triggered a fear response, or the large shadows from the moonlight feeding my imagination. I listened to that wailing sound, a few decibels higher with my window's pane lifted, and it sounded almost animal. Something distinctly different from the cries of a human baby. I locked that 2nd story window after closing it that night.

My curiosity grew as certain peculiarities I could not explain became more frequent. A few days later, I returned from a grocery run. As I pulled into my driveway, I sat in my car for a few minutes, observing the pale blue house of the unseen neighbors. It looked very different, yet the same. It took a while to work out what seemed to be different.

The house appeared to be closer. Just by a foot or two. Something clearly impossible in every regard, of course, but unable to ignore nonetheless. The 30-foot space between our homes looked just shy of that. The dull painted wood siding, flaking with neglect, was more prominent and in focus. I proceeded to unlock my front door, then doubled back to bring my produce inside.

On the east side of my home from out my kitchen window, their house did appear to be closer. Their dark windowpanes looked larger, closer than they previously had been. I consider myself a rational man, so I did my best to ignore the phenomenon. I did a good job of getting lost in my work until the golden sun began to set, a veil of shadow extinguishing its glow.

I did my best to avoid looking out my windows. Getting worked up over nothing is counterproductive, even unhealthy. Still, once it was fully night, that strange cry sounded from next door. Louder, it was so very clearly louder. I exited my study and followed the hallway to the window overlooking the neighboring home. Framed within my windowpane was that of the neighbors. It was undoubtedly closer.

I approached without thinking, walking slowly down the runner carpet. I reached my window and looked through theirs. It was dark, the only sign of life the harsh crying that lit up the corner of my mind reserved for superstition and make-believe. My fingers pressed against the cold glass as I looked into the dark second-story floor of my neighbor's home.

In the void of light that shrouded the interior in darkness, I saw some fast movement. An appendage whipping in the dark from one side of the window to the other. Something impossible to identify, maybe an arm. Maybe.

Fear got the better of me. I briskly walked through my home, locking the windows and doors.

"Out of sight, out of mind." I mused, wiping my hands as if the gesture would rid myself of that tingling feeling of horror from my runaway imagination. I chuckled to myself, finally accepting how preposterous I was being. With a deep exhale, I poured a glass of red wine and plopped down onto the couch to watch something. A comedy. Despite all my efforts, I was unable to ignore the fact that I had to raise the volume a few bars in order to cover the crying from the neighboring house.

That week, work came in an avalanche. I freelance, so I was grateful not only for the money that would come, but for the fact I would actually be busy again. "Idle hands" as the saying goes. Long days stretched into the evenings as I toiled away debugging sloppy code. In the white light of the screen, I kept my earbuds in to drown out the terrible cries from next door.

"It's none of my business." I muttered to myself when pushing the earbuds deeper and raising the volume. I opened a browser window and ordered a set of curtains. That seemed enough to calm my nerves, and I was eventually able to fall asleep that night.

Try as I might to convince myself it was all some optical illusion or lapse in memory, I was unable to. That was punctuated after fetching the mail a week ago. I exited my front door and felt every neck hair raise when I *felt* the proximity of the house next door. When I turned my head, I just stood there stunned. It was roughly 15 feet from my home, undeniably closer than it previously had been.

Just to allay my worries, to ease these unnatural fears lurking about my mind, I decided to meet the neighbors. Just a friendly introduction and maybe mentioning the peculiar phenomenon. They might think I was crazy, but at least I'd have a face of the mother or father to put my mind at rest. Maybe a glimpse of the baby creating those hideous sounds all hours of the night.

After a deep breath, I walked along the concrete path to the sidewalk. It was only when I'd nearly reached their pathway that I realized something I hadn't before. There was no car in the driveway, nor had there ever been. I swallowed the lump that grew in my throat and tried to calm myself. It was a sunny day, lovely in all regards, aside from the large blue home that loomed overhead, casting a stark shadow.

I knocked and waited. Nobody answered the door, but someone was clearly home.

I heard a muffled scampering sound from behind the door. Despite the sounds from inside, nobody answered.

"Hello? I'm Mitchell, the neighbor, just wanted to apologize for not greeting you earlier!" I tried to maintain a chipper, neighborly voice, but it came out shaky. The sounds of movement from within the house left my insides cold. Something was quickly darting about and then stopping, as if listening. I flinched when I heard a heavy thud from somewhere deep within.

Curiosity led me closer to the tall, narrow windows on the sides of the door. I just wanted any sort of visual confirmation of the neighbors. Just some sign that things were normal. I leaned in closer to the dark glass, peering in. Every light was off, and the sunlight that gave sight to the interior was strangely dim. I could barely make out anything at all. Just the general shape of a staircase like mine. A pink wallpaper that looked to have a glossy sheen.

It looked wrong somehow, but I couldn't place it at the time. In retrospect, I think it was that the walls and stairs had an irregular texture. I quickly recoiled from the window, running back along the grass towards my home. I tried the police, but was lost for what I would say. I settled on a wellness check, mentioning the sounds of a neglected infant from within and no vehicle or sign of the neighbors. I left out the most peculiar detail; the fact the house seemed to be getting closer to mine every day.

I watched from my window when the police cruiser arrived as the sun dipped beneath the mesh of tree branches. I saw the officer step outside his car and walk down the path to their front door. He knocked, waited, and looked in the window. He circled the house and vanished from view, presumably to look in other windows. I watched for a while, for any sign of him reappearing, but he did not. Eventually I was so creeped out I had to stop looking at that house. I occupied myself with the internet as the sun sank and evening came. And then I heard the gritty crying that's not quite human.

I walked downstairs to refill my water glass, and when I peeked out my kitchen window, I let out a gasp of shock. The neighbor's window was right there, just feet away from mine. I could even see into the shadowy home. The fuzzy darkness supplied a little insight into what was within, and that crippling fear lurching up from the crevices of my mind returned.

I could see the walls, slick, wet and lumpy. An organic hollow form with fleshy walls that jittered and twitched ever-so-slightly. It was like looking into the beaded fat and veiny muscle of a freshly gutted elk. Bone-like support beams were visible through the translucent membrane I'd previously mistaken as wallpaper.

I screamed, and it screamed back. The infant cries, coarse and distorted, bellowed from deep within the impossible structure. I panicked then, gathered a few belongings—phone charger, wallet, jacket, cash—and descended the staircase. I'd rent a hotel and call the police, recommending backup. I played through the actions in my head, thinking of the cheap hotel off the highway just 15-minutes away.

My skin crawled as I reached the first floor. I tried to ignore the undeniable sight out my kitchen window. It looked directly into that fluid-glazed organic interior of the neighboring home. I focused on the front door, trying hard as I could not to register the fact that the horrific house next door now appeared to be directly attached to my own.

I was jogging by the time I reached my front door, undoing the deadbolt with nervous digits. My mind was screaming at me to move faster. "Get to the car!" but then I opened the door. A dark, red interior lay beyond my door. A continuation into a cubic, bodily cavity with viscera and veins. There was a stink of coppery meat. The smell of a butcher's shop in the dead of summer, humid and rank.

I slammed closed the door to the impossible horror that had somehow encompassed my home. My feet sprinted, carrying me to the basement door, which I locked behind me in a frenzy.

Here, I wait in the dark basement, as the screaming and gurgling sounds draw closer overhead. Wooden beams creak and groan. Glass occasionally shatters. I dialed emergency services again, but the signal is blocked by what has encased my house.

A matchbook I found on the shelf rests in one hand, a tin of gasoline in the other. A last resort, quickly becoming the only option. I made my peace and accepted my fate. I only have one request for anyone out there who might see a house ablaze on Mulberry Lane.

Make sure they don't put the fire out. I'm begging you, let it burn.

THE PROBLEM WITH LAB-GROWN MEAT

The numbers could not be ignored. After adding vitamins and bio-active compounds, lab-grown meat would be 70% healthier than meat harvested from livestock. It would cut greenhouse gas emissions by over 90%, prevent rainforest depletion, and even reduce shipping costs and subsequent pollution. It was by far the most humane option as well, ending the suffering of billions of animals each year. Quickly approved by the USDA and FDA, the meat made itself home in grocery stores and butcher shops across the globe.

Jim Dougan—a resident of Harrison, Michigan—ignored his stomachache for the first few weeks. He attributed the stomach pain to his decades-long battle with acid reflux. It always went away on its own, but after a sixth day of stabbing stomach pain and crimson stools, he decided to make an appointment with his physician. Though only a week away, the appointment was never met. When they found him screaming and writhing in pain on the cement floor of a Home Depot, an ambulance was called, and he ended up in the ER instead.

An X Ray was performed after painkillers were administered to Mr. Dougan. The illuminated film showed what appeared to be a large number of calcium deposits in the swollen stomach of the unconscious man. Before the anomaly was even identified, hospitals across the globe had become flooded with an influx of suffering people. Excruciating abdominal pain was followed by the expectoration of blood and multiple hematomas. It was clear an epidemic was unfolding. Emergency surgeries revealed strange tissue growth throughout the digestive tracts of the ill.

By the time the link was made, thousands had already died from organ failure, suffocation and internal bleeding. Those unlucky enough to survive soon lay immobile with massively swollen stomachs and engorged purple limbs as they wheezed their numbered breaths. Fleshy, pink filaments grew like ground meat through stretched skin pores and other orifices when real estate within the epidermis quickly ran out. The problem with lab-grown meat became apparent far too late to address; it simply would not stop growing.

MY SISTER WEARS A PILLOWCASE

My older sister Carly left for summer camp on July 15th. I said something along the lines of "good riddance" when she stuck her tongue at me after delivering one of her go-to insults, but it was all in good fun and I was finally free. Despite being able to sprawl out on the couch and hog the remote, the days began to grow long and dull without Carly there to antagonize me. By the time the month of freedom crawled towards an end, I kind of missed her presence in a masochistic way. My ears perked up when my mother informed me she was off to pick up Carly from camp.

I perched on the sofa and watched out the window as mom drove off, and time slowed. I was eager to hear all about the camp, and I waited with my nose pressed against the pane for what felt like an eternity. Eventually I saw mom's station wagon appear between the pines. The car slowed to a halt on the grumbling gravel and my mother exited the vehicle. She then circled back and opened the back door for my sister, and I cocked my head in confusion when she emerged from the back seat. Carly was wearing a light lavender pillowcase over her head, concealing it completely.

I watched dumbstruck, wondering if it was some kind of planned joke or makeover-reveal setup, but my mother was not smiling as she assisted my sister slowly out of the vehicle. I wondered if another girl was beneath that hood, but I recognized Carly by the way she walked. My mother then aided my blindfolded sister down the pathway to our front door. Upon entering, a gust of hot air swept in as the two walked slowly into the living room.

"Carly?" I asked my hooded sister as she shuffled in, but she didn't respond. Her small fingers twitched as if she'd meant to speak, but she only continued trudging along the carpet. My mom slowly guided Carly towards the staircase, supporting her every step with an extended elbow. Once they passed by and their backs were to me, I could see a faded brown stain on the pillowcase my sister wore. I shivered at the sight of it but was too stunned to speak.

I stayed downstairs, staring wide-eyed at the dim stairway leading up to our bedrooms until my mother descended alone. She didn't say a word as she headed into the kitchen and began chopping vegetables for dinner. I remained on the couch, my eyes fixed on the shadowy staircase. I listened to a faint, rhythmic sound coming from the darkness upstairs. It was Carly's wet breathing, raspy and bubbling, and it turned my stomach.

The clatter of metal pans and sizzling oils brought onion and garlic smells from the kitchen. But any appetite I might have had vanished once those stairs creaked, signaling Carly's presence. I looked up at her darkened figure at the top of the staircase, looming above. She was slow and shaky, gripping the banister so hard I thought it might splinter during her descent. When she walked closer and passed by to enter the dining room, she dragged a faint stink through the air with her. It was the smell of spoiled meat.

I remained motionless until mom commanded me to join them at the dining room table. I approached the table with a racing heart, and I sat down as a thick silence filled the air. I picked at the vegetables on my plate, unable to stop staring at the disquieting scene of my sister with a cloth bag over her head. Every few minutes, my mother would stand up with a fake smile and approach my hooded sister. She would lean over her and feed forkfuls of food under that cloth hood, each time careful to hide any glimpse of Carly's face. When my sister chewed, she created a sound that roiled my guts.

"What is wrong with her?!" I finally blurted out as hot tears streamed down my face. Carly's thin hands clenched the table's edge until her knuckles whitened, but she didn't respond. My mother shot me a molten glance of fury, her dark eyes and fake smile twitching as she struggled to maintain her composure.

"Carly," my mom paused to swallow, "Is under the weather, honey. Eat your meal." The scowl accompanying her statement derailed any further questions I had. I looked back at that stained pillowcase hiding my sister's face. The concealed head twitched, and I shuddered in response. That awful odor crept into my nostrils once again, and I jumped up and ran from the table, knocking back the chair in my wake. I raced up the stairs into my bedroom and slammed the door. With my face pressed into my mattress, I cried until the sheets were soaked. The sun eventually sank, and the room grew dark and cool. I tried not to imagine what horrible things lay beneath that pillowcase. But then my door creaked open just a sliver. Just enough to see that pillowcase and the bony white hand on the door frame.

I curled into a ball against the opposite wall, wishing to fall back through it to get away. That deep wheezing magnified as I lay still with bated breath.

The door creaked open wider. My eyes adjusted to the cloth which hung loose enough to make out the slope of her forehead in the pale moonlight from my window. The top ridge of her nose jutted out at an angle that didn't look right at all. Then the fabric began to move.

Things fluttered beneath the pillowcase where cheeks and eyes should have been. A wet, sticky sound whispered as the fabric came slowly alive with new ridges and valleys that no head should have. That stench of putrid meat permeated my room and my heart raced as I watched; terrified. Carly took a step into my room, her wheezing breath thick as tar. She lurched forward in a shaky step, and the peaking horror finally became too much for me to take. My vision clouded black as I lost consciousness.

I awoke today to the appetizing smell of eggs and bacon sizzling. I groggily rose, the muddling transition to consciousness causing me to reassess what exactly took place the night before. It all might have been a nightmare, I thought. It had to have been. I had nearly convinced myself of this in order to preserve my threatened sanity, but when I approached the stairway and looked down over the railing, my heart sank.

There Carly stood, hooded in that awful pillowcase that looked even filthier than before. Blossoming patterns of gray and ochre blotched the fabric over. Her arms hung by her side, pale and veiny. My mother stood by her side, wearing a forced smile as she extended an open palm to the full breakfast on the dining room table. My eyes quickly drifted to the suitcase standing near the front door.

"Make sure you eat up, honey," my mother spoke in an apathetic voice. The fake smile slid off of her face and I looked away from her, back to the suitcase by the door as she continued. My suitcase.

"Today's your first day of camp."

SWITCHED LUGGAGE

I groggily watched the silver carousel turn until it finally spat out my suitcase. I lugged it down and rolled it outside to the cab queue, too tired to haggle the inflated flat rate. Once in the cab, I nodded off until I arrived at my hotel. I checked in quickly, eager to finish the nap I'd started on the plane. Upon my head hitting the pillow, I was out.

When I woke hours later, I licked the film on my teeth and winced in disgust. I got up, desperate to brush, but when I unzipped my suitcase to fetch my toothbrush I stared down in confusion. There were stacks of neatly folded dress clothing and a leather-bound book embossed with the word "memories" within; nothing of my own.

I cursed, realizing I must have taken a nearly identical suitcase from the luggage claim by mistake. I dialed the airport's customer service number and listened to the automated list of departments, pressing the "lost and found" menu button as my anxiety built. No lost or misplaced bags had been reported. Try back later.

I searched for a phone number on the luggage, but there was no sticker or bag tag anywhere to be found on the ringed zipper pullers or the handles. Hoping to find a number, or at least a name, I removed the photo album and opened its clinging plastic pages.

Upon opening the creaky leather book, I was greeted by black and white photos of smiling faces and rows of text. I tried to ignore them as I scoured the inside jacket for contact information, but I found no number or name of the luggage's owner. I only saw the word "missing" in the bold, black text of headlines. I turned the page to see more smiling faces on various newspaper clippings.

I flipped through laminated pages of missing persons from numerous states, reading details of their last known whereabouts, and large cash rewards promised for their safe return. When I turned the page marking the last of the news clippings, I dropped the book in shock. Teeth. Meat. Flesh so butchered I didn't at first understand it was human. Dozens of Polaroids—original photographs; not clippings, prints or copies—revealed images that shook me to the core.

I reached down to slam the book closed, eager to protect my rattled mind from the horrors documented within. As I did, the naked truth of the situation set in as a headband of panic tightened.

The person responsible for the atrocities photographed in that book had my suitcase. My suitcase, which I'd thoughtfully tagged with a little looped label where I had written my name, my phone number, and my home address. That person now had my suitcase, containing my photos of my wife and eight-month-old daughter.

WHAT MY GIRLFRIEND'S BEEN PAINTING

I met the love of my life on my lunch break.

I was cramming a BLT into my mouth while leaning forward on the painted wooden bench in the park near my office. The weather was perfect. Lush green leaves were swaying in the whispering breeze; but I felt like I was being watched. I glanced up from my meal, which had coated my hands in dripping mayo and bacon grease. I then noticed her on a bench to the left of me; a fair-faced girl in a ratty hoodie with the most stunning eyes I'd ever seen.

I gave a small smile and waved a grease-slathered hand, instantly cringing at how awkward I was. Though my coworkers find my impression of a drunken Orson Welles funny, charisma is generally not one of my strengths. The girl in the oversized sweatshirt just smiled at me. She was absolutely beautiful.

A pixie cut of dark hair peeked out from under the large hood. She had a dusting of freckles on high cheeks. A small, yet elegant, nose was reminiscent of Audrey Hepburn. Her graceful lips curled up at the corners, but her eyes are what sped up my heart in my chest. Wide windows of wonder fitted with beautiful brown irises. They were looking at me in curious fascination. Not judgment, but intrigue.

As I gulped down a bite of my messy sandwich, I felt butterflies stir in my stomach. I tried to swallow the large morsel of food before speaking.

"Nice day, I love this park," I said, but the words were muffled by the large chunk of sandwich I'd attempted to force down.

And then I felt the ball of bread lodge in my throat. I sipped my cardboard cup of soda, only to find it was empty. My face felt hot, and I wheezed out but was unable to breathe in. I was choking.

She watched me for a minute as I staggered from the bench before taking charge. She then ran up to me and wrapped her slender arms around my torso, heaving up under my ribs as pain shot out from within me. On the fourth painful constriction, the clump of greasy bread was ejected from my gaping mouth: a cannonball of carbs that rolled onto the grass. She'd saved my life.

"Thank you," I gasped as she led me to the bench by an elbow. "I must have tried to inhale my sandwich" came out. I'd battled with, and firmly decided against, a corny line about how she'd taken my breath away.

"Tina," she said, extending a slender hand that poked out from the cuff of that sweatshirt. "Your drink's empty." She glanced at my cup, then back at me with her captivating eyes. "Can I… buy you one?" Her voice was like honey in warm water. Yes, a hundred times yes.

"I'd love that," I said more sincerely than at any other time in my life.

We went to a local bar and drank the afternoon away. I emailed work saying I had a health emergency, and Tina told me about her dreams of moving out of her parent's house and becoming a famous artist. She was a painter, but between day jobs and living with her folks while she sorted things out.

I told her about my mundane existence of coding for a communications company, and my passion for golden age cinema. I expected her to dash out of the booth and through the pub's door at any moment. Based on the looks of interest of other patrons, I wasn't the only one who thought she was stunning. Yet she only smiled and widened her lovely eyes as she expressed a similar passion for classic films.

I was head over heels. With each word, she spoke about the fast-lived romance Ingrid Bergman had with Gregory Peck, or about how Rock Hudson had been blackmailed for his closeted lifestyle. My heart rushed with blood. I tried to brace myself for it all to suddenly end. I expected her to look at the time and excuse herself, realizing her mistake, but she only watched me with wide-eyed wonder. As if I was interesting too.

After a few rounds of drinks, Tina looked up at me with her big eyes during a pause in our dialog.

"My parents are home, and I really don't want to be there right now. Can we go to your apartment?"

My mind shifted into worry. What if this was some long con? What if she was planning to rob me? I weighed these things, but my heart was already firmly decided. I nodded my head 'yes' and smiled, and though she offered, I paid our tab.

We then walked hand in hand to my apartment. We spent the evening on my couch, chatting about politics, pets and everything under the sun. Eventually, she leaned over and kissed me.

"Let's go to bed," she whispered coyly. I'll spare you the details of the best evening of my life.

She stayed the night. I still kept waiting for it to end abruptly, but she stayed, naked and curled next to me. She seemed truly happy, just as I was.

We were together nearly every day that week. She'd wait for me in the park, a worn book in her hands as I typed through lines of code and daydreamed about her. My coworkers noticed my glow and even made some comments about how I must have gotten laid, but they didn't deserve to know. Each day I stared at the clock, counting the minutes, the seconds, until I could go out and embrace Tina. I was well aware after the fourth day we spent together that I was in love.

She was smart, an old soul with classic beauty. And she saw beyond my receding hair and belly fat. She was the only person who seemed to really see me for who I was, not just the superficial details everyone else always seems to fixate on. I even mentioned this to her one evening as we watched Hitchcock's "Rope" cuddled on my couch.

She raised her head to give me a kiss on the cheek and said something that stuck with me. "We can change who we are on the outside. It's what's inside that counts. You can't alter that."

I found the statement a bit strange. Tina wasn't one to wear makeup of any sort. It's not like she needed to; she was stunningly beautiful. There were also a few other odd things about her that I couldn't quite figure out.

Though I frequently expressed interest in seeing her paintings, she adamantly refused to share them. She also made it very clear she did not want her photo taken, mentioning often how photos never accurately depict people. She didn't have Facebook or Instagram either, and refused to join social media, despite me explaining that she'd need to get both herself and her work online in order to advance in the art world.

Secondly, she always seemed a bit nervous at the mention of her parents. "They're very particular," she might say, or "I want you to meet them, but only when it's the right time."

After two months of dating, I asked her to move in with me. She told me she'd agree if her parents did, and asked me to join them for dinner at the end of the week. I nodded, dabbing the sweat on my brow. I'd never been in a full-on relationship before. Meeting the parents sounded intimidating. I got a haircut and a shave and purchased a crisp new dress shirt for the occasion.

When Friday arrived, I skipped my morning cup of coffee; my heart was pounding the entire day. When I finally left the office and met Tina in the park, she assured me with a sweet smile and a soft kiss that they were very agreeable and there was nothing to be concerned about. She held my hand and guided me past the park to the street, and we began walking.

She led me past block after block of businesses to a residential area filled with row homes. They were colorful and quaint, albeit less upscale than those in the surrounding areas. I was surprised she spent so much time at the park near my office, as she lived a good 20 minutes away. Soon enough, Tina was tugging my hand up some concrete steps to a home that looked to be a bit of a relic; old, peeling paint on wooden siding likely installed in the 60s.

"Stop being nervous!" She smiled that beautiful smile and led me through the threshold into the house. "Mom! Dad! We're here!"

A musty odor filled my nostrils as she led me across old carpeting, deep into the long, narrow home. It was a railroad-style house, and the decor was bizarre. Old porcelain dolls festooned every available surface. Ceramic figurines once popular in the 60s smiled and watched from the mantles and dressers.

It was unnaturally humid in that dimly lit residence, and I felt the dampness cling to my hands and face as Tina led me through room after room of endless dolls until we reached the entrance to a dining room. I could soon make out two still figures seated at a table, watching us intently.

Something was very wrong with them. Some uncanny valley effect that triggered some primordial fear within my brain. As Tina's gentle hand led me into the dining room and closer to them, I understood what was wrong. The seated, life-sized figures were not flesh at all. They were dolls; painted on flesh tones and rosy, smiling lips. Two mannequins watching with unnerving painted eyes.

"Tina, what's going on?" I asked, hearing the crack in my voice.

"Meet my parents, Ron and Barb. I've been telling them so much about you." Tina sounded genuinely engaged in the charade. I smelled it then. The sweet stink of decay emanating from the seated figures whose waxen, painted hands rested on the table. There was a dark stain on the tablecloth under each hand. The figures had been leaking.

"Don't be rude, say hello," Tina whispered under her breath.

"I-I'm—" I gasped, realizing then these figures were not simply mannequins. A wave of nausea and horror washed over me as I fully comprehended what I was seeing. They were, in fact, Tina's parents. Dead and glazed over with a thick shell of paint as they decomposed from within. These were Tina's paintings. I gagged, unable to hold back my reaction.

"You're just like the rest," Tina sobbed from behind me. I twinged in agony, feeling a sharp sting in my shoulder. I pawed at the aching muscle, and my hand brushed across the slim plunger of a hypodermic needle. My vision blurred, and I immediately understood that Tina had injected me with something.

"It doesn't matter, really. After a coat of primer, you'll be a fresh new canvas."

My heart pounded as my eyesight dimmed, and I staggered out of the reeking dining room as terror washed over me. I was going to die here.

I fought to stay upright as I waded through the dark rooms in a panic. Tina was complaining and accusing me of something, but her words were hazy, phasing in and out so that only a few were intelligible. I was lost; all sense of direction gone, as the array of closed doors on every side left me trapped. I reached one and twisted the knob, feeling my rubbery hand slip and fumble before finally opening the door.

A wave of nauseating stench caused me to retch. My blurry vision struggled to make out the looming figures in the room, all watching me with painted, lifeless eyes. It was a room of men, some seated and some standing. Painted-over corpses of those who'd come before me.

"Please don't be jealous," a bodiless voice spun around my head. The seven posed bodies all watched me with unsettling smiles as my vision darkened. This is where I would die and rot, I realized. A painted carcass among the rest of them. The adrenaline finally kicked in.

I blindly swung a numb arm, connecting with Tina who emitted a yelp, and I stumbled back through the spinning room to the other hazy doors. I tried to speed up, but my body was barely obeying. I felt a sharp sting on my bicep and looked down to see an open gash leaking red. Tina had a knife. I struggled to get away from her, staggering through the stained, carpeted hallway back towards the murky entrance.

"Don't worry, I can paint over the cuts," Tina's calm voice stated from behind. I raced to a door that emitted a sliver of daylight through the cracks. Another stabbing pain in my back hit me as I tripped out into the evening's dark sky. "Get BACK here!"

I stumbled down the few stairs, collapsing onto the street with a fleshy smack. I lay there, unable to move a muscle. I was totally paralyzed. Yells and shrieks called from outside my view. I stared at the branches above me until they dimmed, and the world went black.

I woke in the hospital to see a concerned-looking nurse hovering over me. She informed me gently that I'd been rescued in the street by a UPS worker. He had fought off a knife-wielding woman that had to have been Tina. My blood contained a mix of GBH and Tetrodotoxin, and the nurse explained that I was very lucky to be alive. If I'd arrived a few minutes later, I likely wouldn't have made it.

The disturbing details of the investigation came in snippets during my recovery. Tina had fled on foot and her home had been raided. The rotted bodies of seven missing men were discovered within; painted over with thick layers of oil paint and sealed with polyurethane.

Tina was still missing, but not just her. Her parents were not in that home either. The only sign that they had been there were the dark stains at the dining room table, and two sets of fetid black footprints leading across the rotted carpet and outside into the street.

THE GLITCHING

A constant banging startled me awake. I sat up confused. There was a steady hammering noise coming from down the stairs. The clock read 2:45 AM. I had absolutely no idea what could have been making that sound.

The fridge or the washing machine malfunctioning? A trapped animal?

I slipped out of the sheets and onto the cool wooden floor. That quick knocking continued with a speed that filled me with unease. I slipped into a t-shirt and sweatpants, listening as the urgent banging continued. It was steady and unrelenting, like machinery hammering away.

I worked up the courage to head down the stairs, slowly making my way towards the living room where the sound seemed to be coming from. There, above the couch, the gleaming framed photos of our kids and parents rattled and shook from that intense thumping; about six per second. It was coming from the outside of the house.

I leaned over the couch to look out the window to the moonlit yard outside. Barely visible through the edge of the window frame stood a night-gowned figure. She appeared to be standing against the outside of our home, spasming in place.

I watched for a few seconds before realizing it appeared to be Mrs. Arlington, the elderly woman two houses over. Why was she at our house at this ungodly hour? And why not at the door?

My fingers reached up and grabbed the heavy Maglite flashlight from atop the dusty fridge, and after a deep breath to steady my nerves, headed outside into the cold night air. My feet carried me closer to that constant, aggressive knocking. I rounded the edge of the house and froze when I saw her.

There was Mrs. Barrett in her nightgown, her soap-white arms jiggling at her sides. She wasn't banging with her fists, but with her head. I was dumbstruck as I watched her puffy curls of silver hair shake as she pounded her forehead against the wall of my home. Her movement was so rapid and with such a steady tempo, she looked more machine than human.

"Mrs. Barrett," I called out to her, but she didn't respond. "Mrs. Barrett … are you alright?" I asked as I approached, knowing damned well she was not. My bare feet tread through the dewy grass as I stepped closer to her impossibly animated body. Each step closer revealed details that sent shivers down my spine. There were dark flecks on her nightgown as well as a large spot on the dented aluminum siding of my house where she was ramming her head impossibly fast. It was blood.

She didn't move like a human at all. It was at the speed of a hummingbird's wings. An alarm clock clapper pummeling a bell.

I can best describe it as watching my son Jeremy playing video games; when one of the on-screen character bugs, and the movement is rapid and twitchy as they slip into a wall. She moved like that; like a glitching character in one of those games.

I turned on my Maglite and shone the beam on her and shivered. She was glistening red from a shocking amount of blood that was dripping from her head down her face. Those wet sounds of the speedy banging of her skull on the aluminum siding made my stomach churn.

"Mrs. Barrett!" I yelled in desperation. I instinctively approached to pull her away from harm but froze. Her head was bent inward, dented like a punctured soccer ball. She couldn't have possibly been alive. Her nose was flattened, and the skin of her forehead was cracked and frayed, exposing layers of raw, red flesh beneath.

I stood there and watched for a few seconds, too stunned to move. Blood trickled down from a crimson crater where her skull was bashing in the weatherproof vinyl siding of my home. I then heard the sound of crunching behind me, causing me to jump in my skin.

I turned to see Dan, my neighbor, but I screamed at the sight of him. His head was twisting around and around, his neck crunching and bulging out more from each revolution. His eyes were foggy, unseeing marbles. It was clear that he was dead. I watched his head spin, tightening the wrinkled skin of his neck as the grinding of shattered vertebrae cracked and popped.

I screamed and stumbled backward before dashing back into my house and sliding the door shut, locking it with trembling hands. I watched from the window as Dan approached the glass window, his head dangling backward at a sickening angle. His neck was ruptured and bruised, the skin twisted and bunched from the mess of vertebrae bulging out from within. His pale hand began 'glitching' and slapping the door in a vibratory manner.

I stumbled back into the kitchen table as I frantically dialed 911. I squeezed the phone until I thought I might crack it as I listened for the dialing sounds that never came. No service. I peered out the reflective black pane into the night, seeing more neighbors approaching in the distance, and my skin rose in rigid goosebumps.

I could see the Davis's kid, Tommy, in his room by the window, staring down at me. His hands were straight out to the sides, but the flesh between them and the shoulders was rippling and snapping so fast they were just snaking, fleshy blurs.

The malfunctioning bodies of the neighbors continued to vibrate and snap as they began encircling my house. Some were naked, some in pajamas and nightgowns. Some I knew, and some I did not. They approached in jerky motions as their bodies were manipulated. It was as if they were being puppeted violently by some impossible magnetic fluctuation.

Soon, flailing arms moving far too fast began squeaking against the windows of my home before slapping hard into them. I ran into the garage when a window shattered inward from a bloody fist, flopping around on a cracked arm faster than any human had moved before. I locked the garage door, feeling as if my heart might explode.

I've been sitting in the dark garage inside my locked car, shaking uncontrollably. I scoured the web for answers, but there is nothing to be found.

I twisted the radio dial tuner with shaky digits until hearing a muffled signal that sounded like intercepted radio communication. Though weak, I could hear an authoritative man transmit through the static. I could hear numbers being read, and it sounded like a list of coordinates, each followed by the word "confirmed."

The shattering of glass from my home began just moments before the machine-like hammering on the garage door to the house separating them from me. The static from the car radio was broken one last time with three clear words before bleeding into static: "Test one complete."

MY BROTHER MADE HIMSELF DISAPPEAR

My brother and I weren't exactly popular in school. All our father had given us before taking off was red hair and pale, freckled skin. Mom raised us solo after he left. I was an introvert and spent my time lost in music and video games. My chubby brother Danny, one year younger than I, was obsessed with magic.

He was always trying to get me to watch the latest trick he'd learned from whatever Chris Angel or David Blaine video he'd just watched. He had posters of all the greats: Penn and Teller, Lance Burton, Apollo Robbins. He was becoming a somewhat impressive magician, but of course, growing up with him I fully understood sleight of hand and the basic gist of how he was able to guess my card or make a torn dollar bill magically restore itself. I humored him as much as I could, but reminded him he was just securing his virginity for all time.

As we wallowed through the hazing and constant misery of middle school, I expected Danny to drop his interest in magic. It was, to be blunt, nerdy. And being nerdy means gathering the attention of bullies. I'd been shoved into lockers and had my bookbag spilled in the halls plenty just for being his brother.

I reminded Danny that he might want to keep his hobby to himself, but my advice fell on deaf ears. I'd see him at lunch in the cafeteria, showing off the cup and ball trick to the snide smirks and jeers of other students.

I confronted him one day after school, selfishly driven by the unwarranted attention that kept making its way to me, the brother of "magic boy."

"Danny, you are making my life hell. Can you fucking quit it with the magic? NOBODY is impressed," I said, or something to that effect. I watched his big brown eyes glaze over with tears. I'd hit a nerve, and I hated myself for antagonizing him. He wiped his nose and then smiled a wide, goofy smile.

"I'm going to impress you all, you'll see." He stormed away, that strange grin on his freckled face.

That week, I didn't see much of Danny. He kept himself locked in his room, watching an endless playlist of YouTube magic videos. One night at dinner, I tried to apologize for confronting him that day in the hall, and his response was a bit off, even for him. My mom smiled in appreciation of my efforts, but Danny just brushed it off.

"Watch me make this chicken disappear!" he said in a sarcastic tone, and he began to devour the baked thigh and leg on his plate with greasy fingers. Mom chuckled, always a good sport.

But something was off. I'd seen it in his eyes. It was like a switch had been flicked. Something that set boundaries in the logic-handling part of his brain had been toggled. Danny devoured his meal and rushed back to his room to watch his videos without a word. After washing the plates clean, I walked past his room and heard faint voices coming from his door.

I stepped closer and listened to an odd, muffled tone coming from his computer speakers. Rather than a squeaky-voiced teen explaining how to palm a coin or guess a card, I heard a droning voice in a language I didn't recognize.

I leaned closer and listened to odd pronunciations on what sounded like a scratchy, old recording. It was hypnotic babbling. Like someone reading scripture in a foreign language. I went to bed that evening with a welling feeling of unease. A feeling that would only intensify after what happened the following day.

It was Thursday, and I was anticipating the weekend. I'd already been picked on that day by my personal antagonist, Ron, the bully who stood a foot taller and 50 pounds heavier than me. I was opening my locker when Danny walked into the hall, fiddling with a deck of cards like it was the coolest thing on the planet. I tried to will him with my mind to put them away before Ron noticed and locked his aggression onto him, but it was too late.

Ron turned his thick neck towards my brother and snorted. "Ha, look here, David Lame and his magical baby fat" I cringed, knowing very well Danny was about to be humiliated in front of all the students in that bustling hallway. I looked away, wishing I could squeeze into my locker until it was over, but then I heard the gasps.

"What the FUCK?" Ron's deep voice shook as he emphasized the expletive. It was the first time I'd heard him sound scared. "J-Jesus fuck,"

I heard the squeak of sneakers and watched Ron barrel through the crowd. He was pale, every bit of blood drained from his face. He rushed past me and out the door. I approached the cluster of kids gathered around to see what could have possibly set him off.

And there was my brother Danny. Most of him, anyway. Danny's pale hand spouted out pumps of deep red blood onto his cards that were spilled on the linoleum floor of the hall. His index and middle finger were gone.

I remember the ambulance and my mother crying as we followed it to the hospital. I remember the news van and the reporters pushing to get the scoop on what had happened. I remember Danny's expression in the hospital bed with his bandaged hand. The cunning smile on his pudgy, freckled face.

They never found Danny's fingers. The doctors and school administration concluded he must have cut them off outside and discarded his digits off of school property. A far grimmer theory was that he'd bitten off his fingers and swallowed them.

Danny was in the hospital for the better half of the week. He underwent a psychiatric evaluation, but whatever he told those shrinks to get them to let him out was a lie. He soon returned to school. Back in front of a crowd where he wanted to be. That's where Danny performed his next "vanishing act."

The entire week before, he looked like he was on cloud nine. He wore a perpetually smug grin, like he'd figured out the secrets of the universe. He'd learned something locked in that room of his, that's for sure. Something he was savoring and reveling in before his big finale. And he needed an audience.

It was a Wednesday after the bell rang when I exited the school doors to see a gathered crowd. I expected a fight as per usual. I peeked over the heads of students, working my way slowly through the group. I winced when I heard his voice.

"Gather around, ladies and gentlemen, for if you like magic, have I got a show for you! I'm going to make myself disappear!"

I heard the heckling of the crowd. Jeers of "Freak!" and "Make your virginity disappear, fatty!" boiled my blood. I pushed past the giggling teens who had all suddenly hushed, staring ahead in shock and awe. It was quiet aside from the sounds that will resound in my head each night until the day I die.

Gurgling sounds. Wet, squelching noises. Popping and flapping. The sound of rending meat. Screams erupted and people shoved past me, running from the spectacle of whatever was taking place.

By the time I made my way to the front, he was gone. On the sidewalk lay what was left of my brother. A few kinked hairs and scattered teeth in a fresh puddle of blood.

There are conflicting accounts as to what occurred, each one more bizarre than the last. Mass hysteria is the default explanation for the bizarre testimonies of the students who were there. Some theorize he was abducted, and the witnesses were drugged. Others claim spontaneous human combustion.

Four kids in the front row ended up in the state psychiatric facility, their minds broken from what they'd witnessed. Two others committed suicide within the week.

Lisa, a girl a year older than me, became a target of humiliation. She changed her name and moved away because of the teasing she received after testifying to what she'd seen. In an interview shown on the evening news, she said Danny had disappeared before her very eyes. That he peeled away into nothing, layer by layer, like an onion.

The one thing that gives me peace at night is what she said about his face. However he did it, Danny won the audience that day, and he knew it. She said that before his face unwrapped to reveal a collapsing skull, and then a shrinking, folding brain… Danny was smiling.

JE TE VOIS

I found it in a box of old VHS tapes I picked up from a flea market. I hunt for deals there; sellers are often just looking to unload the crap that sits around off their hands. I buy in bulk, then check the goods—tossing out duds and ensuring items work, are clean, and include the necessary pieces—before jacking the price and selling them on eBay.

Videotapes are usually a minimal profit at best, but I've found rare items; first releases, black diamond edition Disney's and rare cover versions that collectors eat up. At any rate, I picked up a large box of tapes that looked to be in great condition for $5, and it wasn't until I got home that I started checking them thoroughly. When I did, I found a standard black video cassette tape missing a box.

Normally, these don't interest me because they're usually unsalable. Secondly, this had no standard label, so it was likely some home movie. What stopped me from tossing it right then and there was the black strip punch label stuck to the back that read "23/2/11" in blocky white raised numbers. I suspected from the dating system it was European and when it didn't play on my NTSC VCR, that confirmed it. I huffed as I returned to my closet and fetched the European PAL deck. It was only 6 PM, and I had time to kill, so I popped the tape into my old VHS player and pressed play.

The footage was black and white, shot high up from the center of a room where the wall met the ceiling. The camera was pointed down to a thin woman hunched over in a wheelchair. Based on the angle and the stillness of the footage, it was clearly a surveillance feed. The footage was grainy, but I could see the seated woman looked disheveled; her gray, chin-length hair was matted and messy, and she appeared to be dressed in a filthy hospital gown.

The way the woman was positioned looked still and unnatural. I quickly realized her wrists and ankles were bound to the wheelchair with straps. Both the walls and floors were padded with quilted square cushioning, and the door behind her had a slot in it, resembling something out of a mental hospital or a maximum-security prison. Just a second after the recording began, the bound woman raised her head and looked directly into the camera.

I immediately felt a growing sense of dread as the intense stare of the woman burned into my retinas. Some primal part of my brain awoke and implored me to get away, but I just watched as curiosity and fear mingled into an all-encompassing wave of building anxiety. The woman just sat in her chair staring, but I felt my mouth begin to dry and my breath felt abrasive. My sinuses burned, and soon I felt the patter of liquid onto my lap from my nose; but I couldn't turn away from the screen.

I heard a rapid tapping, and it took a few seconds to understand the sound before I realized it was the chattering of my teeth. I was shivering, and my arms and legs trembled as I watched the woman on the screen tilt her head to one side as if observing me through the screen itself. That feeling of impending danger heightened, and I wanted to turn it off at that point, but I just kept watching as the woman began fidgeting in the wheelchair's restraints. She was becoming progressively more agitated; thrashing until the chair began to rock between the two large wheels. After a few minutes, she opened her mouth and began to scream.

The tape was silent, but I swear I could hear her faintly, though not through the speakers. It was like she was screaming from inside my head; small and muffled from deep under the folds of my brain. I felt my lips crack in stinging slivers. I began to wonder just how long I'd been watching the tape, but I was enthralled by the unsettling footage and unable to stop it.

Eventually, the door to her room opened and two large men in white uniforms entered her padded cell. One was shorter, with a shaved head and stocky build, the other taller with a slender frame and face framed by dark bangs. The tall man began holding his head in apparent agony, screaming and then dropping to his knees on the padded floor. He remained there as the shorter guy struggled to remove the cap from a syringe.

I only then noticed the subtle relief my own body experienced. It was as if whatever had taken hold of me—the intense dryness in my throat, a pulsing headache, and the palpable dread—had redirected its focus. The man on his knees began to shiver and soon enough his nose streamed down a dark rivulet of blood.

The shorter character with a shaved head had uncapped the syringe, but was clearly struggling. His right arm drew it closer, needle first, towards his own eye. His left was gripping his other wrist, struggling to redirect its course. I watched in horror as the tip punctured his eye just a centimeter or so. He seemed to regain control and quickly removed it. He then stabbed the needle into the bound woman's shoulder and pressed the plunger fully down.

The feeling of intensity seemed to wash away from both the on screen characters and myself. Euphoria set in as my previous state of dry, labored breathing and chest pains left me. The two workers at the hospital, prison or other such facility both seemed to recover as well, the one helping his cohort to his feet. The two men left the room, securing the sturdy door behind them.

I watched for a few minutes as the woman in the wheelchair slouched and then dropped her head. She looked to be asleep, or at least heavily sedated. She remained that way for a good minute or two after the men had cleared out. I watched her slack body for a few more minutes in utter fascination until the tape reached the end and stopped with an audible click.

The intense anxiety dissipated completely, and I only then realized how absolutely drastic the shift in my own state had been. I felt as if I'd been desiccated. Every ounce of water in me sucked out, yet my nose was wet and dribbling down my chin. When I wiped it instinctively with the back of my hand, I saw that it was blood. There were dark red spots on my lap as well from where it had poured out during the viewing of the tape.

I stood up on muscles that ached and groaned. I glanced at my phone for the time and stopped in place, my jaw agape. The time read 6:00, the same time I'd started watching that tape. I was about to chalk it up to a glitch when it changed to 6:01. There was no shadow of a doubt in my mind that I'd watched that tape for a good 10 minutes or so.

I stretched my aching muscles and walked to the bathroom to clean my bloodied nose. I downed a quart or so of water, dying of thirst. I waited a few days before even considering watching the tape again. When I did, everything that secured my knowledge of the world I knew seemed to crumble.

It was a sunny afternoon a week later when I built up the courage to watch the tape again. I just felt the urge to confirm what I experienced was real and not some effect of delayed food poisoning, an allergic reaction, or some other bizarre coincidence. I popped the cassette tape and rewound it, which took only seconds. When it stopped, I pressed play.

The woman bound to a wheelchair once again appeared on the screen and a foreboding feeling of dread began to simmer inside of me. Something was different though. The woman was askew, facing the camera still but at a slightly different angle, as if her wheelchair had shifted. On the floor behind her, black spots where the guard had yet to collapse were on the floor. It was as if the tape was showing a continuation of what had previously been recorded.

My palms began to sweat, and my throat dried like an arid desert as I watched the woman staring into the camera once again. Her hair was shorter, trimmed down unevenly as if someone had hastily clipped the matted patches and knots. I knew it was impossible, but the tape appeared to be now showing a different recording altogether. Then she looked up at the camera and I felt it again.

My throat swelled and dried, and my breath began to burn. Her dark eyes locked onto mine through the screen. I felt a spasm in my arms and legs as they began to shiver. My sinuses flooded and my nose began dribbling out a thin stream of blood, which dripped rhythmically onto my shirt. I watched, unable to peel my eyes away as the woman in the wheelchair yanked her spindly arms, snapping her restraints. I let out a yell as she stood up fully, revealing her filthy hospital gown.

She walked slowly towards the camera and her wrinkles came into view through the fuzzy tape. Her features looked young, but her pale skin was wrinkled and speckled with burst capillaries. Her eyes were milky with cataracts and looked wild with excitement. She drew closer, getting larger on-screen until her face was clear, and she mouthed something I swear I could hear inside of my head. She spoke the words "Je te vois," and a hint of a smile crept onto her face before the tape clicked to a stop.

I attempted to make a copy, but it showed nothing but a black screen when played. I even tried recording it with my phone, but the TV screen in the video is black aside from a flicker. What I just couldn't shake were those words she'd spoken that resonated from deep within my skull. They're French, and they translate to "I see you."

For over a week, I kept the tape boxed up and hidden in the back of my closet. I tried hard to forget it existed, but it echoed in my every thought. I wanted to burn it. To break it up into a thousand pieces and bury it deep in the field in the back of my house, but that niggling itch to find out what I had witnessed kept building until I couldn't take it any longer.

I finally broke down and fetched the tape. I felt my eyes water and skin itch just touching the black plastic. Visions of that sinister face flashed behind my eyes like a film negative, and the fear returned. I realized this was bigger than myself, and I called my old pal Carl. I asked if we could meet up, hoping he could help me figure it out, and he agreed.

"The hell you mean it changes, a tape's a goddamned tape. It's recorded, it can't change." He scratched his balding head and frowned. "You sure you OK man, not hitting the sauce too hard?"

"Damn it, just humor me, OK? I just need to know what you see." The desperation in my voice dripped with every word. I hated how I sounded. Weak and cowardly, but there's no way to explain what viewing that footage did to me. I felt like I was dying, rotting from the inside out as an old woman stared at me from the fuzzy screen.

"Hell, if it shuts you up, I'll watch it." Carl took the cassette and stared at me with baggy eyes, his brows furrowed with concern. "I'm worried about you, man. Promise me you'll ease up on whatever you've been up to."

There was no way to convince him I was dead sober and scared half to death. "I promise, OK? Thanks, Carl." I walked back to my truck and drove home. It took two days to hear back. Carl knocked at the door, breaking my attention. I'd zoned out, having been staring at the wall. I got up, shuffled to the door, seeing Carl's leathered face through the pane of glass. I unlocked the deadbolt and opened the door.

"Did you watch it?" I asked, eager for answers.

"Yeah, I watched it. It's just an empty room. Looks like a suicide watch room in a prison or something. What is the big deal?" He handed me the tape, and something twisted in my guts. A primal fear awakening once again.

"What do you mean empty?" I asked.

"An empty room man, except for a wheelchair near the open door. That's it. No woman or anything else you mentioned in your text." Carl handed me the videocassette and raised his eyebrows. "Look, man, you can talk to me. I've had my share of demons too. There are support groups. Meetings."

My heart was pounding in my chest. Carl's words muted out, and I pictured her face, lined with wrinkles and glowering stare. The room was empty. The door was open.

"I've gotta go." I walked back into the house, turning away from Carl's concerned face. The hair on my neck raised. She'd gotten out.

Carl shook his head as he walked back to his car. I watched him from the window as I locked the door. Once he'd driven away, I raced from window to window, locking them as well. As I did, I stared out into the night, to the empty field of dead reeds. To the service road rumbling with a steady stream of traffic. I finally gathered the courage to pop the tape into the VCR. It began to play.

Black and white static filled the screen before clearing to reveal an overhead security feed of a convenience store. Some large signs on the windows advertised specials in English. Aisles of candy, snacks and office products were warped from the wide-angle lens. There was a scrawny twenty-something guy at the register staring at his phone.

Then the veins in my temple began to throb. My throat swelled closed, and I began to sweat. A figure approached from the darkness outside the store. Barefoot and wearing a filthy hospital gown covered in blooming stains, she shuffled her feet, one after another, until she pushed open the glass door and entered.

My nose began dripping blood. The coppery taste filled my mouth, and I heard it pattering onto my floor, but I couldn't turn away. The clerk was shaking, a tremble at first that grew more exaggerated until he was wobbling like his limbs were made of rubber. He reached down into a container of pens and grabbed one with a shaking fist. I couldn't look away, no matter how hard I tried.

He brought the pen up to his face in a violent motion, jamming the metal tip deep into his eye socket. Blood splashed outward onto the counter as he forced the pen deeper into his orbital cavity until it vanished completely. The clerk then collapsed to the floor, leaving only his twitching sneakers visible on screen. Though the tape was silent, I soon heard a scratchy whisper that echoed out from deep inside my skull.

"Je te vois," she repeated in a hushed growl, followed by a raspy giggle. I see you. The hunched woman then cocked her head up and stared at the security camera of the convenience store. My vision dimmed slightly as the woman approached the camera.

Her damaged, wrinkled face was patched with small veins that showed under her translucent skin. Her wild eyes, foggy and marble-like, widened as the corners of her mouth raised in a smile. The tips of her jagged teeth came into view through her parted lips. Just as I felt my head might explode, the tape clicked to a stop.

I collapsed to the floor and wheezed labored breaths as that all-encompassing horror rattled around in my brain. My muscles ached and my sinuses were clogged with congealed blood. My throat was dry and rough, and I coughed crimson drops onto the back of my hand.

I was eventually able to raise my sore body and down a few pints of water, which burned my dried throat. I was unable to sleep, hearing her growling whisper that simply wouldn't go away. It was there the next day as well, and the day after that. I didn't dare watch that tape again, yet I could still hear her voice in the recesses of my head.

I panicked. I drove that videotape nearly an hour away to the National Park. I hiked out a ways and buried it deep in the cold ground with a shovel and my two shaking hands. I covered it with black soil next to a gnarled, dead tree, packing the dirt hard on top of that tape. I hiked to my truck and drove back, watching the dense forest shrink in my rear-view mirror. I even counted the mile markers, praying for evidence it was over as the distance grew, but I could still hear her awful whisper from deep within my skull.

After three days, I could still hear her creaky voice. It began as a distant, breathy sound, but it gradually grew louder and more distinct, hour by hour. There was no doubt in my mind anymore.

She was getting closer.

I scoured the news hourly until finally stumbling across a recent article detailing the violent death of a cashier while working his shift at a convenience store. There were few details, but the ones mentioned chilled me to the bone.

VA. (AP)—Authorities in Richmond say a convenience store clerk was found dead after a grisly suicide. Emergency responders pronounced the man dead at the scene. His identity wasn't imme-diately released. Investigators say it's unclear what transpired due to a faulty security camera, though foul play is not suspected at this time as his wounds appear self-inflicted.

I read and re-read it again. The words "faulty security camera" sent me into a panic. I was positive then; I'd watched that man die. Worse, the article was from Virginia, just two states over.

That whispering voice continued to echo in my head. It was clear enough to understand, and it repeated things I needed to look up to translate.

"Si proche," it growled in that distant whisper. "So close."

I tried earplugs and blasting music, but nothing would drown out her menacing voice. She was taunting me, playing with me like a cat with a cornered mouse.

I made a few wild searches, casting a net far and wide online. Escaped French patients or inmates turned out nothing of note. Finally, after digging deep into the rabbit hole of conspiracy theory sites, I stumbled across a page mentioning a woman called Nathalie, which set alarms off in my head.

Nathalie had been a patient at a psychiatric hospital but had been transferred to a more secure facility after a significant in-crease in the number of violent incidents and deaths in the weeks following her admission. Seven patients and two staff members had died under very gruesome circumstances, and rumors had also circulated about secretive experiments as well as a military pres-ence at the hospital shortly before she'd been transferred. No other mention of this Nathalie was available.

What made me shiver was reading the last recorded location of Nathalie. It was when she was transferred in February 2011. The tape that had started my endless nightmare was labeled February 23rd, 2011.

I called my old coworker Darren and asked him to meet up for a beer. It had been almost two years, but he was the most tech-savvy and pragmatic individual I knew. I explained it all, well-aware of how insane I sounded. The whole time that tormenting whispering continued in my head. Darren listened until I'd finished recounting what happened before speaking.

"Sounds crazy, as anything but the coincidences are some-thing." Darren pushed up his glasses and perched his chin on the tips of his fingers in thought. "So, if you aren't crazy—no offense—and you somehow witnessed a live feed through that tape, you could watch again and see where she currently is."

"That tape is what drew her attention to me. Whoever or whatever she is, that's what started this damned thing." I saw the faces of patrons in other booths turn towards me before I even realized I'd raised my voice from heightened stress. Darren continued in a hushed tone.

"Hypothetically speaking, when you watched the tape, she latched onto you. You were the first person to view the recording, opening a window to her after what, 8 years? She clearly isn't going away. If this is real, I don't think watching it anymore can hurt. On the contrary, it might help you know this individual's location, which can help to keep you safe." He polished off his mug of light beer and smiled, proud at solving a theoretical problem, but it was only hypothetical to him. For me, this nightmare was very real.

"If you were in my shoes and were experiencing what I am, what would you do?" I asked, gripping my knees to stop them from shaking.

"I'd get some friends together and watch it."

The next day I drove back out to the National Park. It took some time to retrace my steps, but soon enough, that large, dead tree with twisted branches where I had buried the tape came into view. I dug it up, tasting metal in my mouth the second my fingers touched the muddy black plastic.

I drove back with the radio on as loud as it could go, but that tape seemed to act like an

antenna all its own, magnifying that horrible voice.

"Plus proche." Closer.

After a two-hour round trip, I was home again. I called Darren and Carl, who, after some convincing, agreed to view the tape with me.

I watched as Darren set his phone upright to record my television. I explained that I'd already tried that, and it wouldn't show anything but a black screen, but he clearly wanted to witness the phenomenon for himself. More likely, he simply didn't believe me.

Darren smiled, thinking this whole thing was entertaining, but Carl just slouched into the cushions of my old sofa, silent. He looked nervous. I took a deep breath, tried to remain calm, and popped the tape into the player.

I watched as dancing static filled the screen with a cold glow. My insides squirmed at seeing the image. It was a recording of a black television screen.

"OK, so this is the hospital room?" Darren asked. My heart sped up in my chest at what he claimed to be watching. "There's no woman, though," he continued. "Room's empty."

"What the hell, it's a convenience store feed, guys, stop fucking with me!" Carl yelled in frustration. He sounded scared, but not nearly as bad as me. I couldn't even make a sound. I was frozen in absolute horror at what I was watching on the screen.

On the TV screen was my television set, the open wall and the view of the kitchen behind it. It was a live feed from Darren's phone, aimed at the black reflective glass of my television. In the recorded screen's reflection, Darren, Carl, and I were seated on my couch. My stomach twisted as I noticed a fourth figure standing behind us.

My blood began to burn in my veins and my temples pounded. I tried to scream but was paralyzed with fear. The woman drew closer to the couch behind us and grinned, baring her jagged, stained teeth. Darren began to yell and shake me by the shoulder, but I was frozen in place. His shaking caused me to fall from the couch and onto the floor. He's the reason that I'm alive.

From the carpet out of the corner of my eye, I could see Carl shaking violently. He then let out a scream that will haunt me until the day I die. The smell of cooking meat filled my living room. It smelled like bacon sizzling in a pan. After a few endless seconds, the screaming stopped. Darren stumbled off the couch and crawled to the VCR, stopping the tape. He called the ambulance after I blacked out.

I woke up in a hospital bed, an IV pumping fluids into my arm. A nurse explained to me I'd nearly died from extreme dehydration. Two police officers came in to question me about what happened. Carl was in a vegetative state. The detective who spoke to me was trying to understand how his eyeballs had ruptured. How his head appeared to have been microwaved, and how part of his brain had oozed out of his nose and onto his lap. They suspect foul play, and honestly, I can't blame them.

I'm not supposed to leave town, but I don't think I have any choice. Not after what I saw on the hospital's television in the corner of my room. On the screen played a grainy black and white feed of the hospital lobby. Patients filled intake forms and flipped through magazines, seemingly unaware of the barefoot woman in a filthy hospital gown.

She stood in the corner, staring into the camera with that crazed smile. Her lips moved and the creaky voice from deep inside of my brain spoke louder than ever.

"Je te vois."

OUR PILOT IS CRYING

"Welcome aboard" the blonde stewardess grinned perfect white teeth. "Seat number?"

"14B," I read off the folded ticket, delirious from the early morning scrambling to JFK. I was exhausted and eager to nap on a long flight to the UK. *Just a few more hours and I'll see Phoebe,* I thought. I'd only known her for two months, but I was flying overseas to see her again after a week apart. I'd also never been in love before, at least not like this.

"Down the right aisle, middle seat!" the chipper stewardess sang in a soothing tone. I hauled my hefty carry-on behind me down the aisle, careful not to kneecap anyone. A businessman in front of me was taking his time removing books, neck pillows and Kindle from his bag, causing a traffic jam. It was nearly a seven-hour flight to Heathrow, plenty of time to do that later. Still, I waited patiently until the people behind me began to shove.

"Ahem!" I cleared my throat, hoping he'd take a hint. He didn't. I groaned and lowered my head in frustration before clearing my throat a little louder.

The middle-aged businessman holding up the rest of us gave me a sneer, squinting down the end of his upturned nose. Finally, he slid into his seat.

The man huffed some whispered insult under his breath as I'd passed, but I brushed it off. Though we hadn't left the ground, I was walking on air at the thought of seeing Phoebe.

I squeezed down the narrow aisle, lugging my heavy bag as an infant's cries grew in volume. I glanced at the numbers as I shuffled onward. Upon spotting my row number, I stopped in my tracks. This couldn't be right. Surely there was a mistake. I checked the ticket a few times to confirm I was seated between a loudly squealing baby and a snoring, overweight man.

"Pardon me," I said to the large man spilling out of his aisle seat. "Sir," I continued before the wide man wearing a Hard Rock Cafe T-shirt and shorts finally woke up. He glowered at me with a face red from rosacea and covered in wild, gray whiskers. He grumbled as he struggled to his feet and then extended a large arm to the dreaded middle seat, as if angrily presenting the last of his possessions to a repo man.

I squeezed into the narrow seat and clicked my belt on before plugging my earbuds in to drown out the wailing baby's screeching with music. The large man spilled back into his aisle seat and his sweaty belly enveloped my forearm like a hairy amoeba.

The plane continued to fill up and overhead compartments were stuffed to the brink of bursting. Eventually, the passengers were all seated, and I breathed out. *Finally.*

"Welcome aboard British Airways flight 2135; this is your pilot speaking. Thank you for your patience, we are now cleared for takeoff," a robust voice said through the speaker. The plane soon rattled as we accelerated down the runway. I clenched the armrest, trying to convince myself the amount of shaking was completely natural. My body pressed back against the seat as the plane tilted and lifted. The city beneath fell away. I watched it shrink into grids of urban planning, then crop fields and pastures.

Eventually, we leveled, and my firm grip on the armrest relaxed. I'd nodded off for some time when the seat belt sign shut off and the pilot spoke.

"Good afternoon, passengers. This is your captain speaking. We are currently cruising at an altitude of 33,000 feet at an airspeed of around 400 miles per hour. The time is 9:00 pm. But none of that matters. None of it fucking matters."

With a click, the announcement was cut short, but everyone had heard it. Concerned whispers spread throughout the cabin.

"What the hell was that?" a man huffed from a few rows behind me. I tried to chalk it up to a joke that went south, but my twisting stomach made it clear I didn't buy that. The pilot came back on as the murmur of concerned passengers grew.

"You put in your time being the perfect husband and they just fucking run to someone else. It's like you never even existed, except as a stepping stone and a wallet. They take everything you have to give, and still move on to some other asshole." He then began to wail, sobbing loudly into the speaker. I was no longer simply concerned. I was terrified. Everyone on board was.

Shrill screams erupted from toppling passengers as the plane banked left at a 45-degree angle. A few overhead compartments unlatched, spilling out hard-shell luggage that smacked into a few passengers in the aisle seats with audible thuds. The copilot was shouting and banging his fists on the cockpit door; he'd been locked out.

More screaming. People mashed the flight attendant help button, but they were all gathered at the locked door to the pilot's cabin, trying desperately to force it open. It only took one panicked man from first class shouting "Oh my God, we're going to die!" and absolute hell broke loose. The pilot took the speaker once again.

"When they scavenge the black box out of the smoldering wreckage, I hope to God you listen to the recording. This was your fucking fault, Phoebe. You and the asshole you texted you'd pick up at terminal 3. Riding aboard *my* fucking plane." The pilot then broke down into an awful, tearful wailing, unable to coherently speak any longer. My stomach flipped as the plane pitched downward, tossing the standing passengers forward down the aisle like rag dolls.

A din of guttural screams has nearly drowned out the pilot's distorted crying from the overhead speaker. The jagged peaks of Newfoundland's Long Range Mountains grow ever closer as I type, but I've been frozen in my seat since the realization hit me like a cinder block. That 'asshole' she'd texted was me.

IT ONLY AFFECTS CHILDREN

William, my neighbors' son, was the first I saw it happen to. It's an image that's now etched into my mind, despite my sole desire to forget it.

I came home from the supermarket as per the wife's request. She was working late, so I was unloading paper bags that were spilling over with produce and artisan cheese. The sun was finally setting, and the heat was receding with it. I balanced two grocery bags in my arms as I walked from the driveway to my front door. I climbed the steps but slowed when I heard a peculiar sound coming from under the porch. A crackling, then a rustling. I thought maybe a neighbor's dog had crawled under there as they do before they die. That sound didn't sit right in my stomach.

I crouched to lower the bags to the porch, then stepped down the 5 creaking stairs and rounded them to take a peek. The latticing of my porch makes little diamond windows to the shadowy space beneath, so I leaned in to get a look. I heard it clearer then: a crackle, a wet squelch, and then a wheeze. It didn't sound like an animal.

"Hello?" I called out. I squinted to try to adjust my eyes to the dense darkness of the shadowy crawlspace. I could just barely make out the shape of a crouching figure. Small, skinny, shirtless. It was a boy, crawling slowly on shaking, lean limbs. One of the neighbors' kids, most likely.

"You alright in there?" I asked, hearing a raspy wheeze in reply, and then the rustling of old, dead leaves that had accumulated in the space. Before I could say another word, the scuttling sound rapidly approached and the dimly lit figure scrambled towards me faster than should be possible. I screamed when the head came into view; a ghastly face was pressing against the lattice wood dividing us.

It wasn't a boy, at least not anymore. It was something out of a nightmare; sickening and warped like putty melting in the sun. Large, purple lips sagged to reveal whitish-pink gums that poked teeth in every direction. It lacked symmetry or structure. A smudged painting manifested in strained, twisted flesh. Its skin was creased and folded, stretched so thin in some patches it gave view to the veins and tensing musculature beneath. The eyes made it all the worse, however.

Bulging from sockets like plump hard-boiled eggs popping with veins, those wide eyes stared at me with a blend of both hunger and horror. Ice-cold dread poured down my back when those eyes shifted outward to the sides with a crunch, followed by a wet sucking sound.

"Heeelp," it gurgled a whimpering plea in the high voice of a child.

With a grisly crack, the left corner of the horrible mouth twisted violently upward into a slanted wound. It looked as if the muscles beneath the skin were forcing it to, acting on their own accord.

Small fingers bent in all directions before clawing violently at the wood between us. The latticed porch began splintering and snapping as that child-thing tore through the skirting with ravenous fury. I fell onto my backside and scrambled back a few feet as horror feasted on my sanity. The rapid disfigurement was happening before my very eyes, shifting the boy's features into foreign and grotesque arrangements. He was trying to get to me.

I staggered backward, then raised myself back to my feet as it burst through. I raced up the porch stairs and that scuttling boy chased after on all fours, so fast it was like watching a sped-up film. I barely closed the door in time, then heard the heavy thud that shook it from the other side. I quickly locked the deadbolt with shivering hands.

I thought of the groceries which sat on the porch and the rest in the back of the open hatchback. I tried breathing deeply to slow my thumping heart. I tried desperately to forget that horrifying face, but then the door began to shake from slapping limbs from the other side.

Fear piqued, and I spun around wildly to look at my home's entry points. The thin glass windows gave view to the trees, neighboring homes and the rapidly sinking sun on the horizon. A shrill scream called my attention to the window facing the Jeffries household. It was the mother, Carla, who screamed. I watched shadows dance on the walls that were visible through their windows as the shrill wailing stopped. A few seconds passed and then I saw their kid Tommy scuttle out the open front door. What had become of him?

His head was buckled in like a crushed can in places. Meaty, swollen pockets of fluid-filled skin sagged outward in others. A red, pulpy hole was all that remained of one eye, and the other was swollen and pendulous, jiggling about as the child-thing rapidly crawled outside. Its stance was unnatural and unsettling. It moved with the torso low to the earth and the limbs high at the joints like some ghastly centipede. The stretched mess of a mouth was glistening red and wet.

A small hand slapped against the windowpane directly in front of me and I screamed. The digits were angled in odd directions as if broken at every joint, and each fingertip popped and twisted against the pane, bending independently of one another. I staggered back, unable to peel my gaze away until the small, broken hand squeaked down, leaving a bloody streak as it vanished. I stepped backward and removed my phone with a shaking hand. I managed to dial 911, but my neck hair rose as I heard a busy signal.

I redialed, holding the phone to my sweaty head with a shaking hand. My heart froze as I heard another distant scream. Whatever was happening was affecting multiple households. Still busy. I raced around to each window, making sure they were locked, and I froze, hypnotized by the horrific sight of one of those child-things on the edge of my other neighbor's lawn.

Its skin had sloughed off in places, exposing the squirming musculature beneath, reminiscent of writhing worms. The prostrate child, if it could be called that any longer, writhed in pain as the glistening red fibers flailed about, arching up from the shiny white bones of its bicep. The child's long, curled neck swiveled up and cracked in place as it faced me. The face was bloated and blue, almost like an infant's pudgy face. I watched in horror as the jaw lowered, widening that awful mouth until the cheeks stretched thin and then split. Those orbs of terrified eyes pleaded at seeing me, but the body moved fast and instinctively. It began scuttling straight towards me with terrifying agility and impossible speed. It shrieked a child's scream.

My eyes glazed with tears from a horrifying possibility. That while this affliction was ravaging the bodies of these children, their brains were locked inside, in excruciating pain and without any control. That grating, child-like screaming drew closer, and then another mangled hand slapped against the window behind me, hard enough to crack it. They were surrounding my house, and the glass panes would not stop them.

I raced upstairs and dialed 911 again; still busy. I locked myself in the bedroom and barricaded my room as best I could.

Through the bedroom window, I saw horrible things. I've seen those child-things overtake a large man and tear him open like wild hyenas. I've seen them crawling up the vinyl siding of a house, insect-like with elbows and knees pointed outward, their faces dangling flesh clinging to hijacked muscle. I've heard gunshots and sirens and screams that rattle my psyche.

I called my wife repeatedly, only to receive voice mail. I was about to text her when I received one myself, and I breathed out a sigh of relief. The text simply read:

"Driving, can't talk."

The shattering of the downstairs windows drew my attention to the immediate threat. I heard them scurrying inside, up the stairs and outside my door. The drumming of little hands and feet that twisted and popped as the corrupted muscle beneath warped them. I heard gurgles and sniffing. They were following my scent.

I breathed as quietly as possible as I searched online. There were very few emerging details, just a couple of other accounts as well as speculation about possible chemical attacks or military testing. What I saw out there wasn't chemical, however. It was something straight from hell.

I was in the midst of typing a message summarizing the immediate danger and to stay clear of the neighborhood. I was typing as quickly as my fingers would allow, instructing my wife to stay in her car and away from people no matter what, but then I received a second text:

"Home late, a kid had a seizure and 911 is busy. I'm driving him to the ER."

MAMA TAKES PILLS SO HER EYES WON'T HATCH

Mama takes pills so her eyes won't hatch,
so her limbs don't stretch and her skin won't peel back.
Mama takes pills so her teeth won't grow,
so her hair won't shed and her fluids won't flow.
Mama takes pills so her spine won't sprout,
so her jaw stays hinged instead of jutting out.
Mama takes pills so her skull won't swell,
so her ribs don't crack and her body won't smell.
Mama takes pills so her hunger stays gone
and her strength stays low even after the dawn.
Mama takes pills so her face won't split,
so she won't howl deep and her tongues don't spit.
Mama takes pills to keep papa and me safe,
but she's not in her bed and papa won't wake.
If you see my mama you'd best keep away.
Mama hasn't taken her pills today.

TIME'S UP

It started just like any other day. I woke up as the sun's golden rays peeked through my blinds and onto my eyelids with a comforting warmth. I sat up and stretched with a shiver and a yawn, then shuffled into the bathroom. I groggily brushed my teeth and stepped into the shower, hoping the warm water would help wake me up.

My mind was already three hours ahead of the pre-lunch scrum meeting. I shuffled my feet down the strangely dim staircase and slowed my pace on the wooden steps, realizing just how impossibly dark it appeared to be down there. A faint whisper of worry stirred as I realized the power seemed to be out on the first floor of my modest home.

Something was wrong, but it took a moment to understand. It was far too dark down there, as if the first floor of my home was lacking any natural light. It was morning time, but the kitchen was dark and painted with cold shadow as if it were midnight.

I looked back at the warm sunlight peeking from the top of the stairs and I stood there for a moment, dumbstruck. My fingers tapped the wall blindly, fumbling for the light switch, and found their target with a click. The bulb flickered and kicked on to light my small kitchen, which looked every bit the same, aside from the fact the black glass of the windows showed nothing but a dense, dark void. Again, it looked like it was nighttime. My brain scrambled to understand what was going on, and I flipped the lights off once more and peered out the dark glass windows to see the silhouetted maples at the edge of the park, swaying beneath the stars.

"How—what?" I mumbled to myself aloud, as if the kitchen might realize its mistake and correct it. I removed the phone from my pocket and double-checked the time. 7:55 AM. This made absolutely no sense at all. It was midnight outside my kitchen windows and daytime upstairs. I flipped the light back on and walked to the kitchen window, unlocking it and sliding up the aluminum frame with a bit of muscle. The cool breeze brought in the crisp aroma of the night. Crickets chirped quietly in the darkness. As I mused over what could possibly be happening, a static burst of a walkie talkie sounded from the tree line.

I squinted and peered out into the darkness, spying the firefly glow of a cigarette ember swelling from a drag. Barely visible were men in partial cover behind the trees and bushes. The cold air and the strange sight caused a shiver as I realized the men wore camouflage army fatigues. They were all watching me.

My eyes followed the perimeter of the park across the street, spotting more of these uniformed men. There were dozens of soldiers roughly 30 meters from my house, surrounding me in a wide circle, staring intently at me in the midst of my morning routine. My eyes squeezed to slivers to see more clearly, and my jaw hung at the stark realization they all held rifles, which were pointed directly at me.

My heart thumped heavily in my chest as I crouched low, away from the windows and low onto the linoleum kitchen floor. I swallowed dryly and felt my stomach rumble. I half-expected gunfire to shatter the windows, ripping into my body. Was America being invaded? Was this some Red Dawn nightmare? Was I about to be corralled into a fenced area? Panic permeated my brain. Why the hell was it so dark outside? Nothing made any sense.

I tried to steady my breathing and think of any possible explanation. I opened my phone, scouring the news feeds for breaking headlines, and found absolutely nothing of interest about Michigan, an invasion or manhunt, or anything even remotely similar. I slowly lifted myself and peered outside into the dark woods to try and understand. It was like some strange dream, but I was wide awake.

I looked at the stoic faces of the soldiers studying me. There were at least a few dozen of them. I could make out the familiar patches on the shoulder of their uniforms. Red and white stripes, they were American. Any relief that the country wasn't being invaded was quickly replaced by the dreaded question as to what they were doing at my house, guns trained on me. Was there a fugitive loose? Was an armed killer holed up in my house? I looked nervously back to the stairs, at the glowing sunlight bouncing off the stairway walls. My head hurt trying to understand how it was daytime upstairs and nighttime down in the kitchen.

I peered out the open window to see the stars twinkling in the onyx sky above the trees. 8:20 AM, my phone read. I stared back at the stairwell and then made a break for it. I scampered upstairs into the glowing sunlight of my second story. I felt the warmth as it shone on my face and constricted my pupils. My legs felt weak as they carried me across my sun-drenched room to look out over the green lawn to the tree line.

There were camps of soldiers out there milling about, as if in the midst of a daily routine. Large trucks and wooden barricades that were not there before. A cluster of troops conversing over tin cups of coffee noticed me and quickly scrambled behind trucks and houses into cover, yelling into their radios and fixing their rifles on me. I raced from the exposed position back to the cover of the stairs.

I looked down into the shadowy descent to the first floor of my home that appeared to exist in the nighttime. I descended the stairs again slowly, peering out into the impossible night. My house was surrounded by soldiers with binoculars, walkies and aimed rifles, but fewer of them, and none of the trucks and tents I'd seen from upstairs.

"What the fuck is going on?" I whispered to myself in a shaky voice, warbling with emotion. I felt my face flush, then bitter tears rolled down my face as I slid down the wall to the floor. Nothing made any sense. Trying to comprehend the surreal paradox gave me a headache. I wasn't asleep. This was all too real. The need for answers built until I marched to the front door. I swung it open slowly, feeling vulnerable and regretting my decision almost instantly.

The metal clicking of guns sounded from multiple directions. From open windows across the street, I saw the reflected flash of rifle scopes. Yellow tape cordoned off the perimeter, and the other driveways were missing cars. I poked my head out into the cool air and craned my neck to see the yellow tape continue, carving out a large circle from the vacant suburban street around my home. It looked like it had become a ghost town overnight. I watched the shaky hands of silent soldiers watching me and waiting. The whole suburb seemed to be evacuated. All eyes and guns were on me. I shouted out to the soldiers in earshot.

"What is going on?" I pleaded.

They stared back, radios chirping muffled conversations. All eyes were on me. I felt like an animal in a zoo and only wanted to leave. Nothing made any sense. I took a barefoot step onto the cold brickwork of my front steps and a booming, deep voice shouted over a megaphone.

"Return inside your home immediately or you will be shot." It took a moment to identify the soldier speaking. A thin man, serious as a bullet, standing behind a kneeling soldier who stared at me through the scope of an assault rifle.

"We will not ask you again, return indoors." the man spoke, his voice distorted through the loudspeaker.

I backtracked inside my home on shaky legs, ducking behind the vinyl-sided wall, well-aware it wouldn't hinder the large-caliber bullets from their automatic weapons. My heart was racing, and I felt lightheaded as stress twisted my face into a crying fit. I hugged my knees on the kitchen floor, only wishing to be at work listening to Adam's complaints about deadlines and deliberating on which lunch spot to frequent. Anything but this. As I nervously paced, I walked by the back windows, stopped in my tracks, and gawked.

A crater the size of a small car had carved a half-sphere out of the back lawn. It was a frilled ring of exploded soil which scarred the earth just feet from my home. Then I saw an oily trail of circular impressions, deformed fingerprints of varying sizes, spidering up the glass pane of my window, leaving a residue black and foul. Something had come from the crater. A scattering of light thumps from upstairs caused me to lurch backward as I understood: The military was not there for me.

My attention shifted from the threat outside of my house to the threat within. As scared as I was of the soldiers surrounding my home with rifles pointed at me, the creaking floorboards and scuttling sounds now coming from the second story were far more terrifying. Whatever crash-landed onto my lawn was now inside of my home.

I walked lightly over to the sunlit stairs and looked upward. A large shadow sped across the upstairs hallway wall. I let out the faintest gasp and, in that instant, it appeared. It scuttled quickly like a crab, but its limbs looked like an emaciated man's. They were deformed and far too long and they oozed black fluids that smeared the wall as it pushed its long torso into view. I watched in horror as a face emerged from a sliver in the torso as if being born from the chest. A face that looked like mine. The moment I registered that fact, it began to speedily climb down the stairs towards me.

I dashed back into the kitchen and searched desperately for a hiding spot, settling on the cabinet underneath the sink. There are separate doors, but they all led to the same large space I knew I was able to squeeze into. I closed the door not moments before that thing scampered into the kitchen to where I'd previously been standing. I listened to the horrible sounds it made as it wheezed and drooled and gargled. It sniffed the air on the hunt for me.

I waited for the door to fly off and be plucked up by one of those long, bendy arms. I tried to breathe shallow breaths to remain silent. My throat became dry, and my stomach rumbled loudly. I tried to will it to be quiet, but I was famished. I felt as if I hadn't eaten for a day or so. I heard squishing just inches from the door and placed my hand over my mouth to hush my breaths, and then I felt it.

I had the beginnings of a beard. My clean-shaven cheeks were fuzzy with scruff, and I swear I could feel it growing ever so slightly.

Suddenly, there was an explosion of glass. A loud crack accompanied by a thud. Another crack and a thud, this time followed by the sound of splashing liquid and a bizarre roar that quivered my guts. It was deep and layered with a higher, frantic squeal. *They are shooting*, I realized in a panic. Another crack of glass, followed by a pained wailing that receded further into my house. Judging from the sound of the creaking stairs, it had retreated back to the second story.

I lay still for a few moments until I was absolutely positive that thing was gone. Soon after, my fervent hunger drove me out of the hiding place in search of food.

Upon exiting the cabinet, I nearly collapsed. I was absolutely starving. The sharp pains in my stomach were excruciating. I felt lightheaded and fought the urge to faint as I crept over to the fridge and cracked it open, making sure to stay out of the line of fire. My leftover salad was slimy and wilted as if it had been left there for days. I forced it down anyway, well-aware the alternative was a loud microwave, crackers or other items that would draw the hopefully injured intruder back. I downed a few pints of water straight from the Brita and finally felt my strength begin to return.

I slowly stood and saw my reflection in the black glass of the windowpane. I looked like I'd gone a few days without shaving or sleeping. Past my reflection, the view was unrecognizable. About twenty meters back was a chain link fence surrounding my house, topped with razor wire. There was a full-sized Abrams tank aiming its heavy steel barrel right at my home. A platoon of soldiers milled about, passing papers and peeping through binoculars. One soldier, the slim guy from earlier, excitedly called to the others, and the rifles raised once again.

My heart jumped as I ducked for cover again. The fuzz of static-filled my dark kitchen from the radio I'd listen to the news with. Breaking the noise was an occasional voice counting off numbers that seemed cryptic. It seemed to be intercepting some of the military's communications.

I walked swiftly, making sure to remain low as I collected a few supplies. I transferred some frozen food and water into the shelf under the sink in case that thing returned, and I brought the radio closer.

I was able to tweak the knob until the signal strengthened and listened in to the bits of conversation the receiver picked up.

"16T FN 37637 53275. Over."

"16T FN 37637 53275. Over."

I was sure of it then; it was the soldiers communicating, possibly in code. I fought to remain awake, feeling the weight of my lids. I was absolutely fatigued, holding on by a thread. As impossible as it was, that thing's presence seemed to speed up the passage of time itself.

My neck hairs stood on end as I heard a quick thumping from just above me. I winced as I listened to the thing moving about up there. In the section of my home that seemed to exist at least twelve hours ahead.

That thing seemed to manipulate time itself, and whether alien, some military experiment gone terribly wrong, or goddamn Father Time himself, that thing scared the ever-living hell out of me. I decided to try and reason with the soldiers. I needed out or it would kill me, that much seemed certain.

I stood up and went to open the door when I heard the crack of the glass and the thud of the wall behind me. The shot where my head had been not a second before. I slid down as my heart pounded in my chest. There was no doubt at that point. They were trying to kill me, too.

I flattened on the ground and slid back into the cabinet under the sink, my Ajax-filled haven. I lay there, still, listening to the repeated numbers. My hair stood on end as I began to piece the cryptic numbers together. They weren't code, they were coordinates. Coordinates for an airstrike.

The knowledge that I was going to die at any given moment pressed down on me. I was trapped in my home and would be shot dead if I tried to flee. I was surrounded; the barricades and fences were just the first line of defense. There was no way to run.

They wanted both that thing and me dead, that much was certain. Whatever contingency plan they'd drawn up, the elimination of all evidence seemed to be their sole priority. With a single word called in on the radio to a pilot, I'd be obliterated, melted into the scorched earth of whatever new explosive they were itching to drop. There was no way out, it was just a matter of time.

I repeated it in my head. It was like a cosmic joke at my expense, but that anomaly with time was the most fascinating thing I'd ever encountered. Terrifying as hell, but fascinating nonetheless. Then the questions began to trickle into my mind. Questions as to what that horrific thing actually *was*. I was convinced that days had passed since it had entered my proximity. When on a different floor, however, time was shifted, like a ripple after a raindrop into a pond. Whether it was the frantic desperation of knowing I had likely less than an hour to live, or the effects of delirium finally hitting me, I had a theory.

The influence of that creature rippled time in its wake. It sped time up when I was close to it and that meant a few things:

First off, it was harder to kill a fast-moving target. I suspect that the shot taken by a sniper from the park had been a lucky hit. If my theory was correct, he'd seen a blur and happened to hit it on its hunt for me.

Secondly, I had only a short amount of time in its presence until it tore me limb from limb, or I died from starvation, dehydration, lack of oxygen or whatever other horrible death could occur when days pass in mere seconds.

Most importantly, if my theory was correct, I could use that thing to get out before being killed by those soldiers. The last thing I could imagine willingly subjecting myself to was that living nightmare with its elongated face-abdomen and long clawing limbs, but the alternative was clear. Death was coming, and it didn't need a warrant.

I took a few deep breaths as I poked my head out of the cupboard in search of anything that could be of assistance. Knives, check. Metal trash bin, check. Granola bars, in case I didn't die from the few hundred possible selections at hand, check.

I reached out to fetch the broom from its spot on the nail left of the sink. I tucked the largest steak knife into the back of my pants, praying that wouldn't end in a horror story of its own. I gently pulled the metal trash bin close to me, then used the broom handle to slide open the door to the outside without risking a bullet-riddled arm.

It hit me then. This might be my final few moments on Earth. A desperate, poorly hatched plan by a UX designer with a knife in his khakis and a trash can. I wanted to see my ex; to see my mother and father one last time. I wanted to live and breathe, but my window was closing because I just happened to live at ground zero. It was unfair. It was unfair, and I was pissed. I harnessed that anger as I set into motion my crazy plan.

I banged on the metal can like a drum, and immediately after, I heard the thuds of fast and heavy steps as that thing descended the stairs and ran towards me. It emerged so quickly I barely had time to react, brandishing the trash can with the open mouth aimed outward. I stood a little, just enough to widen my legs to brace myself, when that thing came into view.

The long, multi-sectioned arms bent and folded in strange angles, streaking black as they skittered across the walls. The face was a nightmarish bust on a human torso, which emerged from the lumpy, gray skin of its original form. It seemed like it was adapting its appearance to try and hide using my likeness.

They're trying to kill me too, dumbass, I thought, but any comic relief the whimsical notion might have brought was gone as the face split in two with a wet crack. The likeness of me had opened like jaws to reveal multiple glistening rows of jagged teeth dribbling black saliva. This thing could swallow me in a few chomps, and that seemed very much to be its intention. I focused as it ran straight into me.

I lifted the metal trash can up and felt the crunch of my ribs cracking as that thing's mimicked head-mouth nestled into the receptacle. I swung out so my back was facing the open door, and with that, the beast sprinted, carrying me outside on its trashcan-muzzled mouth like some alien rodeo cowboy.

The beast shook and knocked me about as it moved. It was immensely powerful, and the snapping of its me-shaped muzzle banged dents in the metal, threatening to burst it and swallow me up.

I felt my throat dry and then burn. My stomach twisted into knots and my bladder released itself as I was carried by the galloping horror in the moonlit field. I noticed the soldiers, frozen with teeth bared mid-sentence. Some rifles on the perimeter were bright with the frozen illumination of muzzle flare. I was dumbstruck by the surreal sight and felt myself losing consciousness but was jolted awake by the jerking motion as the thing I rode climbed the fence and dropped to the other side. My vision dimmed as I caught glimpses of housing developments, trees and distant highways. I lost consciousness. After that, thing had carried me long and far.

I awoke to the sound of lapping waves, and I thought I was dead. My vision was blurry, and my exhaustion was indescribable. Waves of cold water splashed against my leg, and I crawled desperately to the sea before me, drinking it desperately in. Freshwater. I opened my eyes to see the sunlit sands I'd frequented as a child. Lake Michigan. That thing had taken me over sixty miles west.

I eagerly ate the granola bar from my back pocket as my stomach growled and ached. As I did, I saw the tracks. Long, inky streaks in the sand coming from the scrub and the dunes. They led past a broken piece of metal I recognized as my life-saving trash can and continued into the waters where that thing had headed.

I scoured my phone for news and discovered an article detailing a gas explosion at my property. Apparently, I'm listed as dead, so I'm not quite sure how that's going to work out. All I'm sure of is that it's going to take some time to figure out how to proceed from here. Thankfully, time is the one thing I now have.

THE GAMES WE PLAY WHEN YOU'RE NOT HOME

Papa showed me how to play, back when he could talk. Back when he would smile; his wrinkled lips parted to reveal a rot-toothed grin. But his teeth fell out a while ago, and since his last stroke, he can't speak. Now he drools and wheezes, staring with foggy eyes so wide, it's like he's staring death in the face. I do most of the playing these days, and Papa watches and points at which game we will play.

If Papa points to the dresser, we play Scavenger Hunt:

We take a single sock from a pair out of your drawer, and we keep it. Occasionally something larger, like a shirt or pair of underwear. We watch you to see if you notice—it usually takes a few days—and when you do, we laugh. Papa dribbles down his chin in delight, clapping his swollen-knuckled hands together.

If you don't notice, we'll move on to other things. We'll take a wire or adapter, a thumb drive or a pen. We'll keep going until you notice, and then we'll watch you scramble around your room, looking under the bed and sifting through boxes and drawers in increasing frustration.

It Papa points to the kitchen, we'll play Chef:

We open the refrigerator and find your condiments. Ketchup or hot sauce is easily adulterated. Papa will peel back a fingernail until a red drop grows and let it drip inside the bottle to flavor it. He'll drink from your milk carton and water filter, drooling half of what he swishes around his mouth back in.

He'll take your silverware from the drawer and stir it around the toilet bowl. He'll scrape the buildup from his toes and titter to himself before returning your spoons and forks. It makes me sick when he plays this game, so I only watch him work until I feel dizzy and need to look away.

If Papa flashes a toothless grin and points to the electrical outlet, we'll play Traps:

Traps is a lot more fun to play, but much harder to prepare. We'll shave metal filings and blow them into electrical outlets, hoping to see the electricity make you dance. We'll unplug appliances and gnaw at the wires with our teeth, so you'll think it was rats from the walls, hoping for a fire. We'll sharpen your knives, hoping to see you snip through your fingers.

Traps are difficult because there's a fine line before we get caught and the game ends. Before you stop breathing and there is an investigation. We'll sprinkle arsenic in your coffee, just a bit. We'll streak the floor with a thin film of cooking oil, hoping for a slip. We'll blow out the pilot light and drain the batteries in your smoke detector.

We sit and watch through binoculars, and Papa cackles as he rocks back and forth as we see you stub your toes, or trip and nearly crack your skull into the corner of the table. We eagerly watch as the game progresses, careful to take it slow so you don't see us playing. Not until it's too late.

But recently, there has been a hitch. You rarely even leave your home at all. Nobody does; they all stay locked inside, glued to their screens. It's harder to come in and out these days. So, we've chosen to stay in with you.

It's a lot harder to play these games while you're home. Papa's wrinkled, bone-thin form easily fits snugly within the walls. I cut tiny holes he can watch you through with his bulging, bloodshot eyes. I'm far more nimble, and I get a thrill in switching locations when you get up to use the bathroom.

Of course, it's only a matter of time before you discover us now, so we've skipped the little games and moved on to the bigger games. The games with higher stakes and much more immediate results. The games that can stop you from waking up at all.

The games we play when you're *asleep*.

WANNA SEE SOMETHIN' SCARY?

Bob's gray whiskers twitched under his jaundiced, bloodshot eyes as he asked me that exact question yesterday. He stank to high heaven as usual, as did a few of the patrons of the soup kitchen I volunteered for at San Martin. Bob was a terminal alcoholic, having spent the majority of his life between the streets and jails. We'd had long conversations about our passions in the three years I'd gotten to know him. His was music, he'd been a guitar player in his teens before the needle and the bottle took everything away. As for me, I loved horror, and Bob knew that well.

"Of course I do," I said as a smile crept onto my face. I pictured a cat skeleton, or a creepy doll infested with bugs as I heaped a heavy portion of mac and cheese onto his tray. I expected a smile in return, but Bob just held that lingering stare as if he was witnessing some unseen horror with his sickly, yellow eyes.

"West Bond Street, go to the end, the large container. Beneath it," Bob whispered in a solemn, raspy voice. He shuffled off to a corner to shovel food into his bearded mouth and wash it down with a three-dollar pint of whiskey. I served the remaining guests with budding curiosity. When I finally finished for the day, I pulled out my phone and looked up West Bond Street, seeing the spot where the edge of town ended, and the sprawling New Mexico desert began. It was only 20 minutes away, so I began walking to the street Bob mentioned.

The houses were smaller and showed more weathering and disrepair the further I walked down West Bond towards the edge of town. I began to see rocks decorating the fronts of the houses, then lines of rounded stones that extended entirely around the modest homes. They appeared more superstitious than decorative. Further down the street, the houses began to look completely abandoned. The homes showed blistering paint and cracked windows, sun-bleached toys and a broken swing set as I approached the end of the street; and that container came into view. It was a large metal cylinder, perhaps ten meters high and fifteen in diameter, rusted and brown.

It was likely an old water tower sitting directly on the ground, halfway between town and the nearby military base. I walked up to a swinging gate at the end of the road. Beyond it, the road continued as a dirt path, and I looked over my shoulder before hopping over and approaching the huge structure. I saw the bumpy, eroding rungs of a ladder come into view and I climbed up the side. The rust crumbled in my hands and the wind rustled my hair. I reached the top and stepped gingerly onto the roof to test the sturdiness of the rusted metal. I then walked over to a hole the size of a manhole cover on the other side and peered into the darkness.

A ladder descended into the darkness below. I felt a bit nervous just thinking about the expression on Bob's face and considered bailing. That insatiable curiosity pushed me on, so I aimed my phone's flashlight down into the darkness, illuminating the ladder and barely revealing the curved interior siding. I climbed down, followed by the echo of the sound of my shoes tapping on the metal rungs. The air within smelled musty. I finally reached the bottom and my feet splashed into a few inches of foul, gray water that seeped into my socks.

My phone's light bounced off the rippling water in that dark interior, dancing on the metal walls before I noticed a square slab on the floor in the center. I approached it, shining the light on a thick stone cover pulled aside to reveal an opening. The stone cover looked old and worn, smoothed by what I assumed to be the water the large container once held. I peered into the hole past the raised stone lip to see a chain ladder descending deeper into the ground.

I was looking into a well that looked hundreds of years old, unlike the water tower I was standing in, which was probably built in the 50s, on top of this old well. The ladder, on the other hand, looked new, as if someone had left it there recently. Bob, after scavenging from it, most likely. "What did you find, Bob?" I muttered aloud in the echoing metal chamber. Unease built in my chest as I climbed over the lip of the well and onto the shaky ladder leading down.

A creeping feeling of immediate danger overwhelmed me as I climbed down that swaying ladder into the unknown depths. Each foot lower felt a few degrees colder, and I regretted not wearing a long-sleeved shirt. I climbed deeper into that ancient well, maybe 20 feet before reaching the bottom, and then I heard something rustling. Every hair on my neck rose as I listened to the muffled sound. I aimed my phone's light towards the source, illuminating a stone wall that led back about 15 feet, and where a huddled form lay in a filthy sleeping bag on the ground.

I stared at the shape of the dirty nylon sleeping bag. Someone was clearly inside it. The cold light of my phone glowed on the edges as I approached. It looked like a dead body. As dread swelled out of control, I realized I was no longer interested in seeing something scary, or whatever it was in that sleeping bag. I turned around to the hanging chain ladder and stopped in my tracks as a series of wet cracking sounds echoed out from that short hallway.

My heart pounded as I climbed that portable ladder back up to the top, looking back at that figure's body just as its head lifted and turned to face me with a sickening snap that seemed to come from the neck, revealing the face. It was Bob, but somehow it wasn't. That unmistakable, shaggy gray beard framed a gaping mouth far too wide. The jaw was completely unhinged, tugging elastic skin as it hung there in a silent scream. A bloated, purple tongue spilled down in forking tendrils from the horrible, massive maw under ice pick holes where a nose should have been; between bruised, purple cheeks. The eyes were wide, black spheres under Bob's blue wool hat, eyes that pulsed and rippled from movement within them as they stared at me like a wild animal's.

With a loud crack, the face split vertically. I screamed at the sight of snaking, amorphous black tentacles that unfolded from the center. That cracking sound continued as it twisted its torso completely around to face me, the legs still covered and unmoving. Those pale emerging arms bent and cracked at impossible angles. It howled, shrill and piercing, filling the chamber with a terrible, inhuman cry. I clawed up the ladder as quickly as possible; my phone gripped in my teeth to light the way.

I glanced back in the hole, seeing that opened face crawl into view, skin loose and wobbling, that broken jaw swinging below the bloated, pendulous black tongues. I screamed louder, yanking up the chain ladder as quickly as I could to stop it from following me. I piled the clanging chain ladder at the top of the 20-foot drop, and stomped through the splashing, stagnant water to the next ladder up to the roof.

I ran to the water tower edge and climbed down the rungs, slicing up my hand in my hasty retreat as that echoing howl filled the interior. I finally jumped off onto the dusty ground with a thud of rising dust. I headed back towards town, trying to get that awful face and that sickening, wet snapping sound out of my head as I ran. I nearly screamed again when I saw a man standing at the gate. It was Bob, his face completely intact and clearly waiting for me. His bulging eyes stared into mine, eager to confirm he wasn't crazy.

"You saw it," he stated more than asked, in a cracking voice, grabbing his elbows tightly with trembling hands. As I nodded, nearly in tears, Bob reached down to pick up a red tin of gasoline from the ground beside him. He walked slowly towards that rusty water tower, knowing at that moment, what he'd seen was, in fact, real. What *it* was is a question I hope I never know the answer to.

THE BURIED HAVE BEEN GIVING BIRTH

WOODBRIDGE, NJ.—A 911 call center in Middlesex County said dozens of people had called in to report strange crying sounds coming from St. Mary's Cemetery, Alpine Cemetery and other graveyards as far south as Ernst Memorial Cemetery in Parlin.

Multiple callers reported hearing "animal or infant cries" in the cemeteries on the NY/NJ border, one dispatcher said. Officers initially were sent out to check the surroundings but did not find the source of the reported sounds at that time.

The dispatcher said she alone had received over 30 calls on the subject between August 23rd and the 25th, prompting a second and a more thorough investigation of Woodbridge Memorial Gardens.

"The last call I got, the guy said he'd heard it six times throughout the night, and he swore someone was buried alive in there," she said. "I knew something was going on, but Jesus... not what they found."

Yesterday afternoon, investigating officers pinpointed muffled cries emanating from multiple undisclosed graves. Despite the burial dates on the gravestones being over five years old, the concern over a trapped person or mislabeled marker led to the exhumation of those graves. A paramedic who was on sight recounted the events he'd witnessed to us in some detail.

"I never heard anything like it. Sounded like a crying baby, but much more coarse and gravely. It sent chills down my spine. They brought in the excavator and went to work while we stood behind the yellow tape. Took them a few hours, but we didn't find any answers in that grave, only questions. Workers secured the coffin and pulled it out using a crane, and the first thing all of us saw was that damned hole at the 'feet end' of the box. It was splintered outward, like something had burst out of there. All kinds of dark fluids spilled out from whatever was left of the body."

But as he sucked down a cigarette with shaky fingers, a forensic investigator told us the real horror he found. He said he found a freshly chewed umbilical cord and a recent afterbirth. He claimed the buried woman's skin was decomposed to the point it was leathered and stripped, but he was absolutely certain she had recently given birth, impossible as that is. Makes no damn sense, a decomposed woman seven years rotting in the dirt giving birth. Worst of all, they found those piles of fresh soil just at the wood's edge.

Further investigation confirmed the mounds of loose soil were the result of tunneling from the grave to the surface. Initial theories of animals burrowing into the coffins to feed have been dispelled, after the findings of small fingernails and what they believed was amniotic fluid along the tunnel paths which lead outward to the surrounding wood's edge. Testing of the recovered samples is currently underway.

As of 10:30PM ET, four missing persons reports have been filed in the Edison area in possible connection to the events, after witnesses reported similar sounds of animal or infant crying. There is no confirmation that these disappearances are related, but citizens are advised to exercise caution.

One Woodbridge eyewitness contacted us detailing an encounter in relation to the bizarre events. The retired woman, who wished to remain anonymous, gave an emotional account of what she experienced late last night.

"I saw it, oh God, I saw it. It was out behind the bins when I was taking [the trash] out. I thought it was a baby some young mother had abandoned back there; people these days have no values over what they bring into this world. But that… that thing. That thing shouldn't ever have come into this world.

"Its pale skin was wrinkled and thin. You could see the cheekbones poking out and the lids all purple and glossy. Looked like a man on his deathbed, but it wasn't no bigger than an infant. Those eyes were inky voids too—emotionless like an insect's—black through and through. They had no soul in 'em. I'll see those eyes in my nightmares until the day I go. When I do, you best believe I'm getting cremated.

"I was taking out the trash and came around the back to where the bins were and saw it crawling, tucked in the shadows and only catching a halo sliver from the light behind it. I could make out a fleshy crater where a nose should be over that horrible toothless grin. Those black spheres of eyes flickered and must have noticed me then, cause that thing started crawling towards me real fast. It was slapping those little bony palms on the pavement with fury as it raced towards me.

"I screamed and fell back into my house when I saw it crawl out from the shadows. Oh God. I closed my eyes as I slammed and bolted the door, but the sight of it's been burned into my head. Those small fingers were clawing at the door to get in, that loose jaw and that bulging black tongue, dear God. I wish more than anything I could forget that face."

As of 4:55 AM ET, a fifth person has just been reported missing in South Amboy, NJ in possible connection. Residents are advised to take precautions when entering or leaving their homes. Residents are also advised to contact the authorities upon seeing or hearing anything that could be linked to the phenomenon, and to avoid unlit areas.

I DON'T THINK
I KILLED MYSELF

I grew up a skinny little introvert in the suburbs. I had a few friends, but usually just got lost in books. I went to summer camps, took piano lessons and enjoyed playing soccer. I did OK at school and the 4th, 5th and 6th grades all passed by as I grew into larger clothing and shoe sizes. My reality would splinter into unfixable fragments one summer, when I was ten years old.

I was playing soccer at the park with Jason, the one friend from school who seemed to take a liking to me. He was a stocky redhead who couldn't get enough fart jokes and video games. He had some crazy system that was very advanced, but I can't recall the name. I had to twist his arm to actually get outdoors to play soccer with me.

One day, Jason and I were out kicking the ball for about twenty minutes before he hunched over, out of breath. He complained about being tired of playing and punted the ball hard; it soared over my head. "Asshole!" I shouted, and I ran to get it, watching as it bounced high and barreled towards the road.

I ran fast enough to catch up to it before it went into the street, but I tripped. By the time I heard the loud music, it was too late. I saw the chrome fender of a fast-approaching black car; it was about to hit me. There was no way to avoid its course. Time slowed as I soared into the street and in front of that speeding car.

There was an awful crunch and my ribs and skull pulsed with a shocking amount of pain. I felt pressure inside my head, like it had burst. I never felt such agony, and I wanted it to end. The world went black, and screams erupted before it all clicked off with a snap.

I awoke to a telephone ringing; I was confused as to where I was. I was in a small, strange room I did not recognize, and the stink of stale cigarette smoke and bourbon made me wrinkle my nose.

"Jesse, take out the fucking trash!" The booming, gruff voice slurred the consonants. I sat up on the couch, feeling my head with my small fingers, confused at the length and texture of my hair. I thought I must've been in a weeks-long coma. But I was alive.

"Jesse, I said TAKE OUT THE TRASH, you idiot!" I felt a sharp smack on the top of my head and yelped. I held my throbbing head and locked eyes with the strange man looming over me. He was talking to me.

"Where am I? Who are you?" I asked, feeling tears glaze my eyes. The red-faced man with gray-peppered stubble smirked an awful smile as he stooped to look into my eyes. His were blood-shot, bulging orbs above a bulbous nose and yellow-toothed grin.

"You want me to put you back in a cast, you little shit?"

I rose and quickly scanned the interior of the trailer I found myself in, soon finding the overflowing garbage which was filled with crushed Pall Mall packs, empty flasks and Styrofoam contain-ers. I kneeled to the stained carpet and brushed stinking cigarette butts and food debris into the bag, twisting the top as I made my way outside the flimsy door.

The sun was oppressive in a circle of old trailers rusting away. Was I kidnapped? I thought maybe there'd been a mix-up at the hospital, and my mom was devastated and looking all over for me. I dumped the reeking trash into a dumpster buzzing with flies and then looked around. I needed to get help. I decided I was going to make a break for one of the other trailers to ask for a phone, when I caught a glimpse of myself in the pane of a door window. I stopped dead in my tracks.

There, staring back at me, was the face of a child who looked nothing like me. A shaggy-haired kid with freckles and scared eyes. I held up my hands as my brain swirled in confusion. I tried to think of my mom and only saw a chain-smoking woman with blue eyeshadow who was yelling at the red-faced drunk in the trailer. My head hurt as I struggled to remember what she looked like in the suburban house I grew up in. I could see her blonde ponytail, but her face was a blank oval of flesh. The house was a faint memory that degraded with each detail I fought to remember, like some dissolving recollection of a dream.

My last name—previously on the tip of my tongue—slipped away from me entirely. I couldn't remember it. All I could remember was the name Nelson. My name; Jesse Nelson. I then remembered trips with my drunk dad to the lake to go fishing, and Christmases with IOUs written in folding cards under a plastic tree. Every sliver of clear memory was lost in a hazy cloud; fine brushstrokes of details lacking the big picture, or even the canvas beneath.

I kept a journal as I transitioned into this childhood as another person. I tried to recollect as many details as I could, thinking if I could piece it together, I might be able to get home. I endured my father's endless insults as well as the negative attention from kids at school. I quickly learned if you can't afford name brand clothing, you are a magnet for bullies.

The insults were endless. Trailer trash. Thrift store reject. Redneck. Hick. School was hell, and home life was not much better. No video games, no TV. This new dad would bet on horses, and he'd usually lose. He'd then get really angry, and I quickly learned to leave and take walks along the highway to avoid getting hit.

I struggled in school. The school system I was enrolled in was teaching different courses than my previous one. Despite the difficulty and distraction, I managed to do alright in high school. Flashes of a previous life would still occasionally come at odd moments. Memories of the metronome's ticking as I sat still for piano lessons, or ice cream Sundays with a smiling set of parents. A grinning man behind a steering wheel. Each time the memories flashed into my head they would burn out, soon replaced with new ones. Fresher memories of throwing rocks at beer bottles and my pop's shouting matches with Mr. Nash, the nasty man at the end of the trailer park. They both argued about a woman. My missing mother, I presumed.

Still, I learned to enjoy what I had in my new life. I even grew accustomed to my new face and modest new home. The bullying also became less intense the less I seemed to care.

I developed different sets of interests, which grew as time passed. I knew a bunch more about cars than I thought I did, as if the memories of this child and my own had merged into some slurry that was slowly taking form. I graduated from high school, and with a sweaty hug from my pops, I knew that was as far as my education would go.

My grades were not good enough for a scholarship, and dad was dead broke. I picked up a job at a gas station. That's where I met my maniac of a best friend, Ron. He was a few years older, a metal head with a ratty mustache and a hilariously twisted sense of humor. He made life there manageable, actually pretty fun a lot of the time.

I would drink beers with him and his buds on the weekend and work hard, making my fingers callous as I removed stripped bolts and struggled to save money. I eventually moved out of my pop's place and into a small, cockroach-riddled apartment in the nearby town. I grew into a young man, having fun and enjoying my freedom as I saved up for a car.

Something drew me to it, but I couldn't quite say what. Its sheen and luster, the black powerhouse, was in my sights for months before I put down that initial payment. "You get the car, then you get the girls," Ron always said. I soon was at the dealership, shaking hands with a smiling salesman. I hopped into the new vehicle and smelled the fresh leather interior. I turned her on and my heart purred with the revving of the engine. My new black Mustang.

I shouldn't have been drinking, and I know that. Ron had won $1000 from a scratch-off card, and I was now 21 and had my very own car; he wanted to party. I picked him up, and we drank at a new spot downtown where he insisted all the ladies frequented. He was slurring, wagging a finger at the bouncer until we were kicked out. It was only around four in the afternoon, and we were tanked.

I was driving too fast, metal blasting as Ron shouted, "RIGHT, take this RIGHT!" and the tires skidded as I pulled past a park. He lit a cigarette, and I yelled at him, screaming not to smoke in my car. A glowing ember hit my arm as he tried to toss it. I didn't see the kid tripping into the road before it was too late. I saw his face. A face I recognized immediately.

My heart broke into a thousand pieces before the impact. I knew as soon as I stepped out of the car and saw his bloody head and twitching, broken fingers. He was pronounced dead at the scene. The sirens approached, and I wept into my hands before the cuffs twisted my arms behind my back. It was me dead on the street. The real me.

I've been in prison for a few weeks now. Every day is the same. It's rough here, but if you act tough and fight back, you don't get eaten alive. But I can't unsee my own youthful face staring up at my fast-approaching car. I swear to it, just before the impact I saw it. That little boy was grinning a wicked little smile at me like I'd just lost a bet.

SHE'S TRYING TO TAKE MY SON

I first saw her when I picked up Lucas from school last week. As I watched the kids stream out of the school's front doors, I noticed her standing on the edge of the lawn. Her arms dangled straight at her sides and her wrinkled face was glaring at the children in a way that seemed off.

The woman looked to be in her late 60s, early 70s with white, wiry shoulder-length hair. She wore a long dress that looked vintage and, from her vacant expression, she appeared to be mentally unstable. As the children flooded the school's front lawn, headed to their buses and cars, the woman began walking awkwardly towards the kids; slowly at first. It was then I noticed she wasn't wearing shoes.

My gaze returned to the kids, and Lucas appeared in the sea of ruddy faces, his backpack looking like an over-sized prop on his small frame. I smiled and waved, but he didn't yet see me. When I looked back to the strange woman, I saw she was walking faster, her arms straight at her sides and that intense, unnatural expression fixed on her pale face. She was moving directly towards my son, and my stomach did a little flip as anxiety built. I instinctively opened the car door and exited the vehicle.

"Lucas!" I called out, well-aware this might embarrass him. I'd apologize later. Lucas looked up in surprise. He lowered his head as if to become invisible and shifted his direction towards my car. I looked back at that woman to see she had altered her course too, clearly making a beeline straight towards my son. Something was very wrong.

I jogged over to my son and placed my hand on his shoulder.

"Mom, you're embarrassing me," Lucas mumbled, as expected.

"I'm sorry honey, I'm just in a rush is all."

I looked back up at the old woman. She was closer now, but standing still. She looked unsettling; her unkempt hair was a mess, and smudges of dirt were visible on her spotted, weathered skin. I watched as she turned slowly back around to face the woods at the school's edge. I continued watching as she began walking away. My gaze followed her pale, sinewy legs down to her bare, bony feet. They were dark with crusted stains that looked like blood.

"I thought you were in a rush?" Lucas asked in frustration, but I just stood there and watched the woman traverse the lawn, and eventually disappearing into the woods.

"Let's go, honey." I led Lucas to the car, looking back over my shoulder to make sure she was gone.

Opting to not cause a panic, I didn't notify the school just yet. While it had appeared that she was heading towards my kid, that wasn't certain. I tried to rationalize how she might have just mistaken my son for her grandchild. Maybe she was confused, lost, or homeless. Still, I couldn't shake that awful feeling of dread that had roiled inside of me as that woman approached my son. The following day, I decided to arrive at the school early. I now dread to think what might have happened if I hadn't.

At 2:40, I pulled up to Lucas's elementary and waited in the car. It wasn't until 2:48 I heard the faint crackle of twigs that alerted me to the white hair peeking through the trees. That same disheveled woman emerged, the same mask-like expression of intense concentration fixed on her wrinkled face. The diplomat I was, I decided to have a chat with the woman before letting my emotions take control.

I exited the vehicle and walked towards her. With every step, I felt a tingle in my neck that shouted warnings of danger into my primal brain. I walked closer to her, until I stood about ten feet from the woman, and I lifted a hand up in greeting.

"Hi there. How are you?" I asked. The old woman slowly turned her gaunt face towards me, her wide eyes foggy from cataracts. Her waxen lips hung open and a trickle of drool seeped out from her crooked mouth. She looked deranged, but I tried reasoning with her.

"Do you have a kid at this school? If not, you are not legally allowed to be here." No reply. Anger bubbled up, but soon shifted into fear. Something was very wrong with her, that much was clear. The clamor of excited children began behind me as they exited the school. "Excuse me, ma'am. Hey! I'm talking to you," I tried to sound threatening, but no doubt came across as nervous.

The woman's eyes twitched in her deep eye sockets and a dusty wheeze escaped her throat. I swear I could smell the stink of rot on her breath from nearly three meters back. I tensed up as she began walking towards me fast and determined, and I stepped to the side. The old woman continued walking past me. I then saw my kid; she was walking directly towards my son.

Adrenaline flooded my body as I ran past the old lady towards Lucas. I turned to the old woman. She was drooling heavily, her wrinkled chin was shiny with seeping saliva. I jogged, ignoring the stares of other children as I intercepted my son and ushered him quickly to the car with both hands on his shoulders.

"Mom! What the hell?" he protested, but I kept guiding him to the car. I turned back to see the strange woman fast approaching. I shoved Lucas into the car, well-aware I must have looked crazy.

"I'm sorry, there is a woman who looks very dangerous out there," I explained as I shifted into drive and sped down the tarmac.

I checked the rear-view as I drove; that old woman was walking down the street after us in slow pursuit. I drove cautiously until she was out of view and there was a good distance between us before driving home. I apologized to Lucas and explained what had happened. "Who is she? What does she want?" he asked, sadness creaking in his small voice. I didn't have those answers.

Once home, I dialed the school as well as the police. I gave a complete description of the woman, her direction of origin in the woods, and anything else I could think of. I decided to excuse Lucas from school the following day, expressing the fact I didn't feel safe until this woman was gone. I did my best to sound calm, not to scare my son, and I told him the school was taking care of it. Once I explained we could spend the day watching movies and eating ice cream, he cheered up a bit.

Yesterday I spent the bulk of the day on the phone with the school as well as the police, filing complaints and explaining everything in detail, over and over again.

"Do you know this woman?" No.

"She's not related to your ex-husband?" No.

"Did this woman actually touch your son?" No.

"Did she say anything to him?" No. No. No and no. With every single 'no', I began feeling more like I was overreacting. Both the police and the secretary at the school said no such woman was there, and I began to consider the fact it was just some unfortunate coincidence until Lucas began repeating "Mom" and called me over.

I walked into the living room to find Lucas pointing his small finger to the window, his face pale and eyes watery with pooling tears. I looked out the bay window and there she was, standing in the middle of our street. That same old woman with milky eyes, drool glazing her slack jaw and her eyes wide and cloudy.

I called the police immediately, frantically explaining she was here at my home. I raced through the house, locking the doors and windows. By the time I finished securing the ground floor, she was gone, no longer visible out in the street.

The police arrived quickly, and I explained the scenario from the beginning yet again. Due to the frequency and severity of these encounters, they stationed an officer who parked out front to watch over the house in case she returned. I moved Lucas's mattress to the floor of my room and shut the curtains. After a day of watching superhero films and various cartoons, Lucas fell asleep and eventually, I was able to as well.

I awoke when I heard Lucas scream. My heart raced, and I leapt to my feet. Lucas was at the window being dragged from the wrist by a liver-spotted hand on a long, sagging arm. The old woman was in the open window, her gray tongue flopping out of her wrinkled, toothless mouth.

I rushed forward and grabbed my son's reaching arm, pulling him with all my strength. That woman was far stronger than she appeared, and I was unable to yank my son from her grasp. I grabbed the heavy reading lamp from my nightstand and brought it down hard on her elbow repeatedly with jarring cracks until she released her grip on my son's wrist. Once freed, Lucas rushed to me and cowered behind my legs. I watched in terror as the old woman scuttled out of the window frame, her limbs moving calculated and deftly, almost reminiscent of an insect's. I cradled my crying son, who was now shivering and sobbing. I then peered out the window before closing and locking it. There was no sign of the woman.

I dialed the police and soon heard vigorous knocking from my front door. I let the officer in, and once again found myself answering questions. No, I do not know who this woman is. No, I do not know how she opened the locked bedroom window. No, I do not know how she scaled the side of my two-story home. What I do know is she's trying to take my son, and I'm scared to death I won't be able to stop her.

UNCLE LEONARD'S DISTURBING SLIDESHOW

My uncle Leonard was the oddball black sheep of the family. We'd only get a glimpse of him at funerals. He'd show up with a wide smile checkered with stained and missing teeth, his whiskey breath lingering in the air before him. Thin wisps of gray hair nested on his wrinkled head, which poked comically out of his gaudy plaid jacket. My mom always said he had a screw or two loose, but I loved his crass jokes, strange and paranoid theories, and odd appearance. He was a janitor at some large facility with a bit of an alcohol problem, and he was the last thing on my mind until a few days ago.

My mother called to tell me he wasn't returning phone calls or texts regarding the planning of her 60th birthday party. After trying him on the phone, she found his Facebook page had lacked any updates in weeks. She called her cousins, but nobody had heard from him. Since I lived closest, she asked if I could check in on him. I was recently heartbroken and single, failing out of college and dealing with a haze of lingering depression. I was not only free but in need of a break from wallowing in misery, so I agreed to visit.

When Friday rolled around, I drove out to the sticks to Leonard's house. It was a dilapidated, one-story home that looked abandoned. His boxy Chevy Caprice, rusted and peeling from neglect, sat on deflated tires. It meant he should have been home. Fall leaves piled up from the rusty gutters and onto the sagging roof that was missing half the shingles. The dead grass looked like a cemetery of toothpick tombstones. A sun-bleached, green plastic mailbox leaned at a 45-degree angle, maw agape and spewing old mail. I took a deep breath and exited the car, walking over cracked paving stones framed by weeds to the unwelcoming front door. I realized for the first time that Uncle Leonard had lived in absolute squalor.

The windows were black and speckled with dust and dirt, with no clear view inside. After a quick rap of my knuckles on the door, I reminded myself to wash my hands thoroughly as soon as possible. No answer. I knocked harder, calling out, "Hello?" No reply. I peeked into the dark windows, wiping with my jean jacket sleeve, the dunes of dust in each dark pane; to try and see within.

"Hello, Uncle Leonard?" I called out and knocked again, harder still. The force of my pounding knuckles pushed the creaky door inward. I immediately coughed from the sour air that suddenly escaped the residence. I pushed the heavy door fully open and was met by the foul ammonia odors of urine and the suffocating staleness of mildew.

He was a hoarder, that much was clear. The place was filled with buzzing flies and piled dishes of fuzzy, molded food waste. Soggy newspaper stacks and mildewy mounds of damp clothing gradated the dreary color spectrum from green to gray. I made the rounds, squeezing past piled garbage, trying not to touch the furry growths of speckled mold that reached out from every surface. I covered my nose and mouth with my sleeve to reduce the miasma of sour air as I continued further into the maze-like mess of junk. I saw no sign of Uncle Leonard as I squeezed by mountains of trash, but I noticed a cracked door leading down into the darkness of a basement.

I pushed the creaky door open and peered down the stairs into the blackness. Flecks of old lead paint drifted to the floor like ash as I pulled the door open. My fingers felt around before landing on the switch on the wall, but after a few fruitless flicks, it was clear the bulb had burned out. I turned on my phone's flashlight. The beam of light swimming with floating motes of dust barely lit the rickety stairs descending. There was a light shining through the darkness below.

I stepped down into the darkened cellar, curiosity filling me as well as unease. A plastic, faux wood-grain box from the 80s I recognized as an old slide projector sat on the armrest of an ancient couch that was crumpled and stained. The projected slide illuminated a concrete wall with a rectangle of light, displaying the image of a playground. I coughed as I walked to the couch, to a kinked, black wire leading to a simplistic controller resting on a filthy cushion.

"Are you down here?" I called out, aiming the light on stacked boxes to cast stark shadows. Old standing lamps, stacks of 70s and 80s board games, and old books formed pillars within the labyrinth of junk. I turned back to the projector, the only immediate clue before me, and picked up the wired plastic controller as I approached the 5x7 projected photo of a playground. I pressed down the 'forward' button.

Click

The plastic carousel rotated. The basement went black and cold momentarily before another old photo replaced the playground on the wall. The blurry photo showed a woman pushing a stroller in the playground. Out-of-focus leaves blurred dark green in the foreground, and I soon realized the photo was taken from behind the cover of bushes in a clandestine manner. My stomach squirmed as I pressed forward on the control and darkness consumed the basement between slides.

Click

A new image showed that same woman, likely the mother, leaning over a crib and tending to her child. The voyeuristic nature of the photos made my skin crawl. The photos had been taken after sneaking into the monther's house, that much was certain. It seemed clear my uncle had been stalking this woman at first, but then a creeping dread shivered me into a realization. He wasn't stalking the woman, but her child. Dark curiosity guided my shaky thumb, which rattled the cheap plastic "forward" button as I pressed it down once again.

Click

A photo from above; the shirtless toddler lying down on a plastic-wrapped mattress in the basement I soon recognized by the shape and concrete walls. It was the basement I was in. My skin crawled with horripilation. The photographed child faced away from the camera, but their spine seemed malformed as if from a severe form of scoliosis. Behind the small figure was a metal cage, the kind used to crate dogs. A padlock hung from the gate. My throat closed as dread grew at the unfolding scenario.

"Oh my god," escaped my dry throat in a rattled whisper. Almost immediately in response to my voice, I heard a faint rattling of metal from inside the dark, cluttered basement. I wasn't alone down there.

"Hello?" I called out, spinning towards the sound with the low-powered LED from my phone. Past stacks of refuse and dismantled shelving, I saw a small cage. My heart became heavy and cold as it sank in my chest. I could see the form inside. There was a small child inside the cage.

Time slowed as I walked closer to the small metal enclosure. I averted my gaze from the shirtless body of a frail child within, holding up small hands to block the light of my phone. The foul odors of bodily waste grew stronger as I approached.

"Oh… oh my god, hang on, I'm getting you out," I called out to the child.

A saliva-filled wheezing soon became punctuated with coughs; the child was choking. I grabbed the padlock with shaking hands as my heart pounded in my chest. I breathed out in relief; a small, rusty key was still in the lock. I turned it with a click and slipped the padlock from the latch. I opened the cage door, looking in the dark confines of the crate to the cowering child inside extending a hand. But I soon recoiled backwards as the kid looked up. Something was wrong with their face.

It was that uncanny valley effect of something mimicking a person but not quite nailing it. I then realized the child was wearing a mask. A closer look caused me to cock my head in confusion when I recognized it from my CPR training for my lifeguard job. It was the rubber face of a Little Junior CPR manikin. The child coughed, and I heard the muffled pops of cartilage in joints as long arms unfolded from behind the cowering form.

Unfolding limbs bent in unnatural ways and the poking spine twisted under skin too small to contain it. My dread about the child's wellbeing shifted into immediate concern for my own. I rose and stepped back slowly from the open cage. My heart pounded as I cowered in the shadowy cover underneath the stairs. I felt the floor cling to my sneaker with an adhesive stickiness unseen in the shadows. I covered my mouth with my hand to silence my breath.

I heard wheezing breaths and the patter of damp feet on the cement floor as that thing crawled from its confines into the basement, sniffing and gurgling. I smelled it then. The stench of bodily decomposition wafted up after my sneaker broke the congealed seal of unseen remains under my feet. I looked down into the dim space as my eyes struggled to make out the form of a person. A crumpled corpse lay in the recesses of the nook with me, wearing an over-sized plaid suit. It was Uncle Leonard.

My mind spun in horror as I only then understood he'd kept this child-thing down there in the cage for a reason. The click of joints called my attention back to the cage, to the unfolding form of something far too tall and strangely shaped that was squeezing its way outside the small window near the exposed beams of the ceiling. It had escaped the basement. I stayed in the hiding place for a few minutes to make sure it wasn't returning before I finally breathed.

I nervously approached the slide projector, nagged by the urgent need to understand what that thing was that I'd released. A lump developed in my throat as I continued the slideshow of photos that painted a truly disturbing picture.

The next few slides were blurry action shots of that thing feeding. A shocking tableau of misshapen things only slightly reminiscent of children lit up the wall. There were more of them, different child-like things with different abnormalities that made my skin crawl. Unhinged jaws and two sets of beady black eyes on one. Slender limbs that folded and split into narrower and increasingly branched appendages on another.

Paperwork marked "confidential" was photographed on the subsequent slides, bearing the logo of the facility Uncle Leonard had worked at. The documents were littered with foreign terms such as 'SCNT', 'gRNA' and 'genome editing'. I needed to look them up; they were terms related to cloning and genetic engineering. The anxiety tensing my muscles and spinning my mind crescendoed when I clicked forward. My knees buckled, dropping me to the filthy couch.

The next slide was an old photograph of a boy getting his blood drawn. A boy that looked just like me.

THE JIGSAW PUZZLE

A fisherman found the left hand off the coast of Maine. The palm was pale and bloated, and fish had nibbled most fingers down to the bone. Part of his fingertip remained, and a partial print identified him. It was the hand of our daughter's killer. My wife burst into tears as the detective explained he was likely dead. I was more than skeptical, however. They'd lied when they told us they'd catch him. Still, some relief washed over me knowing the scum might never take another child.

They found his right hand a week later, mangled and broken. It had washed up on a New Jersey shore one afternoon. The officers told us it seemed more than certain he'd tried to flee the country on a boat that had capsized. "Karma," they said, as if a boat accident is a fair price to pay for what he did to our little girl.

Weeks passed and other parts trickled in across the coast. A pair of feet, ears and even a nose. They found the calf and thigh muscles sawed down into shank steaks afloat in Chesapeake Bay. It was then obvious his death hadn't been accidental. They told us he must have been butchered alive, and I had to admit, that gave me some comfort. Whoever killed the animal made him suffer.

We received a few calls with more information about the parts they dragged up in nets from the ocean. His forearms, elbows, and lower jaw. I began to relish these bits of information that would trickle in. I finally got some bounce back in my step and was almost content enough to even bring up the idea of having another child to my wife. Then one night the power went out. As I descended the stairs into the dark basement to find the fuse box, I heard a muffled rustling coming from the back.

I found a hidden seam in the cement wall; a secret door I'd never known about. I opened the heavy panel to reveal a foul-smelling chamber no larger than a small bathroom. I froze when I saw a silhouetted form in the shadows. Its contours were jagged and bizarre. My heart jumped in my chest when it twitched. My eyes adjusted to the darkness, and I could then see the hideous details.

A gargled whimper trembled the tongue, which dangled from a jaw-less mouth. Lidless eyes pleaded, wide with terror. Gnarled stumps of arms raised up in defense. I left quickly, sealing the horror back inside of the wall. I switched on the circuit breaker and raced back up the stairs. I slid into bed and sidled up to my wife, and as I wondered which piece of the puzzle she'd leave next, I hugged her close and smiled.

MY DOG BROUGHT STRANGE BONES FROM THE WOODS

A loud tap on the sliding glass door startled me. I looked up to see Oscar was trying to get in, but he was carrying an odd stick in his jaws that prevented his entry. His faint whine soon let me know he'd requested my assistance in getting his hard-earned treasure from the woods indoors. I sighed and rose from the table.

Oscar is my lovable mutt, mostly beagle-lab mix, or "beagador" as the woman at the pound enunciated through mauve lipstick. Oscar's got a heartwarming, high-pitched howl and wags his pointy tail as he bounds off into the woods behind my property for his afternoon walks. This time, it appeared he'd brought something back.

As I approached Oscar, who was excitedly wagging his tail at the door, I tried to understand the item he'd carried home with him. It had the luster of bone, slick with saliva in those floppy jowls of his. I slid open the glass door but knelt quickly to block his path.

"Drop it," I commanded, and Oscar gave a defiant squint as he clenched down on the long stick. It resembled an antler, but it was thicker and warped. Petrified wood, maybe.

"Oscar, DROP IT!" I shouted louder, and the object fell from his jaws and clattered onto the brickwork walkway. Oscar whimpered as I held his collar and rubbed his fur dry with a towel before granting him entry. I then returned to eyeing that odd form on the ground just outside the door.

It was organic, and it had rounded joints on each end like bone. Points jutted out, and it curved in a way that no bone I'd ever seen before had. It was long too, ⅔ of a meter from end to end. It was like some strange femur that had started to grow out additional branching bones from itself before whatever it belonged to had died and eventually decayed. The calcium formation looked more like a deep-sea discovery than something from the woods.

I peered at the bone on the wet brickwork as I slipped into my jacket. I fetched my gloves from the closet shelf and headed out into the drizzle. I picked it up and rotated it in my gloved fingers. It was dense and heavy. A few strings of black meat dangled from the joint and the stench of rot became apparent as I lifted it up from the ground. I couldn't even imagine what it could belong to. I analyzed it for a few minutes before I cocked back my arm and lobbed it hard back into the thick of the woods.

Last night, exhausted from work, I pulled into the driveway as the sun melted on the horizon. Upon entering the house, I spotted Oscar straddling the kitchen floor, gnawing on some other filthy trophy he'd brought back from the woods. He whimpered softly to himself as I approached him and kneeled. I pet his head and gently pried it from his resisting jaws, trying to understand the form.

It looked like a bunch of skeletal snakes, but they all stemmed from a shape resembling a skinned animal paw. I approached the stinking remains, confused. Even leaning close and holding my breath from the foul odor, I had no idea what I was looking at. It resembled images I'd seen of skeletal whale flippers, five long, tail-like fingers composed of seven knuckle segments, tapering down into pointy nubs.

Oscar then began to growl as I'd never heard before. His paws were spread out and his hackles raised across his arched back as he bared his pointy teeth at the glass door facing the woods. I felt truly exposed for the first time, the blackness of the woods surrounding me as Oscar growled at the trees. With a yelp and a strange cry, he bounded out the gap of the front door and into the woods.

"Oscar, COME!" I shouted, sliding open the door. I heard the rustling of twigs and leaves as he dashed into the shadowy woods. He soon began barking his sharp beagle yelps from deeper within.

"OSCAR!" I called out, following his voice. "COME!" I ordered, but he only continued to sound the alarm. I huffed angrily to myself, fetching the flashlight from the kitchen drawer before walking outside onto the dewy lawn. I followed the circular beam of projected light illuminating bark and pine needles. Twigs snapped beneath my feet as I penetrated the tree line and into the cover of the trees. Oscar continued to bark and growl; he sounded 20 meters or so in.

I sped up in pursuit, ducking under spiny branches aiming for my eyes. The crunching of the leaves and Oscar's barking were the only sounds, as if even the insects were hiding.

"OSCAR, god DAMN IT," I yelled, feeling my face flush red. "COME!"

A yelp sounded from up ahead and my heart sank. "Oscar?" I called out, worried. I ran.

I followed his whimpering as I sprinted into the shadows of the woods, and I nearly fell in. The ground stopped in front of me, opening up into darkness. There was a hole in the earth roughly ten feet in diameter. I aimed the light inside that hole and my jaw hung slack as I saw the beam vanish into the depths.

The air escaping that massive hole was far too cold. It appeared to be a sizable cave recently unearthed due to a sinkhole of sorts. Soon, the thumping of running feet grew louder from the hole and I nearly screamed when Oscar bounded out of the shadowy mouth straight towards me. "Oscar!" I shouted in relief, but it was short-lived. A second set of running footsteps was approaching from within. Something else was coming; something heavy and fast.

I ran, following my bounding dog through the woods back home. I only turned back once, catching a partially obscured glimpse of what was pursuing me. Through the shadows of the trees, I saw flailing white limbs, but far too many of them. I kept running and eventually breached the wood's edge onto my lawn.

My pulse raced as I sprinted, despite the flaring pain in my joints. I raced inside my home and slammed the door, locking it with desperate fingers. Oscar panted loudly, staring at me from under the kitchen table with worried eyes. Outside, through the reflective black windows, I saw movement along the edge of the forest.

Between the trunks of trees, I saw flashes of a long, pale face and then another. There looked to be an assortment of different heads, arms, and legs affixed to the same misshapen torso. Some of the parts looked human, some canine, and some amalgamations of other forest creatures, like cloven deer hooves. Some were slender twisted limbs resembling those bones that Oscar brought back. It was as if multiple animals had been harvested and re-purposed into a twisted collage. It loomed in the shadows encircling my small home, watching with numerous sets of beady, black eyes that flickered as they watched me.

My heart pounded in my chest as I backed away from the windows and turned off the lights. I knelt down by Oscar, resting a shaky hand on his heaving back.

Without warning, a glass pane shattered. I grabbed Oscar by the collar and quickly led him down the narrow stairway leading into the basement, the only place in my home without windows. My mind raced as I slammed the door closed and locked it behind me. After a minute or two of listening to the crunch of stepped on glass, the basement stairs began to creak. Behind the thin wooden door, that thing drew closer, sniffing and huffing as it closed the distance between itself and the door.

My heart sank when I heard a clatter on the cement floor behind me. Dread climbed up my spine and bristled my neck hairs as I turned to the source of the sound. Oscar was licking a skeletal trophy from a small pile of those strange bones he'd apparently been hoarding down in the basement. Bones that thing wants back or worse, wants to replace.

THE WATCHING MOON

Floating in a sea of stars
Left of Venus, right of Mars
Pale and white and always still
Lighting up our windowsill
People watch it every night
Guided by its spectral light
When we close our eyes and sleep
Others open from the deep
From the shadows down within
Right above a crooked grin
In each crater deep and black
Are two eyes that watch us back

THE HOLE IN THE HOUSE

It started after I received a worried call from my aunt. She asked me to check on my cousin Peter and his wife Sharon, because they stopped returning their calls and emails.

I was shocked at the news of the possibility something had happened to them. Thoughts of a home invasion gone wrong, or a kidnapping sent shivers up my spine. Sharon, after all, was six months pregnant. Dread welled in the tips of my toes as I got in the car and drove the half-hour to their development.

It was a newer housing development, built in the 90s with generic, cookie-cutter floor plans. Each home was similar, with vinyl siding and perfectly manicured green lawns. Christmas ornaments decorated the lawns and a few trees glimmered with little white lights. The quintessential suburb. A little, white-fenced haven from the noise and dangers of the city. The pristine two-story houses rolled by as I followed my GPS, and I soon began to feel an unexplainable agitation. The sun was golden and the eggshell-blue sky nearly cloudless, but some primal urge to leave grew until my throat tightened and my mouth dried.

Nearly every house had a car or two parked in the driveway. The lights were on in almost half of the buildings; it looked like a normal afternoon in an all-American suburb. There was no sign of anything amiss, and I expected to see shadows cast on walls through the windows from movement within, but there was no sign of activity whatsoever. The GPS guided me onto Peter's street, announcing the arrival at my destination on the right. Their car was parked in the driveway.

I exited the vehicle and as I did, the silence hit me. Aside from the slight bobbing of a branch or two in the faint breeze, it was unnaturally still and quiet. I walked up the asphalt driveway to Peter's front door and knocked loudly. No reply. I walked around their two-story home, peering into the windows showcasing modern furniture and quaint decor. No sign of him. I tried the back entrance and found it unlocked. I slid the heavy glass door open and stepped inside.

Peter's keys were on the wooden dining room table, as well as a bag of groceries on the counter. The bag was wet at the base, and it stank; the produce within had begun to rot. I began the dreaded action of looking into each room; half-expecting to find them lying on the floor dead or hanging by their throats, blue-faced and glassy eyes bulging in their sockets. But they weren't there. I searched every room and closet. The tub, the basement, and the attic. There was no sign of them at all. It was as if they'd simply vanished.

After a half-hour sifting through their mail for clues, I left, realizing there was nothing to be done; Peter simply wasn't there. I headed back outside to my car. As I was about to get back in, I felt an urge I hope to never feel again as long as I live.

I trembled from a chill that consumed me from deep within. It was a chill you feel in smaller doses when realizing your wallet is no longer in your pocket, or that you've locked your keys in your car. It was that dawning dread that something was wrong, but it was stronger. It hit me when I noticed a house one row back from theirs. It was an ordinary home, the same shape, size and color as all the rest, but once I noticed it, my pulse quickened, and my blood iced through.

I was drawn to it like a fly to festering meat. It was calling me, speaking with perfect right angles and double-paned windows, willing each of my feet forward, one after another. Across the street, over the creosote smells of lawns. Unable to resist the beckoning structure, I wandered along the empty sidewalk.

There was a subtle feeling just under my skin. A tender, vague itch that only closing the distance between myself and that unassuming house near the end of the block seemed to scratch. My eyes itched too, from dryness, and I only then realized I hadn't blinked in minutes; I could do nothing but walk. Soon enough, I stood in front of the modest house with dull vinyl siding. The front door was wide open, sucking inward and pulling me closer. I stepped inside, and as I did, the air grew thicker, and my lungs struggled to adjust. The air was humid and still, despite every window being wide open. It was at least ten degrees warmer within that dim interior. It was a tropical heat. Damp and thick.

The floor was a mess. It looked like the clothing dressers had been dumped onto the floors of every room. My feet carried me over piles of jeans, dresses, shoes, and socks. Among the apparel were coins, keys, wallets filled with cards and cash, and even small toys and diapers.

The piles of crumpled clothing grew more condensed the farther I walked into the home and towards the center of the house. It was hotter with every step and the strange air felt sticky and warm, like hot breath on my skin. I unzipped my coat and undid my shirt buttons as I entered the innermost room of the house. The perimeter of the room was strewn with mounds of clothing. Underwear. T-shirts. Cellphones. Wristwatches. Eyeglasses. Pacifiers. Within the center of the piled possessions was a hole.

It wasn't broken out of the floor. The entire floor of the room was concave, bending inward like a funnel down into a deep, black chasm that tapered inward as it reached down into absolute darkness. A chill ran up my back and caused me to shiver uncontrollably at the sight of it, yet the itch of curiosity grew stronger than any fear.

There was no sign of a struggle. No drag marks or blood. The personal effects were set aside haphazardly, giving the impression that whoever they belonged to removed them willingly before entering that strange mouth into the earth. I removed my phone and switched on the LED flashlight, leaning carefully in to get a look.

It was abyssal, at least a few dozen meters deep into the earth before the light could no longer breech the darkness. The carpet stretched down the narrow tube that the funnel of a floor became. The hole shrank as it reached deeper into the earth until it was no wider than a manhole. It was an abstract deformation. The warping carpet maintained its pattern on the circumference of the tunnel as it descended deep into the ground. It was like a square piece of rubber that had been pulled down from the center by a safety pin.

I felt a rumble within my bones. A thrumming vibration of some sub-bass too low to hear. It was calling me. I was so hot. I removed my jacket and emptied my pockets. The air was sticky and wet, the heat unbearable. I could feel the enzymes clogging my nose hairs and dampening my wrists. I stripped down automatically, removing my shoes and socks, my wallet and phone, my keys. I discarded them all as I drew closer to the lip of the mouth in the earth. I was down to my underwear when the clamor of shouting behind me made itself heard.

There was yelling, gruff and muffled, but it sounded so distant, so unimportant. Flashlights illuminated the dim, breathing room and I leaned forward into the hole, desperate to know what was within. I felt stiff fingers clench my elbows, catching me mid-fall. I heard screaming fade out as my vision darkened. I lost consciousness then.

I awoke in the hospital. A nurse stood over me, checking my vitals. My skin was bandaged, every bit I could see. My fingers looked like a mummy's, plastic tubes dangling out of the folds of gauze. The drips of morphine keep the pain at bay, but not the itch from the layers of my skin that have been stripped away. My injuries were determined to be the cause of corrosive enzymes as well as hydrochloric acid, potassium chloride, and sodium chloride; a gastric acid blend found primarily in the stomach.

Officers came to speak to me, and they had a somber desperation in their eyes and voices. The officers who'd discovered me were missing. Only the EMT who placed me in the ambulance was accounted for. A deaf EMT, they eventually told me. I explained in detail the events that transpired, and they explained repeatedly they had found the home and those possessions and clothing, but no hole. They even dug up the floorboards but reported nothing but bugs and earth beneath the foundation.

THERE'S NO SUCH THING AS GHOSTS

Last Fall, my wife and I moved into a farmhouse about an hour north of the city. Attached were four acres of sprawling pasture on one side and a wooded area separating us from the nearest neighbor's home, ensuring privacy and a stunning atmosphere. Sandy and I knew immediately it would be the perfect place to raise a child when the time was right. The only thing my wife had a hard time with was the reason the listing price had been so low; the last owner had died there.

"It's creepy," Sandy whispered to me when we'd been debating the purchase. "What if it's haunted or something?" She smiled, but her eyes didn't.

"There's no such thing as ghosts," I said, "but if there were, they'd jump at this listing price too."

"There'd better not be," Sandy smiled, nuzzling against my cheek before whispering in my ear. "I wanna be the only one getting freaky in sheets." She flashed a smile, and I swept her up in a hug and carried her over the threshold, dropping her gently inside our new home. She giggled, then sprinted up the stairs, stripping off her heather shirt and cutoff shorts in a winding dance. I followed close behind.

Once at the top of the stairs, I spotted Sandy in the light coming from the bedroom window behind her. She was coyly peeking from the door frame. I kicked off my jeans and gently tackled her onto the cool sheets. She turned away from me, signaling me to undo her bra, but as I reached out to do so, she clenched her hand hard on my wrist. She was squeezing tight, frozen in place, but trembling.

"Something wrong?" I asked. She looked strange in the pale blue moonlight, her arched back tense and the expression on her face hidden. My neck hair rose as her arm slowly lifted and pointed to the wall, shaking uncontrollably.

"Do you see it?" Sandy's whisper was filled with worry. I lifted my head, shifting away from her in order to sit up and see what she was referring to. My heart stopped dead in my chest as I stared at the shadow of a man in the square of light from the window. Someone was watching us from the window.

I quickly turned my head to the pane in horror, but nobody was out there. How could there be? It was the second-story window with no access. I turned back to look at the wall, and the shadow was still there, despite the fact that nothing could have possibly been framed in the projected moonlight.

"I see it," I whispered as every hair on my body stood on end. Filled with compounding horror, I flicked on the bedside light. The flooding brightness of the bulb blinded me momentarily as my pupils adjusted and the shadow slowly faded. I then rushed to the window and opened it wide with a balled fist ready to swing; but the cold air drafted in giving view to the fact that nothing was outside. No ladder, no stilt-walking peeping tom. The view of the field made it obvious nothing could have possibly been out there.

"Maybe it was an optical illusion," I tried to rationalize aloud, but even I didn't buy that. The silhouette had looked exactly like a man. Even large ears had protruded from the sides of that shadow of darkness that seemed to be watching us. It was ethereal and illogical in a way that flickered on every alarm in my brain.

The next day, I tried to understand what that mysterious shadow could have possibly been. I researched shadows without light sources, finding only information on nuclear shadows from the atomic blasts in Japan, as well as an abundance of references to hauntings; nothing that could scientifically explain the dark form in our home. Eventually I gave up my research, hoping it was just a trick of the light despite the nagging voice in my head. I tried falling asleep, but upon switching the light off, that shadow of a figure returned.

I watched it as my heart pounded, but this time I left the light off. I rose from the bed and watched, slack-jawed. A full shadow of a man was visible. The chair, the dangling feet, the lolling head to the side and even the thin line of a noose; it was the shadow was of a hanging man. A suicide imprinted onto the wall in an impossible shadow that churned my stomach. I scampered to the light, fumbling with doddering fingers until finally switching it on and watching with unblinking eyes as the shadow quickly faded into the wallpaper. A cold block of ice formed in my stomach as a concept brimmed into my conscious mind, *into the wallpaper.*

I approached the dull floral print of the ornate wallpaper as if in a dream, fascination moving one foot and then the other until I got closer to the wall. I leaned in close, hearing the faint humming that grew louder each inch as my face came into the area where shadow had been cast. I leaned in until I saw there were small stippling of pores in that wall, like pocked skin. A humming soon filled my ears with a strange, constant buzzing. Curiosity led my fingers to the frayed seam of wallpaper, and I ripped a loose fold down with one sharp tear.

I collapsed then, observing a shadowy mass of squirming insects, each no larger than a millimeter. Hundreds of thousands of small beetle-like bugs clicked and skittered over the wall. They remained in that silhouetted shape of a hanging man for some time before exploding out onto the wood floor in every possible direction.

I felt their tickling pincers and stick-like legs scratch into my toes as they climbed my bare feet in a hectic agitation. I screamed as they bit, gnawing at me until the puffy skin raised hard and pink as dozens more climbed over my bare legs. I smacked at them, screaming and swatting the shadowy socks that buzzed and clicked and raced up my body, each one not much larger than a tick. I sprinted my numbing legs to the bathroom as I fought to stay conscious. With scrambling fingers, I turned the faucet on until the scalding hot water rid the biting insects from my tender legs.

The next few days were spent making inquiries from a budget hotel as Sandy battled a full breakdown. I learned that the building's previous owner had been discovered hanging in his bedroom, but not for some time. For weeks he dangled, rotting from a lamp fixture in the ceiling. During that time, he'd been devoured down to the bone by the aggressive beetles, which had nested in the darkest area of the wallpaper; the space where his shadow had fallen.

WHY I QUIT DELIVERING FOOD

I'd been Dash delivering for a few months and enjoyed the freedom of not having a boss order me around. I could play whatever music I want in my car and take jobs I want and skip the ones that tip poorly. I haven't saved much due to gas costs, but I have been saving, and I enjoyed seeing new places and meeting new people. That changed after I received a notification for a $150 paying delivery. Immediately, I swiped "accept" and then pulled over to read it.

I first expected this to be some out-of-state delivery to some rich individual longing for some Michelin rated specialty. I regretted not checking the distance first, and after reading the address, I found it was a bit out in the sticks, but still very much worth the easy $150. I sighed with relief and pressed the GPS button to bring up the map to a restaurant named "Danny's" that I'd not previously heard of.

The sun was setting early, as it does in October, and I had my lights on by the time I made it to a less-populated corner of town where the restaurant was apparently located. Dinner brings the best tips, but I hate driving at night since it's harder to find restaurants without a boldly emblazoned logo lit up in neon. That, and I've always harbored some lurking fear of a delivery-turned mugging; or worse, some gang-initiated killing. Rare as it is, it has happened.

"You have arrived at your destination," the soothing voice of the GPS alerted me.

I slowed to a stop, confused. I was on a dark, residential street, no sign of a restaurant in sight. Where "Danny's" was supposed to be was a dark gap in-between two homes. I checked it again, even typing the restaurant name into Maps outside of the delivery app; but nothing popped up. I realized then it might've been a glitch. In retrospect, $150 for a 30-minute delivery sounded too good to be true. I sighed and began searching the app for the troubleshooting menu when a loud slap on my passenger-side window caused me to jump in my skin.

A man stood outside my car; his hand pressed against the pane. I rolled down the window only a crack. Just enough to hear him.

"You the delivery driver?" he asked, and my mouth went dry. I didn't want to say 'yes' because the vision of a pistol pulled and a muzzle flash kept playing in my mind. But he seemed harmless enough; older too. Mid-fifties, receding hairline, thin frame. Not quite the gang-initiation type. I was fairly certain everyone knew that delivery drivers nowadays don't carry cash.

"Yeah, I'm looking for Danny's Restaurant. Is it near here?" The man just looked at me with a hollow stare before raising his other hand. The fear of an impending bullet to the brain immediately dissipated when I saw a large plastic bag. I sighed out in relief and lowered the window, accepting the delivery.

It was large, much larger than I was used to delivering. I'd typically receive a Styrofoam container or two, a drink as well. This plastic bag contained a stapled paper sack and was filled nearly to the top.

I needed to use both hands to accept it. I placed the surprisingly heavy meal on the passenger seat, staring at it for a moment before looking up again.

"Thank you," my words tapered off as I realized the man was already a few yards back. I watched him disappear into the shadow-filled gap between houses. I have no idea where he was going or where he had come from. Dark curiosity led me back to the app, to see what I was even delivering. My confusion only heightened when I read the order. "Danny's," it simply said, where "cheeseburger" "fries" and the like would typically be listed for me to check off upon pickup.

Despite the questions that kept tugging at my resolve, $150 for this awkward delivery was the overpowering factor. I swiped the "slide after pickup" bottom bar to continue the delivery. The GPS once again popped up, and I stared at the large green areas encompassing the pinpoint. My insides squirmed a bit at the revelation; the delivery address seemed to be dead in the middle of the woods.

I shifted into drive and followed the directions onto the highway. The sun had fully set, but the tunes from the radio kept me in good spirits. Few people were on the road, so I was making great time and could call it an early night after this gig. The miles counted down; from 15, to 10, to 5. The off-ramp came into view, and the large pine trees on either side of the highway continued to darken the path as I merged onto smaller roads. With every mile further into the wilderness, my uneasiness grew.

More than a few times, my eyes darted over to the suspicious double-bagged delivery on my seat. My heart raced as my mind played tricks on me in the shrouding darkness of the tall trees on either side. I did a double take when I thought I saw the bag rustle. Something within appeared to have moved.

The last turn on the GPS signaled for me to take a left. It was a turnoff of the paved asphalt road and onto a dirt road that cut into the woods. I slowed to a stop and double-checked the app, praying there was some sort of mistake. On occasion, the wrong address was listed. No luck, however. My destination was half a mile into the dense wall of pines.

I took the turn and slowly drove into the dark tunnel cutting through arching trees. I could barely see the sky through the dense copse overhead; just darkness broken by the limb-like branches. With each rocking of the chassis and each bump in the narrow dirt road, that heavy bag on the passenger seat seemed to rustle. I fixed my eyes on the road, deciding not to look at it after I heard a faint noise emitting from the stapled inner bag. A noise that sounded like a faint wheezing.

By the time I arrived at the destination, my knuckles were white from gripping the wheel so hard. I was sweating, despite the autumnal chill that had breached my car and clothing. This part of the woods seemed colder than any part of the drive by at least ten degrees.

I shifted into park and looked at the app screen, the only source of light aside from my headlights, which faded only a few meters out. The address was supposedly on the left, and the instructions read "leave at door."

There was no house in sight, however. It had to be a glitch of sorts. Above all else, I didn't want to leave the safety of my vehicle. This entire delivery was all wrong. Something dreadful about it made me crave a shower. It made me want to run scream-ing from the situation I'd unknowingly gotten myself into.

Crinkle

I saw the bag shift in my peripheral vision, and I let out a glot-tal yelp. I hurriedly opened the car door and got out, eager to distance myself from whatever was in the bag. I then navigated the menu of the app on my phone screen, seeking out the 'cancel order' option. My score would go down. I'd miss out on the money, but I'd be able to get out of this strange gig that I wanted nothing more to do with. I was about to press "confirm" on the cancellation when I spotted the door.

A few meters to my left, illuminated only faintly from the light of my phone's screen, stood a door. It looked ancient, its thick wooden beams bone-white from petrification. The design was archaic, something that belonged on the side of a medieval European church. Black steel hinges and latches ornamented it, but the most noticeable feature was the one it was missing. The door was housed in a frame of charred, black beams, but aside from that, it wasn't attached to anything.

I stared at the structure and felt my heartbeat quicken. Dread and curiosity battled within my scrambling mind as it tried to register what this door was and why it was out there. I took a few hesitant steps towards it and felt the hairs on my body rise. With every step towards the detached door, the temperature dropped. I stepped around the unnatural thing to peer behind it, and sure enough, there was nothing behind it but endless trunks of trees.

I'd made it this far, and I just wanted to get my money and get out. With a few deep breaths, I returned to my car and opened the passenger door. With two hands, I lifted the heavy delivery, which shook in my shivering arms.

It moved. Something gasped and gurgled from within, but I continued carrying the parcel over to that strange door. My teeth chattered from the chill as I placed the large bag on the dead leaves in front of the door. I took a photo to verify the delivery, then swiped to complete it. And with that, I rushed back to my car and got inside as quickly as possible.

I then heard the faint cries of an infant. I saw the bag shift and shake, poked outward from the inside. I shifted into reverse and began to backtrack down the pitch-black road into the heart of the woods, but not before I saw that door creak open.

Not before I saw that rotted, black arm with long, desiccated fingers reach out eagerly. I watched it yank the screeching delivery bag into the impossible space behind the door that should not exist.

I WATCHED A MAN WALK OUT OF THE OCEAN

I run a quaint bed-and-breakfast in Maine. Despite the mild winter, it's been slow, to say the least. Two families passed through, as well as a nature photographer, but aside from them, I've been pretty much alone the past few months. As I was sipping my coffee and staring out at the white sands, I saw a dark shape bobbing in the icy waters.

At first, I thought it was debris of some sort. Litter from partying boaters often makes its way to the shore; bottles, cans and other jetsam are not uncommon. But when I saw the inky black hair float up to reveal a face, my heart sank.

I suspected it was a dead body. A few years back, an elderly woman—later found to have suffered from dementia—washed up after drowning in the middle of the night. I put on my coat and walked out into the cool breeze to check, and I watched as the head rose higher up from the skim between lapping waves. A neck and then shoulders poked through the surface. A man was standing upright in the water, walking in from the sea.

Worry shifted tightly into fear at the unlikely sight. I slowed my fast approach on the shifting sands to watch as a soaked-through blazer and tie, both black, raised higher still. Stiff arms dangled at his sides as he walked out of the freezing ocean.

"Sir, are you alright?" I yelled out to him as the cold wind rippled my hair. I took a few more steps to look for any tracks leading to the water, wondering if I'd somehow missed him entering it in the first place. There were no boats anywhere near the horizon and no tracks aside from the ones he made as he fully emerged to walk on the damp sand.

The man didn't answer. He just continued advancing towards me in a slow stride. His wet, black suit was soaked through, and looked to be an odd cut, a bit out of fashion. His skin was pale and his eyes dark and inset. His narrow face remained expressionless.

It's important to note the water is around 35° Fahrenheit this time of year; just above freezing. There was no way he should have been conscious, let alone walking, after the amount of time he'd have had to be in there for me not to have seen him. Not to mention that the time he must have been submerged would have drowned him. Still, this man was moving quickly as he marched towards my residence. I called out once again as I took a step back to my door.

"Sir, do you need help? I can call an ambulance." He walked closer, closing the distance. 30 meters became ten, and soon he was nearly upon me. I panicked. I stepped back into my house and watched in horror as he drew closer.

The man was pasty and white, his skin bloodless and bloated. His eyes were black as a fish's and his pockets spilled out shiny ribbons of seaweed. Each slow step released seawater from his black leather shoes. The man's white lips parted, and water began to trickle out in a steady stream. He then made a series of deep, throaty clicks; hollow and deep.

I yanked the sliding patio door closed and locked it. I took my phone out and watched as the man walked up to my sliding glass door, stopping only after banging his forehead into the pane with a solid *clunk*.

He stared at me with empty black eyes. His white, waxen hands raised up and pressed pruney fingers against the glass. His mouth widened, leaking out saltwater until his jaw let out a sickening pop.

I watched, frozen with peaking horror, as translucent strands of gelatinous rope spilled down from his mouth, dangling like living cellophane noodles from the rotten teeth in his black gums. The texture resembled jellyfish, but the form was unlike anything I'd ever seen. The man's vacant stare locked onto my eyes and his palms then closed into fists. He began to pound on the glass with jarring slams, and I screamed.

I retreated to my bedroom as those slamming fists beat against the glass. I dialed 911 and listened in horror to the rattling thuds that boomed like a drum.

I explained someone was breaking in and gave them the address to my guesthouse in Moody, Maine. I answered the questions as calmly as I could until I heard a high-pitched crack along with the loud thuds. My heart raced. The large windows were storm-proof but wouldn't hold forever.

I begged them to hurry as I searched for a weapon. I grabbed my old squash racket as I listened to the intense thuds continue for a minute or so.

After a few minutes, however, the banging stopped. I could then hear my heartbeat in my ears as I listened for any sound other than the wailing wind. I approached my bedroom window and stared out.

The frothy waves slapped the sands, misting the air. Soon, the back of the man was visible as he walked back towards the water. I watched, transfixed, as he continued his march back into the ocean, each leg carrying him deeper into the crashing waves until they vanished in the surf. He continued on, shrinking in size and sinking into the declining shelf until only his head was visible; and soon that, too, disappeared beneath the break. I stared for a solid ten minutes in disbelief, but he was gone. I finally breathed a sigh of relief; still rattled and confused.

It took another fifteen minutes for the police to arrive, and by then I knew how ridiculous my story sounded. Regardless, I recounted the strange occurrence, detailing his appearance and demeanor. I led them to the door, which was wet from his pounding fists. A tiny crack was visible in the pane. I received the obligatory line of questioning regarding drug or alcohol use, but they could see I was dead sober, and this was not a prank, publicity stunt, or simple misunderstanding. Additionally, there was a single set of footprints leading to my house and back to the ocean, which confirmed my bizarre story.

I was advised to keep my doors locked and told it was likely some confused renter. They didn't believe me, but the man was gone, and I knew how ridiculous my story sounded. After a small chat about the weather and being told to call back if anything else happened, they took off. I expected it to turn into a bizarre tale I'd later share with my friends at the pub over a pint. As the sunset blazed across the ocean and vanished beneath the horizon, I even began to question whether I'd just missed some obvious explanation.

When night came, I saw the other dark shapes floating on the waves. I watched in disbelief as a dozen pale individuals slowly rose from the water. Their widening jaws dangled strings of jelly from rotten teeth as they emerged from the ocean and onto the sand.

Among them was the man from earlier. He hadn't left to return to wherever he'd come from. He'd left to bring back others.

DAISY CAME HOME

Daisy was my best friend, ever since my mom found her years ago in a cardboard box in the parking lot where she'd worked. She'd tell the story with a twinkle in her eye about how she peeked inside to see that one floppy ear and those glacier blue puppy eyes, and just like that, we had a dog. Dad had guessed her breed to be a pit-bull-husky mix; a beautiful, sweet pup with pistons as legs and a face as sweet as honey. Daisy became my fellow adventurer when we'd play in the yard, and a warm fluffy pillow to lay my head on upon our return. Years passed and her eyesight worsened, but our bond didn't.

When this past school year had finally come to an end, I was beyond excited to hit the beach, camp with friends and just simply relax. When I got home that last day, however, I abandoned any hopes for a decent summer. Mom and dad were waiting for me outside with eyes red from crying. My mom's frown quivered as she walked up and embraced me before sobbing the news into my shoulder. Daisy had wandered into the road and had been killed by a car. My heart broke then and there.

The next few days were absolutely devastating; we buried her in the field at the edge of our property, and I cried so much my nose scabbed over from blowing it. The tears never seemed to end. Summer came and went, and I eventually began to accept that Daisy was gone. She had a great life in her years with us, and she truly enriched ours as well. School started again, and I felt like my life was getting back on track; but that all collapsed when I came home today to see muddy paw prints on the kitchen floor.

My heart pounded as I followed them to the living room, thinking mom must have gotten a new puppy to surprise me with.

My eyes began to tear up with joy, but then an awful stench hit my nostrils. It smelled terrible, both sweet and foul, before I realized it was the smell of death. I held my nose and slowly rounded the kitchen into the living room with growing anxiety; and then I froze. There, standing on the living room carpet, was the decayed body of Daisy, her fur matted and missing in patches to reveal dried-out wounds and white bone peeking out from beneath. Her jaw hung open, unhinged, but worst of all were her eyes, milky white and dead, staring coldly at me.

"Why are you looking at Daisy like that, honey?" My mom's voice spoke from directly behind me and I flinched as tears trickled down my face. I turned and faced my mom to see her wide smile under her auburn curls. "How was your day?"

I blinked, stunned and unable to fully process the living, rotting dog that stared at me from the living room. A deep, rumbling growl sounded through that dog's bared, broken teeth in that mangled jaw. I ducked back a bit into the kitchen, watching the breathing corpse of Daisy in absolute horror. Her dangling jaw writhed with long, wormy pulp, and a glistening stream of dark fluid spilled down onto the carpet. I looked desperately at my mom's smiling face for some sign this was all just a terrible nightmare I'd wake up from.

"M-mom, Daisy's in there. What's going on?" I asked with a trembling voice as tears streamed down. I was shivering from the mix of fear and confusion. My heart pounded rapidly, and my throat closed up.

"Um, yes dear, she's allowed in the living room," my mom said casually as she chopped peppers. I just stood there stunned for a few moments, and then I heard the front door open. "Who's a good girl?" my father's voice warmly filled the house. I peeked into the living room.

Dad was in the living room, down on one knee of his pressed suit, petting the growling, rotting body of Daisy like nothing was even remotely wrong. I watched as his hands massaged her exposed, festering muscle from skin that slipped off to reveal the white peaks of jutting vertebrae. I covered my mouth in revulsion as he lifted his wet hand back up, dripping dark red with congealing blood. My father then brushed his hair out of his face with that decay-covered hand, leaving a streak of dark red and brown on his forehead. Tiny, wiggling maggots crawled along his graying hairline from the red smear, and I began retching.

"Oh honey, are you sick?" Mom called out and put a gentle hand on my shoulder, which I flinched off and quickly away from.

"Wh-what the FUCK is going on?! Daisy is *dead*, she's *rotting* in there!" I shouted. "She's been dead all summer. Are you both insane?" I yelled and watched them through blurry tears; but my mom's brows just scrunched together in anger. "Don't you use that language in this house, young man. Why would you say that about Daisy? Are you on drugs?" my mother snapped coldly before sighing, "James, talk to your son."

"Apologize to your mother now," my dad spoke sternly as he petted a patch of white skull, exposed from the peeling flesh on Daisy's rotted head.

I ran out the back door, and the world spun. I collapsed on the lawn, the knees of my jeans hitting the damp grass as I looked back in the window to see that standing corpse of Daisy, staring those dead eyes at me. My father continued to pet her decomposing body, his hands streaked with dark blood and chunks of meat. They were totally oblivious to her horrific state, and I soon realized why.

I stood on the lawn, watching through the window as my mother turned back to finish preparing dinner in the kitchen with a smile. As she did, I saw a puffy mark dead center on the back of her neck encircling a small hole the size of a peppercorn. I trembled as I watched a thin, red worm slowly emerge from the hole, and realized that Daisy hadn't come home alone.

She'd brought guests.

THE SKIP

12:21 read the nicotine-stained face of the clock on the wall. I sat under flickering yellow lights, swirling burnt coffee in my mug while waiting out the night's rain in a small, roadside diner. At the counter, a red-faced, white-haired man in a flat cap poured cheap whiskey from a plastic pint into his coffee mug as he ranted. He babbled on to a burly trucker who shoveled boiled chicken into his bearded mouth, clearly disinterested.

The rain outside hissed as it beat onto the black asphalt of the parking lot. Roy Orbison crooned from the jukebox over clinking metal on dishware when a bright flash and loud boom startled me. I jerked from the sound and spilled some coffee as my heart jumped with me. I sopped up the black liquid on the tabletop with thin napkins from the metal dispenser, and as I did, I heard the record begin to skip. I looked up then, and gooseflesh textured my skin as I realized not only the song was skipping.

The tired-looking waitress lifted a plastic dish tray of glasses from the counter, but I watched in wide-eyed in confusion as the brown tray jumped back to the counter. She lifted it up again, but it soon appeared back down again to the rhythm of the skipping song. The lush at the counter gulped his Irish coffee, but then the mug in his bent arm blinked back onto the counter to repeat as well. The entire diner was looping; trapped in a one-second span of time.

It was like some masterfully choreographed performance piece. The impossible glitch in time had me gripping the vinyl seat cushion, struggling to tether myself to a reality that seemed to have broken. I spoke, then shouted, to the other patrons, but they didn't respond. When I looked out the window at the skipping cars on the highway, I yelled in shock. Someone was out there, walking slowly towards the diner and staring directly at me.

A grim expression was frozen on his waxen face as he approached. His gray eyes stared deep into mine as he opened the diner's door and walked towards my booth, dripping rain onto the floor from his dark clothing. My heart pounded in sync with the scratchy pops of the record as he leaned over me, then the sound of both stopped.

"Heart attack," a deep, muffled voice spoke from above me. The discolored clock face ticked to 12:22 before fading slowly darker into black. "He's gone."

MEET YOUR MAKER

I've always been terrified of death. I was raised to have faith in God, but I found it impossible with no empirical proof. I desperately wanted to believe in some purpose or an afterlife, but the concept of an intelligent architect of the universe just seemed so abstract and—to be blunt—childish. That changed last month.

I was waiting for the bus, and I saw a man who shouldn't be there. There was no possible way he could've entered the exact location on the sidewalk at that particular time. I know this, as I'd looked up from my phone not a few seconds earlier to scan for the bus. Nobody was on the block but a mother pushing her stroller and an elderly man walking his terrier.

Where did he come from? I wondered. I returned to my phone screen, but my focus was broken. Unless my brain had short-circuited and I was having a stroke, there was no possible way he could be there. I slid my phone back in my pocket and just watched the man.

He looked to be in his mid-sixties. Clean-shaven and wearing a dark blue sweater and black jeans. His salt and pepper hair had receded, showing a significant number of sunspots and wrinkles. His bushy eyebrows rose when his eyes locked onto mine.

I quickly looked away, but it was too late. He'd seen me. The man was crossing the street and walking towards me. In moments, he sat next to me and smiled. He then craned his head at an awkward angle so that his face was clear and visible to me. When he did, I felt the temperature drop and my skin began to crawl.

He appeared as average as the word can convey. Not ugly and not attractive; average with a capital A. The man you might see working the register in the background of a 1960s sitcom. A generic smile and round nose, friendly eyes with wrinkles on the sides.

"Hello there, waiting on the bus?" he asked in an exceptionally generic voice.

"Yeah," I returned and looked to the street to break eye contact with the individual. I could smell him then. A slightly sweet yet foul stink reminiscent of a pig farm. It lingered, delicately but distinctly.

"I know you saw me, so let's drop the bullshit." The man's smile widened slightly, and I felt my heartbeat quicken.

I didn't want to be near the guy, but I was dumbfounded and a bit stunned. I just blinked and looked at him, trying to understand where this was going. His stare grew more intense, his eyes widened and began to glisten wet.

"You want to know how, yes? You want to know how a man snuck into your precious little street where you wait for your bus and take it to 136 Rockwell Road?"

I felt like I had been punched in the stomach. Goosebumps raised on my arms and my mind raced to figure out who this man was. He knew my work address. Was he a stalker? A hitman or a blackmailer?

"Who are you?" I asked, hearing the quiver in my voice.

"I am not a who," replied the smiling man. "Let me show you."

His face began to ripple as if the skin were liquid. Skin shifted and lapped, giving glimpses of muscle and twining veins beneath. Teeth, translucent and sharp, pierced fleshy gums, which opened into mouths within mouths in a fractal nightmare. Beneath the dancing filaments of muscle fiber, the white of his skull cracked and split and his face reached out into a dozen segments like pieces to a floating jigsaw puzzle.

I tried to scream, but it refused to budge; locked in my lungs. I tried to get up and run, but my body refused to obey. The impossible geometry of the broken face leaned closer, and he spoke deep into my mind, no longer speaking through vocal cords.

"I am the first and the last. The creator and destroyer. I built this wretched place to feed off of one thing. The haunting knowledge that everything I provide will be snatched eagerly away once the desire to live is at its peak and the desperation is palpable. I am God, and I populated this stagnant boulder with my seed billions of years ago."

I felt resistance when I tried to scream, but my throat relaxed slightly as I tried to speak, allowing my words to finally come out. "What are you?" I asked, hypnotized by the swaying organic patterns that parted so effortlessly.

"I am what you ignorant people would call an alien. I was born in a galaxy far from this one. I've traveled light years in search of others, but I was alone. It didn't take long to realize it was all my doing. Every star a teardrop. Every planet a ball of phlegm cast from my shapeless throat. I chose to fill my time by terraforming worlds. Earth is far from the first, there have been thousands before. After a few billion years of playing with the squealing life within, I incite an extinction event and lavish in the clamor of screams as all life begins to die."

His two glassy orbs of eyes tethered to a thread of muscle swiveled upward to the sky. "You've all been doing a fine job of that yourselves, though. I'm impressed."

A man in a suit and tie approached the bench. I stared at him with desperate eyes, eager for him to see the monstrosity seated next to me. If it was distracted, maybe its paralyzing grip would release, and I could get away.

The man checked his wristwatch and walked closer before sitting down on the bench next to the horror claiming to be God. He didn't even seem to notice us.

"You were hoping this man might intervene?" Fibrous tendrils of muscle and vein reached curiously out from the warping face towards the newcomer's neck. He began scratching his throat and coughing. I watched in horror as tentacles of meat and vein reached out from the monster's face and squeezed the man's throat. A muffled pop of vertebra crunched from within the tightening grasp.

His neck pulled closed like the end of a sausage link. With a sickening squelch, the victim's head snapped off, dropping to the sidewalk with a heavy thud as blood streamed out. The amoebic tentacles and frilled muscle of the abstract face began to recede, gradually reforming into the nondescript visage of the man I felt I recognized from films. He then spoke.

"No one will ever believe you," the voice gently stated, and with that, he stood and walked across the street. I watched as his body began to slim, his torso, arms, and head narrowing until they vanished completely before my eyes.

I sat there stunned until the ambulance's blaring siren and strobing lights alerted me to their presence. The decapitated man on the ground to the left of me was still there, and the reflective blood pool from his neck had begun to creep down his clothing like red ivy. A police officer's words were muted, but I saw the gun pointed at me and knew he was shouting. I raised my hands and felt the pain in my shoulder as they were twisted behind my back. I was cuffed and thrown into a police car.

They took my prints and then questioned me for hours. The red-faced detective slammed the table as I recounted what happened until he finally stopped asking. Eventually, a woman in a suit took the detective aside and had a brief discussion. He then informed me they didn't have any prints or evidence to hold me there. I was free to go.

And that's the end of it. As much as I wish I could dispel it as a hallucination or a vivid nightmare, but it was real. That encounter was the definitive proof I needed. I now know that God is, in fact, very real. I just pray I never run into him again.

THE HOUSE BENEATH THE BASEMENT

My wife Sandy and I recently moved into a housing development a half-hour outside of the city. We set up most of our things, furniture and the like, though we still have boxes to unpack. When storing a few summer chairs and other less essential items in the large basement, I noticed an acrid smell, one that only worsened when it rained. Before moving in fully, I wanted to fix whatever mildew or animal remains might be causing the issue. While Sandy was at work in her home office, I descended the creaky open stairs wearing a dust mask and brandishing a spray bottle of bleach, like some antiseptic cowboy.

The basement has no windows, mind you. It's just a four-cornered concrete space, empty aside from a few cardboard boxes of old items I'd carried down a week earlier. I began inspecting the concrete walls for mold spots or water damage, but found no source of the foul odor. It was as standard and minimal as a basement could be, aside from the lack of windows. Then, after a bit of following the scent trail, I found it.

Underneath the stairs, in the corner where the two walls and floor met, was a slab of ever-so-slightly mismatched concrete. I stared at the rectangular seam in curious wonder.

I realized there was likely a burst pipe below that had been sloppily fixed by a previous tenant. After living in the city for 15 years, I was used to landlords pulling quick and dirty fixes to avoid out-of-pocket work. This was our home now, though, and I was determined to fully repair it before we settled in.

As the afternoon faded into evening, Sandy was still shut in her study editing books (she's the breadwinner), so I went to work, donning my rattiest pair of jeans and a T-shirt I'd ruined when painting the rooms. I descended the creaky wooden stairs into the basement, ready to bust open the concrete rectangle below them.

It turned out the concrete slab wasn't even sealed, and it lifted easily with my crowbar. I slid it aside with a rumble to reveal an old stone stairway descending to a further level, a sub-basement.

It looked ancient, much older than the rest of our house. Our home was estimated to be from the 1960s, but the cobbled rocks stairs descending into shadow looked to be a few hundred years old. I looked down into the darkness, then climbed back up the rickety wooden steps to my home. I headed into the garage, searching through unpacked boxes of tools before finding my flashlight. Curiosity grew as to what could possibly be down there.

I was well aware that many people built fallout shelters in the 60s in preparation for a looming nuclear war. I first wondered if it could be one of those, but it clearly predated 20th-century construction. My next guess was a hiding spot built to help the underground railroad. I'd seen similar hidden spaces in old Quaker farmhouses. They were there to help hide runaway slaves; something I respected greatly. Once I began my descent, however, I realized that this was neither of the aforementioned. My jaw hung open at the discovery.

There was a room-by-room copy of the first story of our home in that hidden sub-basement. Every dividing stone wall and doorway was identically placed. I stared in awe when I realized the outer walls even held windows in the same locations. Warped, thick glass reflected my flashlight's beam. I approached one in amazement, staring at a worm squirming against a pane that seemed to barely hold in a wall of compacted dirt.

I continued into the familiarly laid out abode, observing the ancient stone walls. Every wall, windowsill, and fixture was similarly placed as in our home up above. Yet everything was archaic and spooled with long-abandoned cobwebs. There were cast-iron hinges on each of the petrified wooden doors. A thick layer of dust clung to every mantel and surface, each looking and stained from centuries of use. Most bizarre of all was the fact that not only was the floor plan of our home above replicated, but every bit of furniture that we'd moved in so far had an antique matching set.

It was like a time-warped version of our home, down to the furniture itself. A pre-Victorian sofa sat in the exact location as our modern one; its threadbare cushions deflated from wear and decay. I nearly yelped when I saw a centipede wriggle out from a hole in the cushions. I glanced around to see stained wooden chests from a bygone era in the exact same locations as the cluster of cardboard boxes that lay unpacked up above.

My flashlight's pale beam danced with motes of weightless dander as they illuminated the most notable difference. Though each piece of furniture was in place, the cold stone rooms were all devoid of lamps or even candles. I walked on to the mirror version of our kitchen. There was a mortar and pestle filled with a congealing black paste on a wooden countertop that was scarred with lines from a heavy blade. It was in the same location as the blender I whir up smoothies in each morning. It was beyond coincidence. It was as if our place had been studied and recreated with furnishings and tools from another time.

My heart pounded in my chest as paranoia built. I darted the circular flashlight beam through the shadows, which raced and jumped behind uneven tables and speckled jars of dried herbs. Then I noticed the dark wood of the front door. It was in the exact spot as our own. I approached it as curiosity brimmed. What could it even lead to?

My pulse quickened. Everything felt wrong, like I was exploring some part of the world that was not meant to be discovered. Some arcane place that had been hidden for centuries for good reason. I couldn't stop my legs from walking forward or my twitchy hand from reaching out, though. The need to know what lay beyond that door was immeasurable. I grabbed the cast iron latch handle, pressing the cold metal mechanism down and hearing an echoing click. I then pulled it open, half-expecting an avalanche of dirt to spill in over me. But only cold air met my face, and I at once sensed the open space before me.

I aimed the flashlight's beam into the darkness and felt a tremble in my bones. On the ground before me was a cobblestone pathway leading out into a vast limestone cavern. I aimed the flashlight upward to the roof, illuminating the long fangs of a thousand stalactites sprawling out, past where my light could penetrate. It looked endless. A massive cave system was hidden beneath our home.

Then I heard something. A clicking noise from deep within the absolute blackness of a space with no light of its own. It was a familiar sound, but not that of the drips from the limestone nor the rattle of debris. My stomach squirmed as my mind made a connection that filled me with a bitter realization. It was the clicking of a tongue.

I aimed the beam forward, reaching my arm out fully as if it would somehow light up the source; and it did reflect off of something. Two gleaming circles from deep in the shadows. Two eyes that were watching me from the cold tunnel. I backtracked slowly, praying my movement would go unnoticed. I tensed with each sound my sneakers made as I stepped back towards that strange, mirrored home below our basement.

Then, fast approaching steps echoed as they became louder. The clicking sped up, too, blending into a gravelly croak. Whoever was down there was racing towards me, and I ran.

I raced back into the copied house and slammed shut the heavy door, which muffled the grating clicking that approached. I ran through the ancient home, only then noticing that the stains on each wooden surface were dark and spattered. Each wooden counter was textured with knicks and grooves reminiscent of a cutting board.

I raced towards the stairwell, turning back at the sound of an explosive bang as the heavy front door was flung open. I caught a glimpse of something that could have been mistaken for a man had I not held that beam which drew features from the shadows. Milky white eyes and a gaping mouth—far too large, similar to the unhinged jaws of a feeding snake.

It wore clothes reminiscent of early North American settlers. Puritan or maybe pilgrim, something that belonged in colonial times. It wore a heavily stained and exaggeratedly large collar, more like a ruff, and matching cuffs caked black with filth. The fingers were too long and swollen at each knobby knuckle. Those eager digits extended like Alaskan crab legs as they reached towards me. My heart pounded and iced over in dread as I climbed the stairwell back up into our basement. I slid the cement slab over the opening just as it came into view, the gaping mouth emitting a bassy clicking that vibrated my guts.

I lay down on top of the cement slab of a trapdoor to keep it in, half expecting it to launch me up and off before those long fingers speared into and eviscerated me. I knew I had to protect my wife, so I lay there, stiff as a board, ready to resist. Then the door above me creaked open. *Sandy*.

I was about to yell up to her to get an overnight bag and to start the car. I expected she'd ask questions, but I'd tell her we were in danger, and I'd explain later. I was about to issue orders, but I closed my throat tight, swallowing the breath that might form the first word. I lay still as I could and hushed my breaths as I watched, through the gaps in the wooden stairs, the tattered fabric of a long, antiquated dress swaying against filthy, buckled shoes.

I laid there, making sure my phone was in silent mode, careful not to shift the keys in my pocket. I have been here for hours now, piecing things together. Like how they might have copied the furniture placement of our home in order to learn it and easily navigate it without sight.

I watch those strange shoes between the top two stairs, praying they'll just retreat back inside to give me a window of time in which to escape. Praying they won't descend the twelve steps between us once my stomach finally rumbles from hunger, or the fetid stink from below finally causes me to cough. I just lie here in silence atop the cement trap door, listening to that awful sound that stopped me from speaking in the first place. That throaty clicking from above.

LIFETIME GUARANTEE

I'd always hunted for bargains to exploit. A '30% off' tag missing that little 'Discounts cannot be combined' sign, and I'd slap down a two-for-one coupon and relish the looks on the manager's face as he parted with his merchandise for a fraction of cost. I'd savor the glares of other patrons. I drank up the glimmer of envy the well-to-do showed in their eyes when they realized they were paying more than four times what I was for the exact same thing.

One deal I'd been particularly fond of was the lifetime guarantee. Some offered cash back, which basically ensured I could use a product until it 'broke', then get a refund of my money. Coats, boots, backpacks and even a few watches. It amounted to free clothing or products once I no longer desired them. I was out hunting for deals and steals today when those two sweet words "Lifetime Guarantee" popped up in my peripheral.

I crossed the intersection in eagerness, like Pavlov's salivating dogs. The suckers at this clothing store were offering a full cash refund, and—best of all—you keep their products. It was sturdy-looking hiking gear, well-made, but for me, a simple sliver on the inside seam and I'd get it free. I grinned at the cashier, whose eyes were dead as marbles, and I put it on my card, well aware it'd be refunded that very week.

I slipped on the expensive jacket, then strutted out of the door with a smile. On the way out, I passed a tall man with a dour expression whose eyes locked onto mine. Something put me off about him. I hurried down the street, looking back a few times over my shoulder to see that he'd followed me out of the store. I sped up my brisk walk until I was jogging, but that man kept close in pursuit. When I glanced back, I caught a glimpse of him, his grim expression, dark trench coat, and black leather gloves.

I tried to lose him, zigzagging a few times down side streets and alleys, but soon found myself in a dead-end. Panic set in. I gasped as I turned back to see him closing in. Before I could even scream for help, he was already upon me, rushing me with the glint of metal.

The blade stuck into my throat, severing my jugular and crushing my larynx with uncanny precision. I gurgled coppery fluid and my limbs felt rubbery, cold and numb as I began to bleed out onto the stain-resistant fabric. The alley is dimming and my shallow breaths sting, but the shop kept their word. This jacket will last for the rest of my life.

GRANDMA'S BONES WON'T STOP GROWING

My grandma suffered from arthritis her entire adult life. Her hands were stiff, and her fingers perpetually curled. Her thick, gnarled knuckles always creeped me out as a child. Back in November, excitement colored her voice as she explained to my father that she was selected to participate in a trial for a new drug that had very promising results for people suffering from Rheumatoid Arthritis.

I spoke to her occasionally after she started the medication, and she sounded thrilled with the results. She would ramble gleefully on about how she'd regained mobility and could fully extend her fingers for the first time in over a decade. Thanksgiving was fast approaching, and we were all looking forward to seeing her. When the holiday arrived, however, we noticed her peculiar behavior.

After noshing hors d'oeuvres and marveling at her newfound agility, we all shared our recent life events as the savory flavors of turkey and stuffing filling the house. It wasn't until we took our places at the table that the tone shifted from warm and welcoming to unsettling.

Our small family was seated at the table, hungrily eyeing the spread when grandma jumped up from her chair and began shaking violently, before erupting in a harsh scream. After a few seconds, she sat down as if nothing at all had happened and turned to me.

"Sweety, do you mind passing the stuffing?"

Grandma was in her 80s, and Alzheimer's runs in the family. Naturally, we worried the medication she'd been taking might have triggered an episode. Dad made a few doctor appointments. After a few cognitive tests and bewildered scratching of heads, they scheduled an MRI. After the scan, they explained that something was peculiar about her skull.

My father showed me the printouts of the MRI. The profile cross-section of her head showed a skull that was very thick, bumpy and misshapen, and the brain itself looked to be pressed inward in one spot near the back.

He told me the doctor was lost as to what could have taken place, but they mentioned Fibrodysplasia ossificans progressiva, FOP. A rare genetic disorder in which tissue is ossified, replaced by bone. FOP doesn't normally manifest later in life, however. Regardless, they ceased the drug trials in case something was triggered by the new medication.

My grandma protested, but eventually agreed and reluctantly surrendered the pill bottle. The doctor discussed monitoring her behavior, and she was given a prescription for Dexamethasone, a more traditional arthritis medication.

I visited with my father a week later. We drove to her large house and spent a relaxing afternoon playing gin rummy. Grandma was in good spirits, but it was impossible to ignore the occasional tic or twitch. Eventually, we said our goodbyes, and both dad and I determined to visit more frequently to make sure she was doing alright. Two weeks later, I was back at her house after promising to join her for lunch. I was startled when she opened the door to greet me.

Grandma looked different. Her face was undeniably longer than before, and her eyes looked out of place, like her eye sockets had migrated upward and outward on her large head. She was a bit taller too. It was shocking. She had to have grown at least two inches since our last visit. After gaping at me, her open mouth showing long, yellow teeth, she finally smiled and spoke.

"Oh, it's so good to see you. Come in!" I breathed in relief at hearing her voice; but only slightly. I had to force myself to smile and not stare at the strange-looking woman in the doorframe. She was taller and lankier, and her wrinkles seemed to smooth out from thin-stretched skin on an elongated frame. It was a truly unsettling sight.

I came in and began to relax as we talked about books and the weather. Grandma would shiver or twitch on occasion, but she seemed to be well, despite her startling appearance. I said my goodbyes and reported back to my father, who seemed concerned.

It wasn't for another month and a half before I saw grandma again, and it would be the last time. My father rushed into my room as I was planning my senior thesis. He informed me Grandma wasn't answering her phone, but he couldn't visit as there'd been a serious accident at his work. I agreed and took the keys as he headed out.

After a short drive, I was at the house. I noticed the lights were off, aside from a single naked bulb up on the second story. I tried not to think of her misshapen head and bizarre growth spurts. I knocked on her front door to no reply. Worry swelled within me as I stood outside in the dimming blue light of dusk, listening for a response. I tried ringing the doorbell. No answer. I called out, announcing my presence.

"Hey grandma, it's me. Are you home?" A muffled, distant thump and crash joined the sound of crickets from the surrounding trees. I tried the door, finding it open, and entered into the dim interior. The house was cold and still; no sign of her. I was startled by the thumping sound of running feet from the floor above me, and I needed to take a few deep breaths to slow my pounding heart.

"Grandma, it's me, Mike. Your grandson. Dad wanted me to make sure you were OK."

I began climbing the winding stairs to the second floor. I just wanted to get out of there as soon as possible. I then heard a faint crackling that grew louder with every step I took upward. I made it to the top of the stairs and scanned the fuzzy shadows, searching in vain for a light switch.

A snapping *click* from down the hallway drew my attention. In the darkness, a tall form moved closer until a silver sliver of moonlight defined the contour of its shape.

It stood roughly seven feet tall. Her now long, slender arms and legs protruded in various places from knobs of sporadic calcium growth that poked out from within her skin. The neck was far too long, like something belonging to a goose. It looked as if half the spine had sprouted out the top of the clavicles. An oversized head veiled in shadow dangled like a grotesque puppet. I was grateful the lights were out; I didn't want to see what the face looked like.

"Grandma?" my voice escaped in a squeaky, shaking plea. I watched in horror as the large head cocked with a crunch. The moonlight caught the eyes, which had migrated to the edges of that strange, terrible head. And then it screamed.

That scream was a howling sound; raspy and deep, confused and aggressive. I stumbled backward and fell as the limber, long arms of that large figure reached out towards me. Reaching, pale branches of stretched skin over knotted, warped bone. I scrambled backward as splayed hands with stick-like fingers fell to land on the carpet with a bassy thud. It was now on all fours, like some unearthly antelope. I watched, and terror spun within my skull as it began bounding toward me. It closed the distance between us in seconds, and I screamed as horror racked my brain.

The long, humanoid form raced by me, followed by a rush of gamey wind. That thing then leapt up and burst through the second-story window, shattering the glass with an explosive crash.

I stayed on the ground, frozen with fear for a few moments before I could finally move. When I gathered the courage to approach the shattered window, it was gone; vanished into the woods behind grandma's home.

My grandma hasn't been found, despite a search of the woods. They theorize whatever I'd seen must have been an animal, and perhaps my grandma was taken by predators. Or maybe she just wandered off into the woods in a fit of dementia.

We did hear about a few strange animal sightings and farmers in the vicinity have reported missing livestock. Despite the incidents, nobody seems to take the account my father and I shared very seriously.

The doctor who administered the medication claimed there must have been some genetic anomaly as the cause. None of the other patients experienced any side effects, and with grandma gone, any chance to study and understand it seems to have vanished with her. At least until today.

I was brushing my teeth when I heard the scream. A shocking animal howl that caused my heart to race. I followed the horrible sound into the hallway and saw my father standing there. He was quivering, convulsing as if in seizure, and his jaw was wide open from emitting that awful yell. His face looked strange, ever-so-slightly different, as if his features had shifted in the night just a centimeter here or there.

"Dad!" I shouted, and he snapped out of the horrific paroxysm.

"Hey there, off to work!" he said, chipper. I shivered, observing his strange features as he grabbed his keys and headed out the door. He made one observation before exiting the house and heading off to work, one that confirmed the dreadful concern roiling in my mind.

"Funny, this shirt seems to have shrunk," he said, and my stomach twisted in knots.

MORE CHILLS FROM VELOX BOOKS

www.ingramcontent.com/pod-product-compliance
Lightning Source LLC
Chambersburg PA
CBHW030137010826
48973CB00002B/599